The Girl with No Sol

KAREN VEGA

THE GIRL WITH NO SOL
Copyright © 2021 by Karen Vega
All rights reserved under the Pan-American and International Copyright Conventions.
This book may not be reproduced in whole or in part, except for brief quotations embodied in critical articles or reviews, in any form or by any means, electronic or mechanical, including photocopying, recording, or by any information storage and retrieval system now known or hereinafter invented, without written permission of the author.

Any names, characters, and places featured in this publication are the result of the author's imagination. Any resemblance to actual persons (living or dead), places, events, circumstances, institutions, or anything else, is purely incidental.

ISBN (paperback) 978-1-7375211-0-5
ISBN (ebook) 978-1-7375211-1-2
For more information: www.karenvegawrites.com

The Girl with No Sol

12/2022
May your future be bright!

KAREN VEGA

12/2022

May your
future
be bright!

Author's Note

When I was thirteen, I had a vivid dream.

I was running in a barren place that looked like Area 51, holding a diamond necklace in my hand. Or so I thought it was me. The sun was shining brightly on the horizon.

It felt so real. I woke up the next day and wrote down everything. Within that first day, I had the names of Kalamiti Sol, Lucas Santiago, The Crew members, Nonna, the setting, and the basic plot of this book divided into three parts. The title flashed in my mind.

And so, ***The Girl with No Sol*** was born.

It took me almost eleven years to write, edit, and publish this novel. At thirteen, I didn't have a laptop. The first few months, I handwrote the original manuscript on loose-leaf paper and a notebook from the dollar store. One summer I borrowed my sister's laptop and typed the entire thing, then transferred it to a flashdrive until I was finally able to buy my own laptop. At that point I thought I was finished with it, so I began querying literary agents. I never heard back from any of them.

During those eleven years, the manuscript collected dust in my closet and sat as a Word document. They were years filled with writer's block, procrastination, and a lack of motivation, all wrapped in hope and sunshine. Editing was tedious and time consuming because I was trying to make sense and organize all of 13-year-old me's ideas. Fear played a role and pulled me back, as well as being a busy high school and college student, working multiple jobs. There were many blockages in my creativity that prevented me from making progress. After graduating college, I cleared those mental and physical blockages, got my stuff together, and the creative flow came so naturally. As I grew older, the project grew with me.

Although Kalamiti is based off of myself and the plot is influenced by my own life events and experiences, this is in no way an autobiography or memoir. Writing this story was very healing to me, and it gave me the opportunity to share my ideas and inspire others. No matter what age you are, what you look like, or how your past played out, you're not alone and there's always hope. A bright future awaits you.

Thanks for reading and believing in me. It's an honor to share my dream with you. More to come soon! And I promise it won't take so many years again.

*For Jungmin Woo
And to anyone who's still trying
to find their place in this world.*

September 18

I'm running.

I'm running faster and faster, until I reach home. My name is Kalamiti Sol, and I am the leader of The Crew. Sometimes I go by K9; the "K" because of the first letter in my name, and the "9" because it's my lucky number. I'm 15-years-old.

The Crew includes Lucas, June, Blake, Jay, and Maci. The only way we can survive is by stealing. So that's why I'm running. I just stole a diamond necklace.

Now I'll give you some background info about everyone in The Crew:

First there's Maci Sherri Brooks, 12. She's like a little sister to me. She has the prettiest blonde hair and baby blue eyes. Maci joined The Crew a couple of years ago. Her parents had abandoned her, so she had no place to go. Although she's the youngest, she's quite wise.

June Aurora Rue is 15 and has been my best friend since the first grade. She was born in South Korea and later came to America. She has shoulder length black hair and brown eyes. She decided to create The Crew with me, so she left her foster family. June loves to read.

Jaylan (No Middle Name) Evans is 13. He goes by Jay and is African American. He's always had a dream to fly, just like a blue jay. He joined a year ago, after having no place to go when his home burned down. He was the only one in his family who survived the fire.

Dexter Blake Sky, 14, goes by Blake. He has Native American ancestry. He has curly, dirty blond hair and brown eyes. Lucas found him begging on the streets. Blake has a dream to someday be in a house, to someday have a family again.

Lucas Isaias Santiago, 16, is my other best friend. He's Argentine American and the oldest member. I may be the leader of The Crew, but in reality, Lucas carries the group on his shoulders. To form The Crew, he left his older brother, Alonzo, who was pretty much his guardian.

I'd prefer not to share my background, but I guess I should. See, my past sucks. The past is something that I'll probably never completely reveal to anyone. I could write a book on all of the near-death experiences, pain, torture, and family issues I've had to deal with. I'd even call it "The Shitty Life of Kalamiti Sol" with the subtitle "Life is Shit." It would probably be the worst selling autobiography because no one wants to read about a girl with a depressing childhood and teenage life.

Anyway, I'm Mexican and Italian. Mom's side is Italian, and Dad's side is Mexican. I have long, wavy, dark brown hair and brown eyes. To summarize, my parents had me when they were both 16. When I was four, my dad was killed by a drunk driver. I still have the gold sun necklace he had given, which I wear daily. Our last name is "Sol," which means "sun" in Spanish.

Shortly after that, my mom went missing. No one knows what happened to her. I was taken to a foster home, but it was pure misery. I left so I could form The Crew. My dream is that someday I'll find my mom.

I like the diversity in The Crew. Each one of us is unique and we all have our own stories. They're like a family to me, even though we all look different and have different backgrounds.

Here's how The Crew was formed. Lucas, June, and I have known each other for quite a while. June and I went to the same elementary and middle schools. In sixth grade, Lucas was a new student at our middle school. He had just moved from California and was a seventh grader. We all became friends. During lunch, the three of us started making plans about escaping our homes. The summer after finishing that school year, we ran away and found The Hideout. And The Crew was born.

The Hideout is our home. We stay in two boxcars. The first one is a black, rectangular one and the second one is a red caboose. They're connected on the railroad track. Trains don't pass along these rails anymore. The cars aren't in the best condition; the paint is chipped and they're both rusty. Both boxcars have ladders on the outside of them. The inside of the black boxcar contains a ladder that connects to a sort of vault, which opens and leads to the roof. We painted the inside of the cars and we adorned them with simple decorations and candles.

We all sleep in the black boxcar. The red caboose houses most of our supplies. There's plenty of space for all of us.

We build fires to cook and we find berries and other stuff to eat. June and I do most of the cooking. Maci helps us occasionally. The boys claim that it's a girl's job to cook. They can be pretty sexist sometimes.

When we're hungry, we even go into different grocery stores and eat a ton of samples. As we walk throughout a grocery store, sometimes we'll open a box or bag and eat some of the item, then leave the rest wherever. The employees don't even notice.

Other times we go dumpster diving. You'd be surprised at some of the stuff people throw away.

This is how The Crew works. We have different jobs. The first one is stealing, and the second is guarding. Guarding means guarding our home when we're away, or guarding around the place we steal from to make sure we don't get caught.

The other day, I was strolling through a nearby park. As I was passing a bench, there was a red brown leather journal left behind, still encased in cellophane. No one was in sight, so I took it.

I've decided to start my first memory book. No, this is not a diary, so please don't call it that. Diaries are written by 10-year-old girls who only write about their crushes at school and fill their pages with poorly drawn hearts. They lack substance.

Finding this journal was like destiny, as if the world wanted to read what I have to say. I'll always make sure to carry it with me, wherever I go.

Ten years from now, I'll re-read my entries and relive memories. My hope is to be able to reflect, to see how far I've made it and everything I've overcome. Things might be completely different by then.

When I'm old, I'll probably place the memory book in a time capsule. That way, someone in the year 3005 can read about my adventures.

Now that I've explained everything, back to the story.

I arrive home, out of breath, clutching the diamond necklace in my hand.

"That's a new record!" Jay yells out. "You got here in 15 minutes, 13 seconds!"

That's how we make things fun.

"Sweet. Now who wants to go sell this necklace tomorrow morning?" I ask.

Blake's hand shoots up in the air.

And if you were wondering how we make money, well, that answers your question.

Lucas comes out from behind the door and high-fives me. "Great job, K9."

"Thanks," I reply.

We all go back inside. Blake, Jay, and Lucas play a board game. Maci paints her nails and June reads. I sit and watch them all.

Sometimes I feel like none of this is right.

September 19

Lucas went to work today, which is another way we make money. He works weekends at a local candy store. Sometimes he brings home candy. Chocolate and sour candy are my favorites.

Lucas is the only one of us who drives a car. We were able to get it because of help from his older brother and gambling. That's all I'm gonna say about it. He drives a '92 coupe, 5 speed manual, with tinted windows and messed-up body paint. It looks like trash, but it's a solid whip.

Today is a school day. School days mean we spend almost the entire day at the local library. The librarians already know all of our names. Since none of us go to an actual school, we just read as many books as we can over whatever subjects. There's fiction. Non-fiction. Ancient Rome. Cars. Facts about Siberian Huskies. Maps of the world. Recipes. Computer programming. Metaphysics. Origami.

Some of it is useful, but we also fill our brains with a lot of random information. I've learned more from reading books than I ever did in school.

For the past few school days, I've been attempting to learn Italian. I only know a little bit. I'm actually fluent in Spanish.

I like school days. I like learning. I just don't admit it to The Crew.

September 21

Tragic Sun.

That's pretty much the meaning of my name.

Did my parents name me Kalamiti Sol for a reason? Am I going to be a tragedy? My life has been tragic so far. Maybe they knew exactly what I was going to experience.

This is the kind of stuff that runs through my mind. It's like a leaky faucet. No matter how hard you try to close it, it won't stop leaking.

My mom's name was Geneva. According to her, she was named after the place in Switzerland. Geneva was a place that my grandma would frequently visit, and it became one of her most favorite places in the world.

Names are important and symbolic. Whether mom's background about her name is true or not, it's still a big deal.

I'm a calamity.

I peer below the caboose and grab a wooden box out from underneath. Damn it, I'm out.

So I smoke weed. Lucas does, too. He doesn't do it as often because he doesn't want to bring that kind of stuff around the rest of The Crew.

I don't consider weed a drug, but I've experimented with different kinds of drugs and pills and stuff. My relationship with drugs is like a one-night stand. I do it once and then I never touch it again. I'd never try heroin or meth. Screw those.

Weed is the only thing I'll continue doing. I kind of stopped with the experimenting after I almost died one time. I didn't end up in a hospital, but I felt like I was dying. That was around a year ago. I don't remember much. All I remember is lying on the floor of one of the boxcars and seeing angels surrounding me, as if they were rescuing me. If you ask me, there really is a God and spiritual beings out there.

I wish I would've died. But I guess there's a reason why I'm still here. I don't really regret any of it. It's all part of growing up on the streets and learning.

A couple of weekends ago, I started sneaking out in the middle of the night. Usually I go to alleys around town. I go by the name Roxy. I make up a completely different life and hang out with a bunch of different people. Then I never see them again.

Nighttime arrives. I take out the last of my money from the wooden box.

I walk to an alley and approach a goth chick who's sitting on a dumpster. She has bloodshot eyes and tons of piercings.

"This is all I have." I take out the very last few bills from my pocket.

She puts her drink down and we exchange. I hand her the money, and she hands me the weed.

"You want a drink?" Her words are slurred.

"Sure."

She grabs a plastic cup out of the dumpster and pours some of her drink into it.

"Thanks," I say. I sit down next to her on the dumpster. "I'm Roxy."

"Ginelle."

After talking for a bit, Ginelle pulls something out of her pocket. "Here. Have these." She hands me a little bag, containing a couple of pills. I'm not sure what they are.

"Um, thanks."

"I'm here every Friday."

"I'll be here."

A goth guy comes up to Ginelle. "Who's this?" he asks her.

"Roxy," she tells him.

"I'm Damien, Ginelle's brother."

Ginelle passes him a drink. I feel kind of dizzy and I'm starting to get a headache. Without me asking, she pours more alcohol into my cup. I pretend to drink it. Whatever she gave me is hella strong and tastes like garbage.

Suddenly, flashing lights illuminate the alley. Panic ensues.

I jump off of the dumpster.

"Come on." Damien tugs at my arm. I follow him.

We dash through the maze of alleys.

He guides me through an unfamiliar neighborhood. We cut across the lawn, and he leads me to the front door of one of the houses. He unlocks the door. "Get in."

Who knows what trouble I'll get into once I'm on the other side of that door? I can't trust this guy.

"I think I'm just gonna head home." I try to walk off, but he grabs me and covers my mouth.

"Do you want to get caught?"

His breath reeks of booze.

I don't show any response.

He stares at me, studying me closely, his hand still firmly clamped over my mouth. "You're on your own." He finally lets me go and shuts the door behind him.

I run into a nearby forest. I can't see anything. It's too dark. I trip over a branch. I fall. I can't think straight. The alcohol is overpowering.

A neighborhood park is at the edge of the forest. I hide in the playground, in a tunnel on the ground.

Footsteps strike my ear drums. I cover my ears and bury my head between my knees.

How did the cops track me down?

"Kalamiti," a familiar voice whispers.

I remove my hands from my ears and look up.

"Lucas? How did you know I was here?"

"I heard you leave in the middle of the night. I've kind of been following you around. What were you thinking?"

"I came to get weed."

"Next time you want weed, just let me know and I'll get it for you." Lucas lies down. "Come here."

I lie down next to him.

He touches my face. "There's a scratch on your cheek."

"It's probably from a branch. I fell."

"You're safe now. We'll have to leave later. The cops are probably still out." He brushes my messy, tangled hair out of my eyes. "Promise me you'll stop wandering around at night on your own?"

I swallow. With all this trouble, I'm done. "I promise."

He kisses me on the forehead.

Lucas? Kissing me on the forehead? That's a first.

If you were wondering by now, Lucas and I are NOT a thing. We're just friends. And it's not one of those things where I like him, he doesn't like me, blah, blah, blah. You get the point. I don't like him that way. I don't even know if he likes me. I doubt it.

To tell you the truth, when I first met Lucas in middle school, he wasn't very attractive. Then he got older, and damn. He turned handsome and shit. I don't know if I just forgot about cooties or if I actually thought he was attractive. I bet he can get any girl he wants, so why would he want me, just the average girl?

Anyway, back to what's going on.

"Go to sleep. I'll let you know when the coast is clear," he tells me.

"I can't, Lucas. I'm dizzy."

He sighs. "You shouldn't be accepting random drinks from strangers."

I shut my eyes, but I can't sleep. My head is pounding, and I can't stop thinking about what just happened.

Who knows how much time has passed?

Finally, Lucas speaks. "Kalamiti. Time to go."

We crawl out of the tunnel and begin making the hike home.

The barely rising sun peeks through the trees.

As we walk alongside a stream, something falls out of my sweater's pocket.

Shoot. The pills.

Lucas picks the bag up from the ground. He looks me in the eye.

"So you weren't getting weed. You lied to me."

"No. I did. It's in my other pocket." I bring out the other bag.

"It doesn't matter, Kalamiti. You have pills, too. Do you really want to go down that road again?"

I don't respond.

"Let me guess. You're popping oxys and doing lines again."

"No, Lucas. I'm not. Besides, I only did that stuff once. Believe me."

He sighs. "If the cops would've caught you, you would've been in a hell of a lot of trouble for breaking curfew, underage drinking, possessing marijuana and pills, and the list goes on."

I put my hands on my hips. "What are you, a cop now?"

His expression instantly displays even more anger. He turns away from me and hurls the bag of pills into the stream. "Don't talk about cops like that."

I don't get what made him mad. It was a joke, and he's the one who mentioned cops in the first place.

He continues. "I'm really disappointed in you. These are the kinds of things we need to keep away from The Crew, especially Maci. You're going to really screw up your life if you don't stop playing around with this stuff."

"I think my life is already screwed up, don't you think?" I say softly.

He sighs. "Don't say that, Kalamiti. It's not true."

That's because you have no idea what I've been through.

He puts his hand on my shoulder. "Come on, let's get home."

At last we reach The Hideout. Time to try to get at least some sleep.

September 22

It's nighttime. We're playing board games. As usual, we all have a bit of a competition. Jay wins every round. No one can ever beat him. He's the ultimate champion.

We set up our sleeping bags. I'm about to blow out the candles, when Maci asks me a question. "Hey, Kalamiti?"

"What's up?" I reply.

"Do you miss your parents?"

I despise talking about the past. It's just way too complicated and intricate. I take a deep breath. "Why do you ask that, Maci?"

"I notice you don't seem very happy. You look upset a lot of times."

"I do miss my parents," I say slowly, "but I don't understand how that has anything to do with my happiness. That happened a long time ago."

She switches the subject. "Don't you ever feel like what we're doing is bad?"

"What do you mean by what we're doing?"

"Stealing. Shoplifting. Don't you think it's wrong?" she says, a bit too loud.

I'm about to reply, when June, Blake, Lucas, and Jay get up from their sleeping bags.

"What's going on?" asks Jay.

Before Maci can say anything, I announce, "We need to talk."

"What's this about?" asks Lucas.

"I'm tired," says Jay.

It's 2:30 in the morning. I scan the room. Lucas has his arms folded across his chest, Blake and Jay have their heads held down, and June looks like she's about to fall out of her chair. Maci's just sitting there, staring at me. She has a blank expression.

"Okay, everyone," I start. "The reason why we're arguing is because Maci and I were discussing stealing. You see, Maci was asking me if I ever felt bad or guilty about it." I pause for a second. I don't know what else to say. I'm not good with speeches.

As I pace around the boxcar, the words come to my lips. "What do you guys think about all this? Do you guys think it's wrong to steal? What do you guys think about our lives and the way we're living?"

I think. I think really hard these few seconds I have. Then I add, "I think we've all realized that we haven't given this much thought."

"I have an opinion," June starts. "I think stealing is bad if you're rich, but if you're not, then it isn't bad."

Then Lucas speaks. "Like Robin Hood. He stole from the wealthy to give to the poor."

After that, Jay adds, "If people really do need to steal, then they do it. That's why we take things, or else we wouldn't have anything."

Blake says, "Someday I'll give my stuff that I stole to someone in need. But right now we need it as much as them."

I nod in agreement. "Without the stuff we have, we would have nothing. We need to steal to be able to survive. If I hadn't have found all of you, I'd probably still be in foster care. We need to continue doing what we do to survive."

I look at Maci. "What about you, Maci? Give us your honest opinion," I speak gently. Everyone turns toward her.

"You know what I think about it? It's wrong. You guys, it's a crime! We're delinquents. I mean, look around. We take more than we need—"

"Maci—" Jay interrupts.

"Listen to me! Everybody! We don't need board games, decorations for the boxcar, or any of that stuff! If we do steal, we should only take clothes and food—"

"Maci, why don't you think about what you just said?" Lucas interrupts. "Why are you complaining about this? It's a privilege to be a part of The Crew."

Why is he being so harsh?

"Yeah, but think about it. We won't be here ten years from now. Criminals don't always get away."

Outbursts ensue as soon as the word "criminals" comes up.

Her eyes now watery, she continues, "Someday we'll all get caught and go to jail. Then our lives will be ruined. K9? Listen to me! Don't you agree with me?" she pleads.

Everyone's eyes are now focused on me. "Maci, I'm sorry. The Crew will never get caught."

Tears stream down her face.

I hate seeing her like this, but I don't want to side with her if I don't agree. "Goodnight, everyone," I say.

They all return to their sleeping bags.

What Maci says a lot of times is deep; you can't understand what she means.

Why is it bad to have all of this? It's just luck. We're pretty good stealers to have all the stuff we have.

My question will remain unanswered.

I blow out the candles. I lie down and stare at the ceiling. It's covered with glow-in-the-dark stars and a couple of planets. The first star I see, I make a wish. I wish that things in The Crew would get better and that life would get easier.

I'm not able to sleep. The whole night I can only think about that one wish.

September 23

I'm exhausted. I didn't sleep at all.

Today is a Sunday.

If you're wondering about our religious beliefs and whatnot, some of us believe in God or some form of higher power. Some of us don't believe in anything. I'm not going to go into detail.

There isn't much to do. I walk around the forest for a bit. After that I read a historical fiction book that I checked out from the library.

Maci approaches me. She just got back from church. "I need to tell you something."

I look up from my book.

"I will no longer steal. I will do everything else here. I just won't steal."

I nod. "I understand."

At that, she turns around and heads to the caboose. Talk about rebellious.

Ever since last night's argument, Maci isolated herself in the caboose. What does she even do in there? I wouldn't be able to stay locked up in a room for a whole day.

I just hope tomorrow will be better. I just hope Maci will understand that we are here whenever she needs us, that she can trust us.

I don't know if that will happen any time soon.

September 24

Maci and I are hanging out all day. I like to have bonding time with each person in The Crew.

Today's activities include visiting a local park, then the mall, and eating at the food court.

Chicago is huge. We rarely go to the downtown area. The Hideout is located on the outskirts of a suburb on the west side. Right now I'm dying to go to Millennium Park and visit the Bean.

We're home. The bus ride back from the mall felt like an eternity.

I want to get a car. I hate walking and taking the bus or train everywhere, and Lucas can't always be my chauffeur.

I'm about to take a drink from my water bottle, when Maci says something unexpected. "You're different now, K9."

Wait, me? Since when am I personally involved in her anti-stealing rebellion?

She continues, her eyes wide open. "The Crew is drowning in deep, dark water. If all of us are not careful, and if we don't swim back to the surface, it'll cost us our lives," she says.

I rest my chin on my fist. "Are you saying we're all going to die?"

Through the boxcar's open door, she stares at the sky, as if she's reading dialogue off of the clouds. "What we do now will affect our futures. Why won't you guys listen to me?"

I don't know what to say. It's not like I don't listen to her. I just don't agree. "Will you excuse me?"

I need to get away. I follow where my legs take me.

Maci scares me. When she predicts things, she's always right. What she said keeps me wondering. Are we all going to die soon? Will we all be killed? Does my future truly depend on my actions today?

I stop. I'm at a junkyard.

Where would I be right now if I wasn't with The Crew? I would be living alone on the streets or back in the system. What would things be like without The Crew, the only friends I've ever known? I would be lonely. Very lonely. Probably miserable. How lucky am I to not be in juvie right now? Very lucky. How lucky am I to have the stuff I have right now? Very lucky, indeed.

A gas station sits across the street from the junkyard, its light green and pink paint faded. Lights flicker on and off. Graffiti adorns the dumpsters and storefront.

Bingo.

The only people inside are me and the man at the register. After checking to see if he's watching, I slip a bag of gummy bears into my pocket. Stealing is second nature. Items go easily through my hands and into my pocket.

I make my way to the exit.

"Excuse me." It's the employee.

I stop in my tracks and turn around.

"You dropped money."

Phew. I pick up my one-dollar bill and leave.

The sun is beginning to set. I'm not ready to go back home.

My legs lead me to the nearest train station.

I've found a way to not have to pay for a train ticket. All I do is go to the bathroom and hide in there. Since I can't camp out in the bathroom all night, sometimes I walk from one car to another, pretending to look for a seat.

I walk down the aisle.

"Miss, do you have a ticket?"

Damn it.

I give him some change. He hands me a ticket and walks off.

I climb the narrow stairwell to the second floor and sit in the seat at the end. There's something sort of therapeutic and stress-relieving about looking out of the window on a train. Especially when it's this empty. I practically have the whole car to myself.

The train arrives downtown. The city lights are beautiful at night.

We've made it to Union Station. Not gonna lie, it's a tad bit frightening walking around the city in the dark all alone.

Sometimes I just want to get away. Get away from all my problems. It's not like I need a vacation to the beach. I just need a break from reality. Even just a walk to the park helps.

Who knows how much time has passed. The sky is pitch black and I can't see any stars.

I walk down a tranquil street. As I approach the intersection, I notice a woman holding a baby. She's sitting on the ground, against the building, next to a young girl who's probably her daughter. The daughter, who looks about 10, is holding a Styrofoam cup in her hand.

I approach them.

Without saying a word, I unzip my jacket, take it off, and wrap it around the baby. I place my one-dollar bill in the cup and hand the bag of gummy bears to the daughter. They aren't very nourishing, but it's something.

I walk off, making my way back to Union Station. Through the dense city noises, I hear "thank you" coming from the woman and the daughter.

A huge weight has been lifted from my shoulders. I'm as light as a feather. What I did was like Robin Hood, stealing from the rich and giving to the poor. I had stolen that jacket and those gummy bears, and now I've given them away.

Maybe I'll be the next Robin Hood.

September 25

"Do you ever feel like something isn't right, like something's missing in your life?" I ask June.

We're sitting at the top of the boxcar, drinking iced tea we got from the gas station.

"Can you elaborate?"

I move my straw around in circles. "Ever since Maci started with her rebellion, it's kind of gotten to me. But at the same time, I had a feeling that things aren't right, even before she said anything. Does that make any sense?"

She takes a sip. "I understand what you mean. Sometimes I think there's more to life than just being here all the time, struggling to get by. In a way, life seems so stagnant."

"Exactly."

She nods. "Like what would it be like to be in a good foster home? What would it be like to go to school again?"

And this is why we get along so well. We both always have questions running through our minds. "Do you think Maci's right? What if The Crew breaks up? What if we're all separated from each other?"

She takes a second to respond. "We all have the right to our own opinions. She might be right, she might not. Even then, we're family and we can always find a way to keep in touch if something were to happen."

I smile. "You're the first person I've talked to about this. Thanks."

She smiles. "Let's try not to think so far into the future. For now, let's enjoy the present."

She hugs me. I'm already feeling a lot better. Talking to the right person can completely change the course of your day.

September 26

Lucas and I are going to hang with some friends from around the corner.

They're four guys. Two of them are twins Felix and Armando. The other two are Bruce and Nat. All four of them are slightly older than me and Lucas.

We've arrived at Felix's apartment, where we usually have our meetups.

"Duke. Roxy. Welcome back," says Felix.

Those are our go-to fake names.

We take a seat at opposite ends of the table, which were

the last two seats left open. Marijuana smoke crowds the dim room.

Nat brings out bottles of beer and tequila, along with some glasses for each of us. I never actually drink here.

The reason we come over is to gamble and take at least some money home. Usually we play poker or some other card games. Lucas is a pro at it. In the past he has won a lot of money.

Felix places an empty bottle right in the center of the table. Looks like we're playing spin the bottle, something we haven't done with them.

So far, the game is slow. The dares are a bunch of stupid stuff like chug a beer or get locked in the closet for five minutes. The bottle hardly lands on me. I'm bored, and no one has actually bet any money. Must be a pregame.

Felix slams his shot glass down. His other hand reaches for the bottle in the center. As the bottle spins, tequila makes its way around the table, refilling the empty glasses.

The bottle slows to a stop, pointing at Bruce.

"Truth or dare?" asks Felix.

Bruce says, "Dare."

"Alright then." Felix puts his hands together. "I dare you to go into the closet with Roxy. You have ten minutes to do whatever the hell you want with her. And we all know what that means!"

The gang bursts into a storm of laughter.

I'm not about to get locked up in a closet with some dude I barely know. I don't even want to imagine what he might do to me.

Lucas interjects. "What? No. She's not gonna do that."

Felix blows out smoke at Lucas' face. "Why not? She's the only girl here. She's bound to be an easy target."

The intoxicated Bruce staggers out of his chair. His sweaty hand touches my chin. I turn my face away.

"Come on." He grabs my arm and pulls me out of my chair.

I slap his flushed face. "Touch me again and watch what's gonna happen to you."

Another storm of laughter.

"Leave her alone." Lucas gets up from his spot and stands face to face with Bruce.

Lucas gives me the look, the one that means flee and go home. I don't want to leave. What if something happens to him?

He looks at me again, and I know I need to listen. I make a run for it, through the front door, out of the apartment complex. I continue running through the alley, the sound of footsteps close behind me.

I arrive at the library, a public place where they can't do me harm.

"Everything okay, Kalamiti?" It's Bonnie, one of the librarians.

I nod. "Yeah, I just needed to get out of the house for a bit. I got into an argument with my parents."

She smiles. "Let me know if you need anything."

After scanning the non-fiction aisle, I grab a book about scarlet macaws and sit down in a beanbag chair.

I can't even focus on reading. Lucas is still out there, possibly being harmed.

Thirty minutes have passed. I take the long way to The

Hideout. By the time I reach home, the sky is painted with an orange and pink glow.

June is standing outside the boxcars, arms folded across her chest. "You two hung out with those losers again, didn't you? It's not worth fifty bucks."

"Yeah," I admit. "But this will probably be the last time."

Worry fills her eyes. "Where's Lucas?" She covers her mouth with her hand.

I was hoping he would beat me here.

I explain everything to her. The rest of The Crew is inside playing checkers. We decide not to let them know about anything, so they won't worry.

I sit at the caboose's entrance, with my arms and head resting on my knees. It's beginning to get dark.

Too much time has passed. Something had to have happened to him.

A hand touches my shoulder. It's Lucas.

He hugs me. "Hey, I'm okay."

"I was so worried. I couldn't help thinking about what could've happened to you."

He's hurt.

"Your lip." I touch it. He moves my hand away.

"Don't worry about it." He lies down on a blanket that covers the floor. He claims he's okay, but he's wincing in pain.

"Lucas, I'm sorry. This is my fault."

"No, it's not. I wasn't going to let a couple of guys disrespect you."

"You didn't have to do that for me."

"Are you kidding? You and The Crew are my family. I would do anything for you guys."

I sigh. "I owe you. For like everything you've done for me."

"You don't owe me anything. Besides, we're kind of even now. You're not the only one who's always getting into trouble. I guess I get into trouble, too."

I manage to smile. "Do you need ice? I can run down to the gas station."

"No. You could do me a nice favor, though."

"What is it?"

"Lie down here with me."

I lie down next to him. It's been a long day and I'm so relieved he made it home.

We lay there in silence.

Soon we fall asleep. And let me tell you, it's the most peaceful and best sleep I have gotten in a long time.

September 27

"Wanna go on a walk with me?"

I look up from my book. Standing in front of me is Lucas. The rest of The Crew is out and about.

"Shouldn't you be resting?" I ask.

He shrugs.

We close the door behind us and begin walking on the railroad tracks.

"Kalamiti, we need to talk about something."

Compared to last night, his lip looks better. "What is it?"

"I think it's best if you get a job. Money has been tight."

"I don't think I can get one. A lot of places won't hire a 15-year-old."

"Security has been tough. We're more likely to get caught

stealing. Jay and Blake have noticed that it's been harder nowadays."

I stare at the ground. "We have some savings, don't we?"

He sighs. "Yeah, about that, it's gone."

"What do you mean it's gone? I'm pretty sure it was there the last time I checked."

He takes a second to respond. "Please don't be mad, but I took it with me yesterday. And you know, I kind of got jumped and the guys ended up taking it all from me."

"Why would I be mad about that? I'm just glad you're okay."

Seriously, money doesn't concern me. I don't think we even had a lot saved, anyway.

He places a hand on my shoulder. "I'll start saving more from the candy store."

I look around and realize how far we've gotten along the tracks. "Maybe we should head back now."

As we turn around, I trip over a railroad tie and lose my balance.

Lucas catches me. "Got you."

I'm too surprised and confused at what just happened that I don't even know what to say. I'm pretty sure I'm bright red.

He laughs. "Follow me."

We veer off the tracks, heading in the direction we came from.

The boxcars are in sight again.

He sits down under the shade of a tree.

I continue to stand. "The Hideout isn't that far. We should head back."

"I'm tired. Come sit with me."

I do as I'm told. "I told you to rest."

"I know, I know."

I tilt my head back against the tree trunk. I close my eyes and take a deep breath in. Crickets are chirping, bees are buzzing, and a bird's wings are taking flight. Nature is beautiful.

"Kalamiti." Lucas interrupts my thoughts.

I get so caught up with my surroundings that I don't even notice he's been saying my name repeatedly. I open my eyes and look at him. "Sorry. What is it?"

"I feel like I need to tell you this." He looks me in the eyes. "I—"

"Kalamiti!"

Jay, Maci, Blake, and June are running toward us.

I stand up and dust the dirt off of my clothes.

"We found a whole supply of berries!" Blake yells out.

I walk away from the tree to join my friends. Lucas mutters something, but I can't make out what it is.

June says, "You should check if they're safe to eat."

I squeeze one of the berries between my fingers. I hold it up to my nose and sniff it. "They're good. Take me to where you found them."

As I follow them, I turn around to see if Lucas is following, but he isn't. I hope he takes my advice and gets some rest.

Blake, Jay, and Maci lead the way.

June whispers to me, "Is Lucas stoned?"

I laugh. "I have no clue, but he is acting a bit strange."

We've made it to the berry collection.

"Well guys, looks like we're having berries for dinner tonight!" says Jay. We laugh, since we could probably have a week's supply with how many we've found.

We do our signature handshake.

Gosh, I love these guys.

September 28

I take a bag filled with berries and leftovers and I make my way to the park.

I'm meeting up with Alessandro. He's my half-brother. After Dad's death, my mom hooked up with some man. She ended up pregnant and gave birth to a baby boy. The dad has custody of him, but it's a bad home.

I've tried to be there for Alessandro as much as I could. I wish I would've brought him with me when I had formed The Crew, but he was way too little back then, and I couldn't handle all of that responsibility.

I don't even consider him my half-brother anymore, I consider him my brother. I don't care if we have different dads. He's the only family I have left. When they didn't love him, I did. And I always will.

Alessandro sits at a picnic table, waiting for me.

"I brought you food." I sit down next to him.

He's covered in bruises. He's only nine. He doesn't deserve this.

"Thanks, Kal," He opens the bag and begins eating.

"Why don't you come join us? I can take care of you now."

"I can't. What if I run away and they go looking for me? They'll find us all. We might become even more separated."

I sigh. "One day you're going to come with me. You won't be there forever."

"I'm gonna be okay, Kal. You've already helped me enough."

I give him a hug and I kiss his head. "If you ever need me, you know where to find me."

We part ways.

September 29

It's early in the morning. I don't even know why I'm awake.

I'm the only one in the boxcar. I know for sure that Lucas is at work, but where is everyone else?

I step out and stroll around the boxcar. The weather is getting chilly. Leaves are starting to change colors. Fall is here and before we know it, winter will hit and there'll be mounds of snow.

The smell of cigarette smoke startles me.

I walk into the woods and there's a slim figure sitting beneath a tree. As I step closer, I realize it's Blake.

He's holding a cigarette in his hand. A pack is on the ground next to him. Puffs of smoke are polluting the air, like storm clouds. Except storm clouds are good for the environment.

When I'm finally close enough to him, I pick up the pack and confront him. "What are you doing?" I ask.

"What does it look like?" he snaps back.

I hold up the pack. "Where did you get these from?"

"A friend."

"Look, you're only 14. You shouldn't be smoking. It's a nasty habit."

"Stop trying to be so innocent. You're the one who's done drugs. You're a hypocrite."

"But I stopped, Blake. Don't be like me."

"Don't be like you? I wish I could be like you! And June and Lucas! You guys think you're in charge of everyone. You keep everything from me. You keep everything from Maci and Jay. I'm practically the same age as you guys and I'm left out of everything. You and Lucas always sneak out at night and drink and party and have fun. I want to be included in that."

He must've been keeping this in for a while. I didn't know he felt excluded.

"I don't think you want to be like us. The streets are dangerous. We're trying to keep you guys out of trouble."

"Lucas always has to save your ass. You just always have to run into trouble. If something happens to The Crew, it's going to be because of you. You're going to ruin it for everyone."

There's a lump in the back of my throat. Blake has never been this rude to me before. "Nothing's going to happen to The Crew, okay? You and Maci both need to stop predicting things."

"You're gonna be the reason why I'm going to end up alone and begging on the streets again."

"Blake, stop—"

"I'm serious. Get your act together before you ruin it for all of us."

I run off with the pack of cigarettes in my pocket. I walk into the boxcar and June is in there.

"What's wrong?" she asks.

I shake my head. "Nothing. Just, here," I take the pack

out of my pocket and hand it to her. "Blake had those. Can you get rid of them?"

She sighs. "Now I know why you're upset. Don't worry about it, Kalamiti. Blake said some pretty awful things to me, too. He's been so moody lately."

I laugh. "Yeah, it's pretty bad."

"Sooner or later he'll realize he doesn't want to grow up and he sure as hell doesn't want to be like us."

I smile, reminiscing about the days I used to wish I was a grownup. Not that I'm a grownup now, but still. Boy, was I stupid.

I look at June and I can tell she's thinking the same exact thing.

October 1

I'm spending the day with Jay at the Lego store downtown. I've gotta admit, it's pretty sweet.

Talk about a zillion Legos.

Jay's looking at all the different models, when I get a crazy thought.

"Dude. Imagine if there was like a ball pit, filled completely with Legos," I comment.

"Now that would be awesome! Except imagine doing a belly flop in that thing. That would hurt," he says.

We laugh.

"But you know what would be worse?" he asks.

"What?"

"Imagine if the whole store flooring was made out of

Legos. And you weren't allowed to enter with shoes or socks on."

"They'd lose all their customers because no one wants to step on a Lego."

Jay decides to buy one of the models with some money that Lucas has given him.

We arrive home and everyone helps build the model.

You know what they all say: it's all fun and games until someone gets hurt. Unfortunately, Blake steps on a Lego. Everyone thinks it's funny except for him.

Karma.

October 2

For the past few days, Lucas has looked upset and sick. He seems to be doing better today.

"Does it still hurt?" I ask him.

"No," he says.

"That's good."

"Kalamiti, have you been seeing someone?"

I grimace. "What? No."

"Then why have you been leaving a lot lately? And then not explain why? There have been a couple of times you've left with food and come back empty-handed."

I don't want him to know about Alessandro. The past doesn't matter anymore. "I don't want to talk about it."

He doesn't reply.

I say, "Maybe you need some more rest so you can fully recover."

"It's not that. That doesn't bother me anymore."

"Then what is it?"

"It's complicated. You wouldn't understand."

I guess we're both keeping things from each other.

October 5

I want to drive instead of walk or take public transportation everywhere.

At the library, I search on the computer for cars.

"How about that one?" Lucas jokingly points at a brand new, $25,000 car.

I laugh. "We can't afford that."

"We can't afford anything," he replies.

True.

We continue searching. Jay peeks his head over my shoulder to help. All we find are three vehicles that can run. Some are way above my budget. Actually, I'm pretty sure we have like no money since the savings we had is gone.

"I give up," I say.

"You don't even know how to drive yet," says Lucas.

What he doesn't know is that I *do* know, just not very well.

Lucas squeezes my shoulder. "I've gotta go to work. See you guys later."

Who am I kidding? I, Kalamiti Sol, have zero dollars to my name. In fact, if I had to repay all the stuff I've stolen, all the stuff I've taken for granted, I'd be in debt for the rest of my life.

That's when I hatch a plan.

So then, I wait until nighttime. I make sure The Crew is asleep.

I leave home and I head to a rental car parking lot.

A freaking gorgeous black BMW Z4 catches my eye.

I grab the set of keys inside of the car. I start it and drive off. As I approach the exit, a gate is blocking it. I drive around, searching for an alternative way out.

I'm on the road home.

I've only driven with Lucas twice. That's why he thinks I can't drive. For practice, I've secretly driven his car around at night without him knowing.

I step on it too much. Suddenly, I'm going 60 in a 35.

I accidentally move the levers and the windshield wipers start moving. My blinkers are on. I slam the brakes and come to a rough stop.

I'm trying to find a way to turn off all the lights and windshield wipers. Just then, The Crew comes out of the boxcar. I step out of the BMW.

They all have a bunch of different expressions.

Blake's eyebrows are furrowed, Lucas has his hands in his hair, and Jay seems impressed. June looks like she's about to faint. Maci stares at the ground, avoiding eye contact with me.

"Hey," I say, "what's up?"

"If you're trying to make us laugh, it's not going to work," June bursts out.

"What are you talking about?" I ask.

"You think it's funny that you just stole a car? Well we're not laughing with you, Kalamiti!" she yells.

"Who said I was laughing?" I'm trying to keep my cool, but The Crew is really ticking me off. I mean, come on, isn't this at least somewhat funny?

"You're doing that one face. The one that you always do when you're about to laugh." Blake speaks this time.

"Oh, come on, you guys, K9 has a car. Now we can all enjoy it together," Jay interrupts. He joins my side.

"See, Jay's cool about this. Now what about you guys? Are you all just gonna stand there?" I ask.

"Jay! Are you that stupid? Kalamiti won't share that car. She only thought about herself when she stole it. I know you too well, Kalamiti," June says.

"That car only fits two people. Keep that in mind," says Blake.

Jay returns to The Crew's side, shaking his head.

"Criminal!" Maci yells.

All of a sudden, police sirens are blaring in the distance.

Blake gets up in my face and points a finger. "See? I told you! You're gonna ruin it for all of us!"

"Everyone, get inside!" says Lucas.

While June rounds everyone up, Lucas grabs my arm. "Let's go."

He takes the driver's side and I hop in the passenger side.

As we're driving down the road, Lucas says, "I can't believe you had the guts to do this."

I want to laugh but I know it's not the right time to do so.

Lucas looks in the rearview mirror. "They're catching up."

"What are we gonna do?" I finally speak.

"I'm gonna save you. Again."

"You don't have to do that for me. Blake had a point. You can't always get me out of trouble."

"Yeah? Well, Blake is an asshole. I don't care how many times I have to save you or anyone else in The Crew. That's what we do for each other."

We make a couple of sharp turns.

After turning into an alley, we drive into a field. "I'm going to try to lose them. We can abandon the car somewhere and run for it."

We continue to drive through the field; the grass is getting taller and denser.

Lucas slams the brakes. "Fuck."

There's a stream cutting across our path.

We get out of the car and slam the doors.

"Hurry. Let's move," he tells me, as he's making his way through the stream. The water is up to his waist.

I stand at the edge. "No, Lucas."

He stops. "What?"

"You go alone. If we both go, we'll both get busted. I'll stay behind so they won't follow you."

"No. I'm not leaving you here."

"Blake was right. You can't always save me. I need to face this battle on my own."

He walks out of the stream. "I can't believe I'm doing this," he says to himself. "Good luck, K9." He hugs me.

He quickly heads back into the water. This time, he swims off. I watch as he reaches the other side. The police sirens sound closer than ever.

I hop in the driver's seat and wait.

October 6

I'm at a police station. Police officers interrogated me all morning.

Lucas is visiting me before I get transported to a

detention center in Springfield, Illinois. I'm going to be miles away.

A police officer escorts me to a room. Lucas is on the other side of a glass barrier that sits between us.

The officer leaves.

I pick up the phone in my cubicle.

He speaks first. "I'm sorry."

"Don't be. It was my choice."

He sighs. "So what's going to happen now?"

"I'm gonna be taken to some detention center in Springfield. I'll be there for a year."

"Springfield? For a year? K9, I'll bail you out."

"No. We don't have any money. And I don't think I have a choice."

"A year is too long."

"I know," I pause. "They found out I don't actually live with parents or a guardian so I'm going to be set up in foster care again. When I get out of camp, of course."

He doesn't say anything. I can barely look into his eyes.

"I need you to do me a favor, though," I say.

"What is it?"

"You need to find Alessandro and tell him that I'm going to be gone. But that I'm safe and everything will be okay. He lives in the neighborhood near The Hideout. It's a bright blue house. You can't miss it."

"So that's the guy you've been seeing? Why should I even tell him, huh?"

"No, Lucas! You don't understand."

"Then tell me why I should tell him."

The birth of The Crew was the day the past died with

me. "I can't. But I can promise you that if you don't tell him, I'm going to hate you for the rest of my life." Anger is pulsing through my veins.

We sit there in silence. I make eye contact with him for a final time. I slam the phone down and I walk out of the room with the officer.

Time to leave everything behind.

October 7

Day 1 in Springfield, Illinois.

They made me put on an orange suit. Since it's cold, I'm wearing a long-sleeved grey shirt under it.

What sucks is that they took my belongings away, including my memory book, small backpack, and the clothes I was wearing.

The two most important objects in my life are my gold sun necklace and my memory book. At least they didn't take my necklace away.

I miss the feel of the journal's leather. For now, I'm writing in a yellow spiral notebook that they provided for schoolwork. Once I get out of here, I'll staple or glue the pages into the journal.

Hopefully, The Crew will find a way to communicate with me.

I won't be leaving this place until October 7th of next year.

October 8

Fuck this place.

October 13

Sorry I haven't written in a few days. I was taking time to adjust.

Instead of juvie or the juvenile detention center, I'm going to refer to it as camp. Maybe that'll make it bearable.

Here's an overview of things so far: daily activities consist of duties and schoolwork. Community service, group time, one-on-one discussions with a camp counselor, simple worksheets, that kind of stuff.

There's a hall of dorms for girls and another hall of dorms for boys. Most dorms fit four to eight bunks. I'm in a room with eight bunks. We've got communal bathrooms where unfortunately I can't drop a load or shower in peace.

Other than that, there's not much to share. What can you expect from some bland building whose walls are made of white-painted cinder blocks? It's like a combination of jail and a hospital.

I'm angry I'm here, so I don't feel like writing anymore. You get the picture. This place blows.

October 15

Each week I'm allowed one phone call. I dialed Lucas' cell phone number.

He didn't answer.

Maybe the police found them and placed them all in foster care.

I need to stop thinking this way.

Maybe they're safe.

But maybe they're not.

October 17

The one-on-one discussions with a camp counselor are awkward.

During my sessions, I've been making stuff up. There's no way I'm going to share the truth about The Crew, my family history, or experiences. All they know is my real name, birthdate, and any of that government information.

I think my camp counselor can tell I'm lying.

The other day she asked me why I took the BMW. *I don't know, you tell me*, I thought to myself. Isn't she supposed to be the expert? How am I supposed to know why I do what I do?

October 18

No calls.

No letters.

Nada.

October 21

So today I went to some school to do community service.

One word: paperwork. Office staff left a giant stack on the counter. It's the kind you see a cartoon character carry, half the paper being dropped behind them or being lost to the wind.

They didn't explain how to organize it or anything. I asked one of the office ladies for help, but she told me to figure it out myself.

That's when I yelled at her.

A camp counselor pulled out what looked like a Bible, only to immediately skip to a page and tell me that I broke Rule #2: Respect the authority.

I ended up being transported back to camp early. My punishment was to get on my knees, face the wall, and balance two books in each hand for an hour. What kind of 1970s punishment is that?

I have a feeling this won't be the last time I break the rules.

October 22

The food here is horrible.

Breakfast is usually sausage on a stale biscuit. Lunch is a cheese sandwich and fruit. Dinner is usually the same as lunch or something similar. Sometimes we have this nasty looking soup. I'll never try a drop of it. Soup isn't supposed to be some thick, greenish concoction. To drink, we always have water and Kool-Aid. Without sugar.

I hate Kool-Aid. Especially without sugar.

If we're lucky, or if we've been good, we get dessert. Dessert is banana pudding.

I hate banana pudding.

As you can see, I'm a picky eater. I prefer me and June's sizzling, fire-cooked meals and our signature melt-in-your-mouth s'mores. The hand-picked berries always hit the spot. We'd score the jackpot when we'd find unopened to-go boxes packed with restaurant food in the dumpsters, too. The food here can't even compare.

I miss The Crew.

October 24

No calls, no letters. I'm not expecting them anyway.

I officially have no friends.

I officially have no family.

I'm all alone.

October 25

We got banana pudding today. Yuck.

Whenever I have food I don't want to eat, I give it to Isa. She's only eleven. Sometimes I give her my entire meal. Whenever I give her food, she says, "God bless you." We talk to each other in Spanish so the counselors won't understand what we're saying. There are a few other Spanish-speaking campers.

Wanna know why she's even in this place? She stole food

for her family and got caught. Her family had just gotten evicted from their home after her father was deported. Isa's mother had to care for five children. Isa was just trying to help her family. She doesn't deserve to be here.

From the conversations I've heard, some of the people are here because of suspensions or expulsions from school. One of them was for throwing desks at school as a prank. Another person is here because they got caught with their dad's pills at school.

Being locked up in a place like this isn't going to help. I bet half of these people didn't do anything wrong. They're all just victims of life's pitfalls.

God, help them.

October 28

Earlier today I had the chance to call Alessandro. I was happy to hear his voice.

He told me Lucas told him. I'm relieved, or else I really would've hated Lucas.

Other than Lucas, no one knows I have a half-brother. No one in The Crew knows the history of Kalamiti Sol before the creation of The Crew. I'm ashamed of the past, and I can't bring myself to tell them all the details.

Once I get out of this mess, I'll save Alessandro from that awful home. And then he can finally be where he belongs. With The Crew.

October 29

When no one's looking, I get on a computer.

I'm about to log on social media to message June, when someone taps my shoulder.

Great. A supervisor.

She gives me a really long and unnecessary lecture.

It's my second offense. I don't even want to know what happens on the third.

I broke Rule #8: Internet can only be used with permission.

This is bull.

For my punishment, I have to carry three books in each hand. This time for two hours.

I'm not allowed to eat lunch. I can't eat dinner either. What I'm required to do for the rest of the day is stay in my dorm.

That's what I get for trying to contact my family.

For the first time, I actually miss cheese sandwiches, fruit, and Kool-Aid. I'm starving.

I can't believe I'm saying this, but I even miss the banana pudding.

There, I said it.

October 31

It's Halloween.

Camp is the same as usual.

If I wasn't here, I would have been trick-or-treating with

The Crew in the rich neighborhoods. I was planning on dressing up as a cat this year.

They gave us candy after dinner. It's not much, but at least we got something.

November 2

I'm gonna miss Isa. She's leaving camp on the fifth. She'll finally be back with her family.

I wonder what Thanksgiving and Christmas and New Year's will be like here.

I can't explain how much I miss The Crew. I wish I could spend the holidays with them.

Maybe if I behave, they'll let me out early.

November 4

After lunch we're bussed to a nearby community garden.

My eyes hurt from the broad daylight. It's my first time outside in what seems like forever. At least the weather is nice.

We're helping maintain the garden beds. We have to pull out weeds, water plants, help harvest, and other stuff. I don't really see this as a punishment. It's actually quite fun.

I'm surprised at how much work we're putting in. Winter will be here in no time. You would think all of the plants would be dead by now.

While everyone cleans up, I walk over to the far end of the gated area. A beautiful sunflower plot occupies the space.

The sunflowers have dried up and lost most of their color, yet they're still standing tall. They give me hope.

A brief breeze sweeps through. One sunflower appears to wave at me with its fuzzy, heart-shaped leaves. I can't help but smile. That's the first time I've smiled since I've been locked up.

Then I hear the unwanted call, the one that means it's time to board the bus. I guess this was good while it lasted.

November 5

Isa's leaving. I can't believe it's already the fifth.

Lunchtime comes around. She doesn't say much. She's usually pretty quiet.

After we eat, Isa picks up her belongings from the office.

I accompany her as far as they let me. Glass doors come between us and the bus waiting outside. Supervisors and camp counselors stand next to the bus, saying goodbye to campers.

I say, "I guess this is goodbye."

Tears begin to roll down her face. They aren't just sad tears, they're happy ones, too. Freedom. She'll be back with her family.

"I'll miss you, Isa."

A supervisor calls for her to hurry up and board the bus.

She hugs me. While hugging me, she chokes out, "God bless you, Kalamiti. You won't be here very long."

I watch the bus drive down the road, kicking up gravel and leaving a trail of dust behind. I keep watching until I can't see it anymore.

November 8

I can't stand being locked up in this place. If I can sneak out of one of the back doors, I can probably get a few seconds of fresh air.

To my surprise, the door is unlocked. What fools.

The fresh air feels amazing. I stand there for a few moments, just basking in it.

I take a seat in the grass. I don't know how much longer I can put up with this place.

The door slams wide open, revealing a supervisor. He forces me to stand. My arms are clasped together and I'm escorted back into the building.

I broke Rule #150: Only go outside when allowed. I also broke Rule #43: No running outside unless required or told to do so. And I broke Rule #1: Escaping should never be tried; action will be taken. In total I received three more strikes today.

For the first two rules I broke, I had to run a couple of laps around the building. Just my luck, it started to rain.

For "trying to escape," they had me do the obstacle course in the back of the building. I guess this is supposed to be like boot camp or something. To me, it's more like a playground, not a punishment.

I wobbled through tires, climbed a few rock climbing walls, went through these monkey bar type of things, swung down a rope from the top of a telephone pole, and other stuff like that. By the end of the course, my orange suit was completely caked in mud.

Another part of the escaping punishment is that I was

moved to an isolated cabin on the top floor. I can't leave the room unless I'm told to do so. It's like solitary confinement.

Oh well, you only live once.

November 10

At this point I'm not expecting communication from anybody.

I'm upset and worried. Upset because The Crew hasn't contacted me, worried because The Crew might be in danger. They might need my help.

Are they okay? Were they caught by the police? Are they still living in The Hideout? Do they miss me? Did they forget about me?

What if they were trying to get rid of me? What if they were trying to get me busted?

But that doesn't make sense. Lucas tried helping me.

Who knows? Nowadays I just can't trust anybody.

November 12

While waiting in line for dinner, a fellow male camper grabbed my ass.

My reaction? I pushed him into a table, causing it to collapse to the ground.

Guess who got in trouble? I did.

They made me apologize to the punk because he got hurt when the table collapsed. They also made me clean the cafeteria after dinner.

He walked away with no punishment. I hate it here.

November 14

Everyone's required to go through the obstacle course. Apparently, we have to work as a "team." Yeah, right.

I ask Chief if I can go through it more than once and he says not to taunt him.

It's 5 a.m. and it's freezing and dark out.

After waiting for my turn to go, I begin going through the obstacle course. While at the top of the telephone pole, a crazy idea arises. As I'm holding onto the rope, I twist it over and swing down the opposite side.

I use my body weight to push me further, and I barely manage to pass over the barbed wire fence. My hands let go of the rope and I stumble as I land on the ground.

I'm out. Campers inside the fence clap and cheer.

I dash into the forest. I can probably make it to a train station. From there, I can return to Chicago.

And I'll be free!

Footsteps are sounding closer and closer. Flashlight beams appear out of nowhere.

I hide behind some bushes. Security guards run right past me.

As I leave the safety of the bushes and run in a different direction, a beam of light blinds me. I try to run back the way I came from, but two security guards are up ahead.

I'm tackled to the ground, a knee jamming into my back. My arms are pulled tautly behind me. Cold handcuffs tighten around my wrists.

"Alright, let's take her in!"

* * *

Chief's office.

I'm dead meat.

"You know, I've never liked you from the start," says Chief.

I don't say anything. There's nothing to say. I don't care if he doesn't like me.

"I've never had anyone try escaping," he says.

Fluorescent lights reflect off of his polished, bald head. My eyes and attention are drawn to it.

I finally speak. "It's called thinking outside the box."

He stares at me.

I smirk. "I just outsmarted you."

"You've been breaking the rules since day one." He's holding a manila folder that probably contains all of my records.

I switch the subject. "Before giving me a punishment, I could help. There are a few things I'd improve about this whole place so that you won't ever have anyone like me again."

He stops pacing around his office and raises an eyebrow, cuing me to continue.

"For starters, shorten the rope. It's so easy for someone to escape that way."

"Thank you, Captain Obvious."

I want to laugh, but I know I shouldn't. "You should raise the fence a couple of feet, and also make sure that the doors are actually locked. That way escaping is harder."

"That's right. How do you come up with this stuff?"

"Like I said, I think outside the box." *It's called common sense, you shithead.*

He finally takes a seat at his desk across from me. "Thank you for the suggestions. Clearly you've brought awareness to some failures in our security." He shuffles and straightens out the stack of forms from my folder. "You've only been here for a month and you already have multiple strikes. I get it, you don't want to be here. Nobody does. If you keep breaking rules, we're going to have to extend your sentence."

My eyes open wide. I shake my head. "No. No, that's not happening."

"Then I suggest you start thinking before you act. Good behavior can lead to an early release. Your friend Isa was able to leave early."

I nod.

He signs a form, a perfect adult signature in black ink, then adds it to the manila folder. "I'm gonna need you to run two laps every morning at 4 a.m. for the next three days. You'll be assisting with cleaning and repairs around the building, too."

"Deal." I extend my hand, and he firmly shakes it.

"You're a smart girl. Stop getting yourself into trouble. I don't want to see you in my office again."

"Yes, sir."

That was not bad at all.

November 15

Because of my punishment, I've been up since 4 a.m. My day started with two laps around the building, like I was told to do.

I spent my morning deep cleaning. They were shitty

tasks, like scrubbing toilets. I broke a sweat from how much I did.

I'm finally catching a break right now, before doing my schoolwork.

What a day.

November 17

I just thought of another idea for change around here. Chief needs to know.

His office is nearby the cafeteria. Without knocking, I barge right in.

He looks up at me from his desk, then balls up a piece of paper and throws it at me. "I thought I said I never wanted to see you in my office again?"

Under the doorway, I say, "One last suggestion."

He raises an eyebrow.

"About the food … forget about cheese sandwiches and get rid of the banana pudding. Oh, and add sugar to the Kool-Aid. Please. But the breakfast can pass." I can't help smiling.

Shaking his head, he replies, "You know, Sol, I never thought I'd say this, but I think I'm starting to like you."

He grins.

November 19

Starting today, the barbed wire fence is being taken down. The new fence is coming in sometime this week.

For the first time, we're having burgers for lunch.

A few campers have approached me and mentioned my escape. Some of them asked me for tips on how to get on Chief's good side.

Be yourself? Offer ideas and solutions? I don't know, it just sort of happened.

I really don't want to make new friends. The only friend I had here was Isa, but now she's gone. We're all gonna leave this place eventually, so it's not like they'll be around for the long run. I don't want to get attached to anyone.

No matter what changes occur around here, I still have a burning desire to go home. Maybe I can sweet talk Chief into letting me have an early release. I wouldn't be able to return to The Hideout, though. I'd be placed in a new foster home, one that could end up being worse than this place. It's like a double-edged sword.

November 20

Community service for today was picking up trash at a local park.

Some campers and I finished picking up our share, so we walked over to the playground and started playing.

A few supervisors came up and talked to us individually.

"Sol, that's another strike for you." She pulled out a folder. "Oh, you troublemaker," she started. "You've collected a lot of strikes."

"What rule did I break this time?" I asked.

"Rule #96: No horseplay."

"Horseplay?"

"Sorry, Sol, but I'm going to need you to run five laps around the building when we get back."

The other campers on the playground received the same punishment as I did, so we all ran our laps together.

I've already been running in the mornings from my other punishment. Who knows how many miles I've been running every day.

The camp directors should reevaluate their discipline system. This whole rule list makes me want to see how many rules I can break.

I thought the whole point of camp was to educate kids and teenagers to prevent them from committing crime in the future. How are these rules supposed to help us? I don't think I've learned anything from my time here.

Running five laps wasn't too bad. I guess I'm already too used to these punishments.

November 21

Today's my sixteenth birthday. I wish I could celebrate with The Crew.

This is the worst birthday ever.

After finishing my duties late, I return to my cabin. A small cardboard box is sitting on my cot.

I open it, revealing a slice of chocolate cake, a card, and a golden candle.

> To Kalamiti Sol,
> Happy Birthday.

Someone here gives out cake for people's birthdays. That's nice of them.

I stick the golden candle into the cake. There's nothing to light it up with, which doesn't surprise me.

I wish out loud, "I wish someone could get me out of this place." I blow out the imaginary flame.

Within seconds, the cake is gone. It was surprisingly good.

Can't sleep. Sugar rush.

November 22

Knocking on the door, followed by the sound of jingling keys, wakes me up.

I sit up in my cot and rub my half-closed eyes.

The heavy door swings open. "Ms. Sol, pack your belongings and come with me," says the security guard.

Other than the clothes on my back, I don't have much with me.

Why would they need me this early? Someone either snitched on me for something stupid, or I'm being allowed to return to the dorms downstairs.

The security guard leads me to the front office, opens the door for me, then leaves. The receptionist hands me some forms to sign. Still half-asleep, I lazily sign my name on the line. She unlocks a cabinet and returns my belongings to me.

"A relative of yours is waiting in the lobby for you. You're free to go," she says.

A relative of mine? It can't be. Other than Alessandro, I don't have anyone left…

I reach the other side of the door.

It's my grandmother.

"Nonna?"

She gets up from the chair and hugs me. "I have so many questions for you," she starts. "But we can talk in the car."

Once in the car, I buckle my seatbelt and ask, "So where to?"

"To my home in San Jose, California."

What?

* * *

So, apparently, I kind of have to move in with Nonna. That's the only reason they let me out. She's like my guardian. It was noted in the forms I signed, which I didn't bother reading.

"Nonna?"

"Yes?"

"You came all the way from California just to get me?"

"Of course, you're my only granddaughter."

"How did you know I was here?"

"A few days ago I received a call from the Springfield Detention Center telling me Kalamiti Sol was there. Now you answer my question. What have you done to get yourself into that place?"

"I kind of stole a car."

"Kind of? No. You definitely did." One of her hands holds the steering wheel while the other is on her forehead. "So tell me what you've been up to all these years."

"I've been living with my friends. We live in some boxcars on an abandoned railroad. We would steal food and stuff so we could survive."

"Aren't those kids a bad influence on you?"

"No, it's the other way around. I convinced them to steal with me."

"Oh, Kalamiti. This has to end. You need to find a brighter path to walk upon."

"Well, I decided to move with you, so that's a start."

"Because you legally had to, not because you want to."

I switch the subject. "To be honest, I thought you were dead by now."

She rolls her eyes. "I'm 55. My hair may be all grey, but I'm not that old."

We're quiet the rest of the drive.

"Turn here," I say. It feels good to be cruising down familiar streets.

In only a matter of minutes, I'm going to see The Crew again. How am I going to explain to them that I'm not staying?

Nonna pulls over to the side of the road.

"Wait here," I say.

I reach the entrance to the boxcar and I knock.

June opens the door. "Kalamiti?" She gives me a hug.

Everyone rushes to the doorway. Questions stem from all directions.

"How did you get here?"

"Where have you been?"

"Why are you wearing an orange suit?"

"Guys," I start, "guys!" They all stop. "I missed you all too, but I'm not staying."

"What do you mean?" Maci asks.

"Nonna got me out of camp and I'm moving with her to San Jose."

Confused looks cross their faces. "Nonna?" they question.

"Grandma." I'm getting impatient.

"Oh," they say. There's a brief pause.

"Where's San Jose?" asks Jay.

"California," I say. All their mouths drop open. Everyone is silent.

I walk into the boxcar and quickly grab my cardboard box of belongings.

I step back outside. Everyone says their goodbyes and we have a group hug. Lucas isn't in the group.

"Where's Lucas?" I ask.

We all begin to look around. I drop my cardboard box on the ground and I check inside both boxcars. He isn't in either one. He's gotta be on the roof.

I climb the ladder to the top. "Lucas, I was about to leave without saying goodbye to you." I sit down next to him.

He hugs me. "I don't want you to leave."

"I have no choice."

"Will I ever see you again?"

"I don't know. I really hope so."

I'm about to pull away but Lucas holds onto me. "No. I don't want to let you go. At least not yet."

"I wish I didn't have to go."

"It'll all be okay." He pulls away at last. "I remember San Jose. It's a nice place. You won't have any trouble adjusting."

What he doesn't know is that I once lived there, too. My mom was struggling financially, so we moved in with Nonna. Then my mom went missing, I ran away, and I came back to Chicago. It's a long and complicated story. "That's right. You used to live over there. With your parents."

"You should probably be heading out now, huh?"

I nod. We climb the ladder down and join the others.

"I need to go. Nonna's waiting for me," I tell them.

"You will visit, won't you?" asks Jay.

"I'll try." I'm not sure if that'll actually happen.

As I walk through the forest carrying the cardboard box with my belongings, I occasionally turn around to catch a glimpse of my friends. The road appears before me, and I soon lose sight of them.

* * *

We're at an airport in Chicago. It's been years since I've flown in an airplane.

Gate B12, boarding group C. I got a window seat, so I'll be able to see the skyline from miles high.

"So, Kalamiti." Nonna startles me. "Are you ready to start school over there?"

I bang my head against the headrest. "I don't want to go to school."

"Again with the little kid behavior? You won't get anywhere in life with that attitude. You will go to school to get a good education and to get your mind off delinquent acts."

I like learning, but I don't want to be around a bunch of strangers.

The fasten seatbelts sign lights up. Time for takeoff.

* * *

The airplane ride was fun. Someday I'd love to fly again.

We drive home in Nonna's actual car, which she had left at the airport.

"We're almost there," she says.

I peer out the window. "I thought San Jose was a pretty big city?" This area appears to be a small town with endless fields. Among the fields are a couple of neighborhoods scattered here and there. The road is narrow.

"I don't live right in the city. I live about two hours east. No one knows what Patterson is, so I just say I'm from San Jose."

We turn into a secluded neighborhood.

"Welcome to my home." Nonna pulls into the driveway.

It's a mansion. Okay, it's not really a mansion, but The Hideout is a cardboard box compared to it.

"This place?" I say.

"Of course."

Nonna gives me a tour of the house and shows me my room. This is luxury.

"Goodnight, Kalamiti."

"G'night."

November 23

Last night I slept really well. I don't know if it's because I was exhausted or because I was sleeping in a real bed. It's probably a combination of the two.

I love Nonna's house. It's a single-story home with three bedrooms, two bathrooms, and a big backyard. My favorite part about it is the wraparound porch.

Nonna has implemented a new plan for me, which includes a chores list. She wants me to help around the house. In return, she'll pay for my cell phone. There are also rules I need to follow, like no drinking, doing drugs, or engaging in other illegal activities. Curfew is 9 p.m. I need to ask for permission before leaving the house. School is my top priority. Things like that. If I do well, I'll get an allowance of $20 a week.

So far, she seems kind of strict. She's not even five feet tall, but she's still intimidating.

This is beginning to sound like camp. At least Nonna doesn't have a handbook with over 100 rules to follow. And I hope she won't keep a manila folder with my records.

November 24

It's 8 a.m. When I walk into the kitchen, Nonna is expecting me.

"You woke up late," she says.

"Late? For what?" I ask.

"You were supposed to help me with chores. Remember your chores list?"

"Oh. Yeah, I remember."

She sighs.

"I'll get started on them right now," I say.

"I've already finished everything you were supposed to do."

"Sorry. I'll get them done next time." I grab a granola bar and I start making my way to my room.

On my way there, I look at some picture frames in the living room. Lots of different images, ranging from paintings to Catholic figures, cover the walls. She even has black and white images from way, way back.

I open my granola bar and I take a bite.

"Ah, I can see you found a picture of your mother," says Nonna.

I jump.

"Did I scare you?" she asks.

I nod.

She chuckles. "Sit down, Kalamiti. Let me show you some photo albums."

She pulls out two boxes from the attic. We look through a red album, when I tell Nonna to pause for a second.

I point at a picture. "Who are they?"

"That's you as a baby with your parents. I'll be right back." She goes to the kitchen.

I continue flipping through the album.

Nonna returns with two glasses of iced tea. "Come on," she says. "Let's sit outside."

We exit through the back door and settle down at a small table.

"What did you do when my mom went missing?" I ask her.

Sadness spreads across her face. "I contacted the police and some other places. They couldn't find any leads. And then you decided to run away. The police found evidence and they thought you were most likely dead. That's when I knew that I couldn't give up. Every day I hoped you would be back on my porch steps. You and your mom. I didn't lose hope."

"I'm sorry I left." That's all I manage to say. I feel bad. Nonna has been through a lot.

She sighs. "I know someday your mom will return. I know it. Hope and brightness will always shine through times of darkness."

"It just doesn't make sense. Why would my mom go missing?"

"I'm not sure, Kalamiti, but sometimes it's better to not know everything."

She's hiding something from me. Maybe she still questions whether I'm really her granddaughter or if she can actually trust me.

If I would've never ran away, I could've lived a perfectly normal life. I wouldn't have had to worry about food or shelter. But then I would've never met The Crew. I guess everything happens for a reason.

November 25

Dinnertime.

Nonna sets a heaping plate of pasta in front of me, followed by a slice of toasted and buttered bread.

I devour my plate. I haven't had decent food in a long-ass time.

Through a mouthful of pasta, I say, "This is one of the best meals I've ever had."

She furrows her brows. "It's just *penne all'arrabbiata*. Nothing fancy."

While I finish the rest of my plate, Nonna stares at me. Can she mind her own business?

I'm finished. Nonna has only eaten half of her meal. I leave the dinner table and start walking back to my bedroom.

"Kalamiti, you are not done here. Come here, young lady," she calls out to me.

I stop in my tracks.

"Pick up your plates and wash them."

I grab the dishes and scrub them in the sink.

After I finish, she holds a napkin in my direction. "Wipe your face. You have sauce all around your mouth."

I slowly take the napkin from her. As I wipe the corners of my mouth, she places both hands on her hips and stares at me. "Work on your manners. You really did need your mother to raise you."

"What do you mean?" It's not like my mom would've taught me manners in the first place. She was never home.

"Use 'please' and 'thank you.' No elbows on the table. Don't eat like a pig."

How am I supposed to know all of this? I basically raised myself.

November 26

Nonna and I are stocking up on groceries and supplies we need for Thanksgiving.

Too many people are at the grocery store. I hate it.

Our grocery cart is full of all kinds of food and drinks, including vegetables I've never even heard of. Nonna makes me push the cart and I'm sick of almost colliding into others.

Don't even get me started on the long checkout lines.

The cashier scans the items, then says, "Your total is $197.89."

$197.89? How many hours of Nonna's pay is that? I'm not sure what Nonna does for a living, but clearly, she makes bank.

November 28

It's Thanksgiving. Nonna's making a lot of delicious food. Lemon rosemary turkey. Buttery mashed potatoes. Decadent pumpkin pie. Mashed potatoes are my favorite. Especially with a crapload of gravy.

It's going to be just us two, so we're going to have a lot of leftovers.

Nonna put me in charge of the pumpkin pie. I'm surprised it came out perfect from the oven. It looked rather watery when I poured it into the crust.

Aromas from the herbs, lemon, and pie fill the house. My mouth is watering.

Nonna and I serve ourselves, then we sit across the dining table from each other.

As I'm about to dig into my plate, Nonna holds a hand up. "Wait. Not yet. What are you thankful for, Kalamiti?"

I make eye contact with her. I wasn't prepared to make a speech. "I'm thankful for my friends back home in Chicago. I'm thankful to be in a house, to have food, and a bed to sleep on. I'm thankful for warm water. And different clothes to wear." I pause. "I'm thankful for you, Nonna."

She smiles. "I'm thankful for you too, Kalamiti. I'm thankful for a job, a roof over our heads, and being able to spend time with you."

She leads a prayer in Italian, and then we dig in. Everything is delicious. This is probably the best Thanksgiving meal I've ever had.

I'm usually not the kind of person who likes to strike up a conversation or have others talk to me while I eat, but thoughts burst into my mind.

"Do we have other family members?" I ask.

She places her fork and knife down, then wipes her mouth with a napkin. "We do."

"Why aren't they here? Thanksgiving is a holiday that's spent with family. Do they ever visit? Do you ever visit them?"

"I haven't talked to them in years." She clears her throat. "I figure they wouldn't want to visit because I'm old and alone."

"What? If you're family, you should visit, regardless of age. And I'm here now. So you're not alone anymore."

She smiles.

I've learned a lot about Nonna. I wonder how she's managed to survive all those years. No husband or partner, and her daughter and granddaughter missing. But she made it through. She's still here, standing tall.

December 2

Today I went to a lot of appointments. Doctor. Dentist. Eye doc. I received a couple of shots. Nonna made another dentist appointment for me. Apparently, I have four cavities. I'm not shocked about that. At least my eyes are decent.

She also took me to a hair salon. These are all things I haven't done in years.

It's kind of nice doing regular human things again.

December 3

Now that I'm not in camp anymore, I can try to text Lucas.

> Me - Hey Lucas, how are you doing? How's The Crew?

He doesn't reply.

December 5

This morning I made myself pancakes with extra syrup.
Today is pretty dull and boring. There's not much to do.
Nonna works Monday through Friday. Nine to five. I'd hate to work that much. At least Nonna enjoys her job, so it's cool.
She hasn't mentioned anything about school, so I'm hoping she forgot about it and I won't be forced to go.
I'm home alone most of the time. I have the computer and the TV in the living room, but I get tired of staring at screens. I like to be out in nature, taking walks around the neighborhood and observing different sights and sounds. There's a park near the house that I like to go to. Sometimes I cook dinner so it'll be ready when Nonna gets home from work.
Nonna wants me to find an activity to do. She says she'll pay for lessons or classes in something I'm interested in. I can't imagine myself doing gymnastics or ballet or anything like

that. I've never really been into sports. I can't see myself doing anything art related, either.

I need to find my passion. Deep down, there's a talent burning within me that's waiting to come alive.

December 7

Tonight we're having a winter party with Nonna's coworkers. She's hosting. Apparently, it's called a potluck, which seems like a funny name. I've never been to one, so I can't wait to try all the food that'll be served.

Nonna invited her entire department over. She didn't mention how many people were coming.

People start knocking on the door. I welcome them in.

Every few minutes, people knock. Soon the living room and dining area are packed like sardines.

"Nonna? Exactly how many people do you work with?" I ask.

"Oh, not that many. Some of them aren't even here. If you think there are a lot of people, you should see the other parties I've thrown."

I guess Nonna's a party animal. At least the knocking has stopped.

I walk through the crowd to get to the kitchen. The majority of the people are middle-aged. Everyone looks professional. Most have on nice dresses and suits. The men are clean shaven, and the women wear sparkling necklaces and earrings. Although I feel a bit out of place, I'm glad Nonna didn't force me to wear anything out of my comfort zone.

I take a step outside the back door to the porch. Two men are sitting at the table, drinks in front of them. One holds a cigar. They look at me.

"You're Jane's granddaughter, aren't you?" the man with the cigar asks, with a thick accent.

"Yes, sir. I'm Kalamiti Sol."

"The missing granddaughter has finally been found," says the other man.

I guess Nonna told them about me.

"My name is Ricky Santiago and this is Lorenzo Petra. It is an honor to meet you," the first man says.

I extend my arm to them. Lorenzo shakes my hand, and Ricky takes my hand and kisses it.

Maybe this man is related to Lucas. They both have the same last name. "Do you happen to be related to someone named Lucas?" I ask him.

"I have two grandsons, Lucas and Alonzo."

My blood runs cold.

Before I can say anything, he pulls out a photo from his wallet. It's an old family photo of Lucas, Alonzo, and their parents, standing in front of a church. "This is my beautiful family."

I take a seat next to them at the table. "Yes, that's Lucas. I recognize him."

"How do you know my grandson?"

Thinking about him makes me sad. "He's my best friend."

He takes a sip from his drink. "I took this photo many years ago when we were visiting Argentina, my home country." Ricky begins telling us stories about the trip, lovely stories too long for me to completely write out on these pages. He sure is a talker.

The expression in his eyes changes from happiness to sorrow. He then says, "This is the last photo the family took together. Everything changed after Fred's death."

I feel like I just fell off the face of the Earth. "What? What happened?"

He sighs. "Fred passed away about five years ago. He and two other officers were murdered in a drug bust."

"Where's his wife?"

"I'm not sure. She hasn't been in contact with anyone. No one has heard anything from her." His eyes narrow. I'm probably asking too many questions.

"Do you have any other family members?"

"I have my daughter, but she lives in another state."

That's it. "You know, Lucas has been trying to get in touch with her. Do you think you could pass her contact info to me so he can reach out to her?"

He takes out a pen and grabs a napkin within reach. He writes, folds up the napkin, and hands it to me. I pocket it.

"Thank you, sir. It was nice meeting you two," I say to them.

As I'm about to head back inside, Ricky stops me. "Now hold on one second." He blows out a cloud of smoke from his cigar. "Tell Lucas I said hi and that he needs to come visit his *abuelitos*."

I manage to smile. "Will do."

If only I could see Lucas in person again.

Time to investigate.

Let's see. Lucas told me since he had moved with his

older brother, he had to leave behind his parents here in San Jose. That occurred when he was in the seventh grade. Alonzo was 20 at the time, which is why they were able to do the move. Eventually Lucas chose to leave behind his brother to join The Crew.

But why would he lie to me about his parents? Can he not trust me? Can he not trust anyone? I guess Lucas is the same way I am. He might not want to discuss the past with anyone. I didn't even know his dad was a police officer.

Or maybe he hasn't kept in touch with them. Maybe he doesn't know what has happened to his family.

I open the crumpled napkin. The writing is in perfect cursive.

Lucinda Santiago
3434 Stonebrook Dr.
Denver, Colorado

If only he would've left a phone number or email to contact her.

December 8

> Lucas – Kalamiti! I can't believe you texted me. BTW, The Crew is doing well. We miss you like crazy. So how are you doing in San Diego? Text back ASAP

That reply is a few days late, but whatever.

> Me – Took you a while to reply. I miss all of you, too. BTW, it's San Jose, not San Diego :)

I sit on my bed staring at my phone, waiting for a reply. My hands begin to sweat.

> Lucas – Yeah, that's what I meant. I'm sorry I didn't ever reply. I was afraid to talk to you, so yeah.

> Me – You shouldn't be afraid to talk to me, Lucas. You can trust me with anything.

> Lucas – Thanks, K9. You can trust me with anything, too.

> Me – I need to tell you something.

> Lucas – What is it?

I take a deep breath and then I punch in the letters.

> Me – Why did you lie to me and The Crew? Why did you lie that your parents were okay?

Now he's calling me.

"Hello?" I speak first.

"Kalamiti, it's nice hearing your voice again. What exactly are you talking about?"

"Look. Your grandfather was here the other day for some potluck. I guess Nonna works with him."

"Wow. Did you talk to him?"

"I did. He started talking about your family and telling me stories. He even showed me a family photo of you, Alonzo, and your parents."

"Oh no."

I pause. "Lucas, he said your dad was murdered. Is that true?" As soon as I say it, I realize it's a messed-up thing to say. He might not even know he's dead.

Silence on the other end.

Finally he speaks. "This is all a long story. I wish I could talk to you about this in person, but yeah. It's true."

"I'm sorry."

"He was a police officer. After he died, Mom shut us out of her life, so Alonzo and I left for Chicago. We never returned home."

I can't believe it. "How could you not have gone home to her, Lucas?"

"It just didn't feel right. And yeah, maybe I was stupid. I craved adventure." He sighs. "There are some days I feel guilty, like maybe she needed me."

"Have you at least kept in touch with her?"

"No. I haven't. She must've changed her phone number. Alonzo doesn't have it either."

"Your grandfather said she hasn't been in contact with anyone. But there has to be at least one family member who has kept in touch with her, don't you think?"

"She was close to my grandmother and my Aunt Lucinda."

Lucinda's the right person to contact after all. "I'm sorry I brought this up."

"No. It's okay. I'm sorry I never told you or anyone else. It was just hard to talk about."

We say goodbye and hang up.

I need to crack this mystery open and help Lucas figure out his mom's whereabouts. I'll have to convince Nonna to take me Denver. She'll understand, won't she?

December 9

It's dinnertime.

"Nonna?"

"Yes?"

"I'm just wondering, if anytime soon, we could go to Denver for a vacation?"

Nonna puts her silverware down. "Are you just trying to get marijuana?"

"Psh. I could easily get that from anyone down the street."

She doesn't laugh.

"Nonna, please. I've been called to go there." I pause. "I've been having some weird dreams lately. I'm thinking about becoming a nun, and I heard they have a camp over there." Nonna's pretty religious, so maybe I can convince her this way.

She looks at me suspiciously. "You want to be a nun?" Then she smiles. "And at first I thought you knew nothing about Catholicism. I suppose you could go, since I've always wanted a family member to become a nun."

I jump right out of my chair. "Thank you, Nonna."

"Under one condition."

I sit back down. "What is it?"

"You have to keep up with your chores and follow the rules."

"That's a piece of cake."

"Uh huh."

"I'll wash the dishes." I pick them up, take them to the sink, and wash them.

I return to my room.

Seconds later, Nonna walks in. "Kalamiti, do you have a brochure or website for the camp?"

"Uh, let me find it."

She leaves the room. I sneak into the guest room and log on to the computer. With my limited knowledge on making brochures, I create my own. The finished product looks semi-legit.

I hand it to Nonna. She looks over it and says, "We'll leave on December 27th."

"Sweet," I say.

"But if you don't behave, I'll cancel the trip."

"Don't worry, I'll behave."

"And about school…" she starts. "You will start next semester, after winter break."

"Thank you, Nonna, I knew you'd understand."

I'm so glad I don't have to start school yet.

December 10

Christmas preparations have begun.

I spent the morning putting up the tree and hanging Christmas lights. Side note: these are extremely time-consuming tasks.

Last night, Nonna and I made a list of what we're going to make for Christmas dinner. I'm looking forward to it. Instead of a huge gathering, it's only going to be the two of us.

The last thing I need to do is get Nonna a present.

December 12

The mall has everything. Nonna seems to have everything, too. I can't find anything for her. Choosing gifts for people is hard.

I've approached the other side of the mall, which is less crowded. Looks like the end is near.

I walk into a random store.

Perfect. On one of the shelves, there's an angel holding a pearl in its hands. Nonna's last name is DiAngelo, which has to do with angels in Italian. Nonna's birthday is in June and her birthstone is a pearl.

Christmas is going to be amazing.

December 14

It's the weekend.

"Get in the car," Nonna says to me.

"Where are we going?" I ask.

"I haven't shown you around town. Let's go for a ride."

Nonna shows me different parts of Patterson. She buys me some new clothes from the mall, the same one I went to the other day. We drive by the local movie theater and other businesses. She shows me some parks and hiking trails.

We do a lot of driving and walking. Although it can't compare to Chicago, this town's not so bad.

Afterward, we stop at Nonna's favorite ice cream place.

As we eat our ice cream, I strike up a conversation. "Nonna, are you rich?"

She laughs. Hard. "Why would you ask that?"

"Let's see. You have a nice house, a nice car, and you flew to Chicago to get me. Not to mention the rental car, organic food, my new cell phone and clothes, and other things like that."

She smiles. "Oh, I'm definitely not rich. For the last few years, I've only had to provide for myself, so I've been able to save."

"What exactly is this job you work?"

"I'm an accountant."

So that's what she does. Interesting. "Did you inherit any money?"

"Some."

"How are you able to afford all this stuff?"

She looks me in the eye and sets her cup of ice cream down on the table. "Oh, Kalamiti, a lot of these things are basic necessities. Having a roof over your head. Food to eat. And clothes to wear. But you haven't had a stable home. And that's okay. I'm glad you're opening up to me and asking questions."

She has a point. Now another question has popped up. "Do I have a grandpa?"

"Don't you dare mention that man. He's dead to me."

Yikes. My bad, I shouldn't have gone there. I wonder what happened to him. I guess it's none of my business.

December 15

"Hey, K9."

"Hey, Lucas."

"I was thinking about our conversation the other day. About my mom?"

"Yeah, what about it?"

"I need to know how she's doing. It's been too long. Can you go visit her for me?"

"What? I've never met her. Wouldn't it be weird for some random teenage girl to show up at her doorstep?"

"I mean, yeah, but you can just explain to her that we're friends. I think she'll like the company."

"Sure. I'll do it."

"Thanks, K9. I'll text you the address. Talk to you later."

I hang up.

December 16

Getting to Lucas' former house was a struggle. It took an hour and a half in a rideshare, so it cost me almost all my allowance.

His mom's place is in a quiet neighborhood. It's a small,

salmon-colored home with an unkempt yard. All the windows are boarded up.

Every single door is locked. There's a window next to the back door. One of the corners of the wood is slightly raised. I yank the plywood off, open the window, and crawl in.

The house is empty and bare, except for the presence of dust lingering in the air.

I make my way through the entire place. I stand beneath the doorframe of a small bedroom with navy-blue walls. This might've been Lucas' former bedroom. An image of a twin-sized bed appears before my eyes. A nightstand and lamp follow suit. In an instant, the closet fills with clothes and a bookshelf shows up in the corner. A young Lucas plays with a toy car collection.

I scan the rest of the home. Furniture pops up. Color paints the plain walls. The hardwood floor in the living room is now covered with a wool rug. Food and appliances flood the kitchen area. Mom, Dad, and Alonzo appear alongside Lucas. A happy family reunites in the vacant space.

Police sirens and a door slamming shut interrupt my daydream.

I run out from the back door and lock it behind me. From the corner of the house, I glance at the front yard. An old white lady, probably the neighbor, is talking to a police officer.

What a snitch.

I hop over the fence, run down a couple of blocks, and take a rideshare back home.

I call Lucas and tell him the news.

December 18

I'm checking out the course catalog for school. I'm going to be in tenth grade. I can't decide what to take for electives.

"You should take a language," says Nonna.

"Do you really think I need to learn another language?" I question.

"It counts for graduation requirements. You need to take a language so you can go to college."

"Who said I'm going to college?"

Nonna doesn't respond. I continue scrolling through the school's website.

The moment Nonna steps out of the room, I open YouTube. The webpage loads and a featured video catches my eye. It's a song I really like, so I click on it. Except it isn't the original song, it's a piano cover. I'm about to click the back button, but the song starts before I can do so.

I'm so glad I didn't hit the back button because the cover is amazing. I never thought I would enjoy piano music.

Nonna returns. Upon glancing at the screen, she smiles and says, "I actually play piano, but I haven't played in years. Maybe I'll give you some lessons sometime."

On my enrollment form, I write down the four required classes for tenth grade. I circle French for one of my electives.

Hey, it can't hurt to learn another language.

I circle piano for my other elective.

December 20

Nonna and I visited the enrollment center.

The school district is currently on winter break. The receptionist went ahead and gave me my schedule for next semester.

Here it is:

Sol, Kalamiti Locker#: 078 Student ID: 75560
Semester 2
1st hour: French I – Adler, Amy
2nd hour: American History – Knox, Douglas
3rd hour: English – Bold, Bobby
4th hour: Chemistry – Oxford, Tyler
5th hour: Geometry – Johnson, Vince
6th hour: Piano I – Hayley, Tiana

December 24

It's Christmas Eve. According to Nonna, it's a family tradition to celebrate today instead of tomorrow.

Nonna did most of the cooking. These are Italian recipes that were handed down, so it's the real deal.

"This is one of the best meals I've ever eaten," I say, as I eat the last forkful of food off of my plate. The biscotti was my favorite.

She smiles. "I'll have to pass down the recipes to you."

As I clean up our dishes and the dining room, Nonna wanders off.

"Come here." Nonna calls out from the living room.

She surprises me with a small, perfectly wrapped present. "Open it."

I unwrap the box, unveiling a touchscreen phone. "You didn't have to get me this. The phone I have now works fine."

"I want you to have it. You need to have a way to communicate with me. Plus, it's a responsibility and a privilege."

"Thank you, Nonna." I give her a hug. I don't deserve this, but I'm gonna make sure to take care of it.

I grab Nonna's gift from under the Christmas tree and I hand it to her. "I got this for you. It's not much."

She looks shocked. She unwraps the gift and holds up the angel.

"This is beautiful. I love it." Nonna gives me a hug and then she places the angel above the fireplace.

This has been one of the best Christmases.

December 25

Merry Christmas!

December 26

Yesterday I messaged June on social media. The Crew is doing well. They've managed to collect some extra blankets to keep warm during these cold months. I'm glad we have the Internet to keep in touch.

Soon the year will be over. Things are going to be different. I can't wait to see what the future has in store for me.

December 27

Our plane takes off from the airport. I have the window seat, Nonna sits in the middle, and a stranger is in the aisle seat. Endless clouds fill my view outside the window. It's like I'm floating right over them. In a way, I am. It would be amazing if I could hop from cloud to cloud without falling right through them.

Now that I think about it, how am I going to get to Lucinda without Nonna noticing? Sooner or later she's going to start asking questions about the religious camp I made up. I haven't exactly figured this all out yet.

After arriving at Denver International Airport, we take a cab to the hotel. Nonna checks us in and we take the elevator up to our floor.

Lucinda's place isn't too far from here.

I'll tell Nonna tomorrow morning that I'm going on a walk. Something like that. Hopefully it all works out.

December 28

It's 10 a.m. Time to go to Lucinda's.

As I open the door, Nonna asks me where I'm going.

I take a deep breath. "I'm going on a walk."

She walks away and comes back with a scarf, hat, and gloves. "Have a good time." She smiles.

I smile back. I put them on and head out the door.

It's chilly. I've missed this weather.

I cross the street and enter the neighborhood. Stonebrook

Drive is a curved street with a dead end. The house at the end is 3434.

The yard looks like it hasn't been looked after. It seems like the home is abandoned. I'm going to be pissed if no one's living in it anymore.

I want to turn back, but I've already arrived, so I might as well try.

There isn't a doorbell, so I knock. As I wait, I study the linework and details of the carved flowers on the old wooden door.

I start to walk off, but then I hear a voice.

"Hello?"

I turn around. A thin woman with glasses is standing at the doorway. "Are you Lucinda?"

"Who are you?"

"I'm Kalamiti. I'm Lucas' friend. I know this is really weird, but I need answers."

"Come in, come in. You must be freezing out here."

I walk into her home. Should I take off my shoes? I don't feel comfortable sitting down on the couch. I don't even know where to stand.

While Lucinda is in the kitchen, I look at pictures in the living room.

She brings out two mugs of hot chocolate and tells me to take a seat.

"Kalamiti, nice to meet you. How did you find me here?"

"My grandma works with your dad. She hosted a potluck at our house. I talked to him and he gave me your address. I need more information on Lucas' parents. What happened to them?"

Lucinda sets her mug on the coffee table. "Lucas used to

live with his parents in San Jose. His father was a police officer. He died about five years ago. Alonzo took Lucas under his wing and they moved to Illinois. Their mom needed space."

"Where is she now? Have you talked to her recently?"

She hesitates. "She actually lives here. With me."

"How come?"

"She was having trouble holding down a job in California. She needed help, so I took her in."

"Is she doing okay?"

"She's doing better. You know, Kalamiti, I think Fred's death wasn't just hard on Elena, but it was hard on Alonzo and Lucas, too."

My eyes follow the movement of the marshmallows swirling around in the pool of hot chocolate. "Why do you say that?"

"Alonzo and Lucas never went home. I think they're scared to face reality. During those years, they never visited Elena."

My heart hurts for his mom. "I need to tell Lucas that his mom is here."

"Actually, he's going to be driving down here soon. I believe Alonzo gave Lucas my phone number, so he called me last week and told me he wanted to visit."

Perfect timing. "Maybe I can meet up with him before I head back to California."

"I can't believe you came all the way over here."

"I had to. Anything for Lucas."

She smiles.

My phone vibrates in my pocket. It's Nonna.

"Hey, Lucinda? Would you be able to drive me back to the hotel? My grandma is looking for me."

"Of course."

After the short drive, Lucinda parks in the hotel parking lot and follows me up to the hotel room. I unlock it with my key.

Nonna is standing behind the door. "Kalamiti Sol! Where in the world have you been?"

"Sorry, Nonna. I'd like you to meet Lucinda. She's Lucas' aunt."

"Nice to meet you." Nonna shakes her hand. "How did Kalamiti find you?"

"We ran into each other at the park."

I'm so glad Lucinda didn't tell her the truth.

They talk for a little bit, then Lucinda leaves.

"Hey, Nonna?" I ask.

"Yes?"

"Are you mad at me?"

She pauses for a second. "Oh, no, not at all." I'm not sure if she's being sarcastic. Then she adds, "Hey, Kalamiti?"

"Yeah?"

"Next time, don't leave me out of your little mysteries." She grins.

I guess Nonna must not be as strict of a grandparent as I thought she was.

I can't help smiling.

December 29

School starts next Monday. I need to call Lucas to make sure he'll be here in time.

I dial his number and he picks up. "Hey, Kalamiti."

"Hey. I'm in Denver."

"I know. Aunt Lucinda called me. You really went all the way over there?"

"Yeah, I had to help you figure out where your mom was."

"Thanks, K9. I should've kept you updated. I guess I wasn't the only one investigating."

I smile. "Your aunt said you were going to come visit. I wanted to see if we had time to meet up. Nonna wants us to leave soon because I start school on Monday."

"You're going to school now?" he laughs.

I roll my eyes. "Yes, Lucas, so I'd love to be able to see you before I leave."

"I'm actually already on my way. I left last night after I talked to my aunt."

"I'll see you soon, then."

Nonna leans against the doorway to the bathroom. "So is Lucas your boyfriend?"

"What? No!"

"That's not what it looks like. Someone's a little smiley."

I can't help laughing. I'm beet red now. Everyone always assumes that Lucas and I are together. "We're just friends."

She laughs.

New Year's is going to be amazing. Lucas will be reunited with his aunt and mom, and I'm going to get to see him again.

December 30

Lucas is arriving today. I want him to get here already.

It's only been a few weeks, but I feel like I haven't seen him in months.

I stare out the window. The hotel overshadows a busy street, which results in a lot of noise.

And there it is. His car turns into the parking lot.

I quickly slip on my shoes, skip the elevator, and run down the stairs, nearly tripping in the process. I dash through the lobby, sidestepping people. I sprint out the front sliding doors. Now to find where he parked.

I stop in the middle of the road to scan the lot.

"Kalamiti!" Lucas comes toward me and gives me a hug. "I'm so happy to see you."

I smile. "I'm happy to see you, too."

The moment I unlock the door to the hotel room, I say, "Lucas is here!"

Nonna introduces herself. Lucas and I sit down on the couch.

"So Kalamiti, when does that camp start again?" Nonna asks.

I freeze. Before I can say anything, she adds, "Lucas, did Kalamiti ever tell you that she wanted to become a nun?"

Lucas looks at me. "Kalamiti? A nun? That's a little hard to believe."

"That's the reason why we came here. Now, when does that camp start?" She folds her arms across her chest.

"Uh, I called yesterday, and they canceled it. Not enough girls signed up."

"Sweetie, I know you didn't come here for a religious camp." She pulls out the brochure I made. "Did you really think I was going to buy this?"

"Um, no."

She sighs and walks away.

Lucas cracks up.

I shove him. "How else was I supposed to convince her to bring me here?"

"You could've just told her the truth."

He's got a point.

Lucas says, "Let's go for a walk. There's a park across the street."

I get up from the couch and walk up to Nonna. "We'll be right back. We're going on a walk."

She cups her hands around my ear. "He's handsome," she whispers.

I roll my eyes. "Please."

She chuckles.

As soon as we step out of the hotel's lobby, the cold air freezes my body. We speed walk to the intersection and take the crosswalk.

The park contains a playground that's lightly dusted with snow, reminding me of powdered sugar.

No one is in sight. We pass empty garden plots and water fountains, before approaching what looks like a greenhouse.

"Do you think we can go inside?" I ask.

Lucas reaches for the door handle and turns it. "It's open. Let's go in."

The temperature inside is nice and warm. All sorts of plants are thriving.

We take a seat on a metal bench.

I say, "This reminds me of camp. We spent a day at a community garden and there were some sunflowers there. I swear one of them waved at me with its leaves."

Lucas smiles. "Those were my mom's favorite flowers. In

a way, they're sort of geometric. There's something mystifying about them."

I smile. "How's The Crew?"

"We actually don't really steal anymore."

My mouth drops open. "What? But why? How do you guys survive?"

"June started working at the candy store with me. And, well, we kind of listened to Maci."

"You listened to Maci?"

"Well, Kalamiti, she made a very good point."

"How?"

"Answer this question: why do we risk so much for something that won't last?"

I look at the ground. "I don't know."

"Exactly. Maci asked me the same thing. Think about it. The things we've stolen, they won't last us forever. Why bother risking everything we have? We were being selfish. We took so many materialistic things that we didn't need."

"I guess she had a point."

He nods. "It was wrong. And we don't want to ruin our lives."

"I can't believe it was so easy for you guys to just … stop. Stealing is like an addiction. I mean, there was a twenty-dollar bill in an unlocked car in the hotel parking lot and I was so tempted to take it. But I didn't."

He stares at the assortment of plants in front of us. "Sounds like you're a kleptomaniac," he laughs. "I'm playing. You're aware of what you're doing wrong, so it's now just a matter of dropping the habit."

"Nonna keeps saying I need to find a brighter path or something like that."

"She just doesn't want you to end up in juvie again. Everyone figures things out at their own pace. Don't worry about it."

"I don't know. I might always be a thief and delinquent. I'm never going to change." My shoes roll over and kick the gravel beneath them.

Lucas says, "Close your eyes."

Without thinking twice, I close them.

"Visualize a sunflower field in the middle of summer."

My mind paints a picture of a field filled with sunflowers. Fluffy clouds embellish the bright blue sky. I appear in a white dress, standing next to Lucas, who's also wearing white. The summer heat beats down on us, filling us inside out with warmth. A narrow gravel path cuts through the field. As we walk down the path, we greet the majestic sunflowers. They wave at us with their heart-shaped leaves, making us feel like royalty. Yellow petals reflect the sun's light.

Lucas continues. "Do you notice that all of the sunflowers are growing at different rates?"

Eyes still closed, I nod. "Yeah. Some are taller and some are shorter. Some haven't completely opened up yet. But one thing they all have in common is a thick stem."

"You're right. The stems and roots provide a solid foundation. The field contains all sorts of bright and lively sunflowers that represent all the people who have found their purpose and happiness. Among them are small sunflowers, ones that haven't opened up, ones that haven't found the sunshine. Let's say you're one of them. In order for these sunflowers to grow, they need necessary components like water, sunlight, and good soil. So, Kalamiti, you need to find the components that will lead you to make the right choices and to find your purpose. Put all of them together and you've got your brighter path."

I open my eyes. I'm amazed. It makes so much sense. Lucas always knows what to say. "Thanks, Lucas."

He looks down at the ground. "I'm scared to confront my mom."

"It'll be okay. At least you didn't run away from your grandmother. She thought I was dead all these years."

He sighs. "It's just been so long. And my mom's like bipolar and stuff so I don't know how she's doing. Like what if she's aged a lot? What if she's turned into a completely different person?"

"No matter what, she still loves you. And even if she is different, that shouldn't change things."

"Alonzo didn't want to come home. He got comfortable in Illinois, so I stayed, too." He pauses. "I don't know if she'll forgive me for never returning or visiting."

"Well, you're visiting now. Explain everything to her. She'll understand."

"Thanks, Kalamiti. We should head back. I need to go visit my family now."

As we walk back, my mind replays Lucas' dialogue. In order to find my brighter path, I need to add up all my components. But I've begun to realize, I don't think I have any.

December 31

I spoke to Lucas on the phone earlier and he said everything went well with his mom, Elena. They also invited us over for New Year's.

Lucinda opens the front door for us, and we walk right in.

Elena is sitting on the couch in the living room.

Lucas introduces us. "Mom, this is Kalamiti, my best friend. And this is her grandma, Jane."

We all shake hands and talk for a bit. Elena is really sweet.

The adults are in the kitchen, while Lucas and I are in the living room. As I look around the room, I never realized how many Christmas decorations she has up.

Lucinda calls out from the kitchen. "You two can go outside in the backyard if you'd like."

Lucas leads the way out the back door.

Talk about an assortment of Christmas lights. A small white gazebo sits next to a koi pond. The backyard is spacious and well-maintained. Compared to the front, it's a whole new world.

We take a seat under the safety of the gazebo. The koi pond water must be cold. I hope the fish are okay.

"Your nose is red," Lucas tells me.

I look at him. "Yours is too."

We laugh.

"Are you cold?" he asks.

"Just a little."

He starts unzipping his coat, but I tell him to stop.

"Are you sure? I mean, I don't mind," he says.

"Yeah, I'm sure."

He zips his coat back up.

We sit in silence, observing the sights and sounds around us. Snow lightly falls from the sky and sprinkles the ground.

"Lucas?"

"Yeah?"

"You don't know how much I've missed you since I left. You and The Crew."

"And you don't know how much I've missed you. I haven't been the same since then. And by the way, I'm really sorry. It's all my fault you had to go to the detention center."

"You don't have to apologize. I can't always get away with everything. I had to deal with the consequences on my own."

"I'm glad you're not locked up there anymore." He hugs me. I don't want to let go because of how cold I am and how warm he is.

Eventually he pulls away.

"So now that you're reunited with your mom, are you gonna move over here?" I ask.

"No. I'm going back to Chicago."

"But she's your mom. You don't want to stay with her?"

Lucas looks frustrated. "I don't belong here, Kalamiti. There's not enough room for me. I would just be a burden to my aunt. She already does so much for my mom." He looks away, which tells me he doesn't want to talk about it.

I continue, "So? They're your family."

He runs a hand through his hair. "Would you want to be around someone who lied to you about something important?" With that, he leaves.

As I watch him return to the warmth of the house, I can't help but wonder who the liar is: Lucinda or his mom?

I don't really know all the details about them, just like he doesn't know everything about the relationship between me and my mom, so maybe being away from them is a good thing.

I should have dropped the subject.

I run back inside as the fluffy, white snow touches down on me.

Lucas is talking to his mom and aunt. Nonna is sitting on the couch with a mug. I sit down next to her.

"Would you like some hot cocoa?" she asks.

"Yes, please."

While Nonna heads to the kitchen, Lucas joins me on the couch. "I'm sorry I kinda ditched you out there."

"Lucas, stop."

"I was pretty pathetic."

"You don't need to apologize. I'm sorry, too. I didn't mean to upset or push you. You know what's best for yourself."

He puts a hand on my shoulder. "It's okay. It was all with good intentions."

I stare at the mug that Nonna just placed on the coffee table. I pick it up and take a sip. "I'm grateful we're here, under the same roof. That's all I needed. To see you."

He smiles. "Me too."

I hold my mug up. "Do you want the rest of my hot cocoa?"

He takes the mug out of my hands and takes a sip. I laugh.

We sit there listening to Nonna, Elena, and Lucinda going on and on and on about grown-up topics. Mortgages, taxes, employment, and all that jazz.

I'm falling asleep.

* * *

"Kalamiti. Wake up."

It's Lucas, shoving me.

"Huh?" I say.

"It's almost midnight," he says.

I open my eyes to the brightness and sound coming from the TV.

"How long was I asleep?" I ask.

"Forget about that, get up!" Lucas takes my hands and pulls me up from the couch.

Everyone is standing in the living room, New Year's hats on their heads.

"Here's one for you." Lucinda places a hat on my head. "It's almost the countdown!"

I glance at the clock. Less than a minute left.

We all begin counting down. "10! 9! 8! 7! 6! 5! 4! 3! 2! 1! Happy New Year!"

Lucas takes me by the shoulders and hugs me. We all hug one another. The adults sip champagne, while Lucas and I drink sparkling juice.

After the celebration, Lucas drives us back to the hotel. Today was fun, but I'm wiped out.

I hope I'll make better choices. That's my New Year's resolution.

January 1

We're starting the new year off with snowboarding. I'm not, but Lucas is.

He asks me again. "Are you sure?"

"I'm sure," I reply.

"I'll help you," he insists.

"No thanks, I'm good."

"Okay, then. Suit yourself."

He takes off, leaving me on my own.

I kind of wish I would've said yes. I'm burning up, sitting here in all this gear that we rented.

Lucas is a natural at everything. Knowing him, he'd make it look like he's been snowboarding his whole life. He is Lucas, and Lucas is good at whatever he does.

After sitting on the bench just observing everyone walking by, Lucas returns.

"You missed out on all the fun!" He sits down next to me and pulls off his goggles.

"I did."

He laughs. "I'm about to go for another round. Wanna come with me this time?"

"Well … I suppose. Sure, let's go."

I grab my snowboard and follow him to the ski lift. My heart is pounding.

I manage to safely get on the lift. It's like a rollercoaster, the anticipation building for the drop.

If there's anything I'm scared of, it's heights. It's not necessarily the height, but the fact that I'm not able to hold onto anything with my hands.

As the lift takes us up, Lucas says, "This slope is for beginners. You'll do great."

I try not to look down. "I'm scared."

He laughs. "You? Kalamiti Sol, scared? That's unheard of."

I tilt my head to the side. "I'm sure you've already nailed snowboarding."

He laughs more. "No, I definitely haven't. You should've seen me earlier. I kept falling."

I smile. "Are you sure this is for beginners? I could go for the baby slope instead."

"I'm sure. But we've got this."

We're now at the top of the hill. I'm having a hard time believing this is as beginner as it gets. It's a long way down.

A random surge of adrenaline flows through me or something because I just … take off. I'm trying to go straight but I lose my balance and do a face plant.

Lucas comes after me. He starts cracking up, but then he helps me up.

"Let's go again. This time I'll go with you," he says.

Although I have goggles on, my face feels frozen. I shake off the snow.

We're back at our starting point.

"You go first. I'll be close behind you," says Lucas.

I take off. I lose my balance, but I manage not to fall this time. Yo, this is hella fun.

I'm almost at the bottom. I'm getting the hang of this.

Lucas is somewhere behind me. I hear his voice yell out, but I can't make out what he's saying.

He crashes into me and we both go tumbling into the snow.

I open my eyes and Lucas is on top of me.

"Thanks for catching the fall," he laughs.

I shove him off of me. I can't help laughing.

"Let's go for another round, shall we?" He stands up and reaches to help me up.

I smile and take his hand.

January 2

Last night, Nonna and I flew home.

Lucas is still in Denver, spending time with his family. In a few days he'll be in San Jose. His plan is to visit his dad's grave and his grandparents before going back to Chicago.

Nonna offered to pay for his plane tickets, but he didn't want to leave his car behind. It's gonna be a far drive for him, but it's a long overdue visit.

Hopefully his car makes it here.

January 5

Lucas made it to San Jose yesterday. He spent the day with his grandparents and spent the night at their home. He was happy to see them again. Although he's exhausted from the drive, everything went well.

Lucas asks me to accompany him to the cemetery, where his father is buried.

As soon as we step foot on the gravel path, a heaviness encapsulates my heart.

"It's here." He looks down at the grave.

I stand close to him, not knowing what to say.

He closes his eyes. "The last time I saw my dad was before I went to school on the day he died. It was like any ordinary school day. Except it didn't turn out to be ordinary. My dad never made it home from work. Mom lied to me and Alonzo. For a while, she told us Dad was sick in the hospital.

Eventually she told us the truth. Since then, she's never been the same. I wish I could remember the last words I exchanged with him before I hopped on the school bus. I never thought that would be the final goodbye."

I grab hold of his arm. "I'm sorry, Lucas."

"I don't remember the sound of his voice. I don't remember much about his physical presence. It's almost as if time has slowly been erasing the image I have of him in my head."

"You'll always have your memories of him."

"He didn't deserve to die. Why did this have to happen to him?"

"I don't know," I pause. "Sometimes life doesn't make sense. I always question why certain things happen."

"Life would be so different if he were still here. Alonzo and I would've never moved to Illinois. My family would be complete. I would be an average kid going to school. We would have continued spending winter break in Argentina."

"It's crazy how one moment can change everything."

We stand there in silence.

Lucas squeezes my shoulder. "Let's take you home."

I hand him the bouquet of flowers, and he sets them down.

Once we're at Nonna's place, I invite him in.

I give him a brief tour of the house, and then we head to my room. We sit at the edge of my bed, side by side.

"It was good seeing my family again. If it wasn't for you, Kalamiti, I probably wouldn't have thought about calling my aunt. This has been a great trip," says Lucas.

I smile. "I'm glad you reconnected with them. I'm happy I got to spend time with you, too."

Lucas lays back on the bed. I do the same. Our eyes are fixed on the ceiling, which is covered in glow-in-the-dark stars, like the boxcars back at The Hideout.

"I don't want to go back to Chicago," he says.

"How come?"

"It's over a day's drive back."

I smirk. "But you love to drive."

He takes a second to respond. "The Crew is my family, but I kind of want to stay. My grandparents are here, and so are you."

I stare at the ceiling, unsure what to say.

"Um, this is impulsive as hell, but can I move in with you two? I'll even start school with you. If your grandma's okay with it, of course."

I abruptly sit up in my bed. "Can't you move in with your grandparents?"

"I could, but it's kind of far from here. We wouldn't be able to go to the same school."

The sound of a door opening and closing resonates through the house.

I say, "Nonna's home. Let's go ask her."

I hope she says yes.

Nonna greets us, then she looks back and forth at us. "What are you two up to?"

I glance at Lucas. "Could Lucas move in with us? He can stay in the guestroom."

She folds her arms across her chest and raises an eyebrow. "Why?"

"I need a change from Chicago," says Lucas.

"Why can't you stay with Ricky and his wife?"

"I want to be able to go to school with Kalamiti."

"Nonna, please," I interject.

"It could even be temporary," Lucas adds.

She sighs. "Well you're going to need to do chores and abide by my rules, like Kalamiti does."

"So I can stay?"

"Sure."

This all must be a dream. There's no way this is real. The trip to Denver and Lucas' presence are just my mind playing tricks on me, and I'm about to wake up any second now.

While Nonna cooks dinner, I help Lucas settle into his new room. He didn't bring much with him.

"I'm dreaming, right?" I ask him.

He laughs. "No. This is really happening."

"I can't believe she's letting you stay."

"I can't believe it, either. I thought she was going to say no."

Nonna walks into the room and squints at us in a suspicious manner. "First rule: after 9 p.m., you two aren't allowed to be alone in a room together."

We both take a step away from each other.

She chuckles. "Dinner's ready. Afterward, we'll go shopping for school supplies. Tomorrow is the first day of school."

Too soon.

"I'm ready for it," says Lucas.

We're both starting brand-new lives. Time for a new chapter.

Part Two

January 6

School starts today. Yay.

Lucas and I haven't been enrolled in school for a while, so I'm shocked we weren't held back a couple of grades. According to Nonna, we're gonna be required to take classes over the summer to make up missing credits.

We head out the door.

"Are you sure you both have everything?" Nonna asks for like the zillionth time.

"Yeah," we reply.

She waves at us.

We wave back. Our bus stop is at the corner of the street, which isn't too far of a walk.

The yellow bus squeals to a stop and opens its doors to us. Boisterous students fill the cramped bus with talking and laughter. As we walk down the aisle trying to find an open seat, they stare. I try my best to avoid eye contact.

We choose the seat all the way in the back.

A girl sitting in the seat in front of us turns around. "That seat is reserved for Joanie."

"Joanie?" I question.

The bus comes to a stop. The girl turns around to check who's boarding. "You're lucky she isn't here today." She turns back around.

Strange.

The bus pulls into the bus loop.

"Well, Kalamiti, it's officially your first day as a sophomore and my first day as a junior," says Lucas.

"Well, I can't wait for the official last day of school," I mutter.

The bus loop doors lead to the cafeteria. Everyone is sitting at the tables, having breakfast, and waiting for the bell to ring. Lucas and I take a seat at an empty table in the back.

A couple of students look at us.

"When does first hour start?" I ask Lucas.

He glances at a clock up high. "In about eight minutes," he replies.

We stroll down the halls, looking for our lockers.

"What's your locker number?" I ask him.

"079. What's yours?" he asks.

"078."

We reach a desolate hall in the back of the school. Cobwebs and dust linger among the rusty grey lockers.

While testing out our locker combinations, the bell rings.

"We're late," I say.

"Eh, whatever. We're new," he says.

"It's not that, it's the attention we'll get from everyone. I don't want them staring."

"Who cares about that? It'll be okay."

I'm glad we have the same first hour.

Room 106. I take a deep breath, Lucas opens the door, and we walk in.

All talking stops. Students stare. The teacher gets up from her desk and stands in front of us.

"Hello, there! You two must be the new students! Come in, come in, don't be shy! I'm Ms. Adler!" she says.

Someone took a few too many happy pills today.

"Lucas, you can sit behind Amelia. And Kalamiti," she pauses, "you can sit behind Summer."

Our seats are on opposite sides of the room.

All Ms. Adler does is brag about the gazillion different animals she has at home. Is that even legal?

I can tell she doesn't like me, solely by the way she looks at me. It's crazy how much you can learn about someone just from reading their eyes.

Second hour. Lucas isn't in this class. If only we were in the same grade.

"You must be Kalamiti. I'm Mr. Knox."

Again, I get some weird looks from some of the students. At least a few smile at me.

"You can sit next to Betsy," he says.

Betsy's the girl on the bus who warned me about Joanie. She's probably one of those popular girls who wouldn't want to talk to me. She has shoulder-length, dirty blonde hair, hazel eyes, tortoise shell glasses, and a nose ring. A neat tattoo of a bird is etched on her wrist. Red lipstick must be her trademark.

I didn't end up talking to anyone. At least Mr. Knox is a pretty laid-back teacher.

Third hour comes along.

All I can tell you about third hour is that I hate pop quizzes, and Mr. Bold is the oldest teacher in the universe. I lost count of how many times I had to repeat my name to him, not to mention the time it took for him to find my unusual name on the roster. I bet I could throw a party in that class and he wouldn't hear or notice a thing.

Fourth hour chemistry is okay, except for the fact that Mr. Oxford is expecting me to take tomorrow's test. Does he not realize I've been living on the streets and have a very limited knowledge of this subject? That's going to be an automatic "F" for me.

Fifth hour. Geometry with Johnson. Since there aren't enough desks, I get to sit at a table all by myself in the back of the classroom. Minimal human interaction. I'm digging it. This class is gonna be a piece of cake.

Piano class is last.

Let me start off by saying, Ms. Hayley is an awesome pianist. She should be performing live for thousands of people, instead of stuck at a school teaching us.

The first day was decent. I didn't really talk to anyone in my classes.

This school is interesting. It's a predominantly white high school. Don't get me wrong, I love my fellow white people, but I prefer diversity. I had that back home in Chicago. This is a whole new world to me.

So far, none of the groups fit me. There's the group of popular kids, the smart students trying to go to Harvard, the athletes, the hipsters, the band geeks, the goths, the drama kids, the average students, and so on. It's only my first day and I already know where all the stoners go to light up, the part of the parking lot where all the country dudes compare their trucks, and even the little space under a stairwell where people have the nerve to make out. I now know which bathrooms I need to avoid because there are either a bunch of annoying girls gossiping, attempting to give themselves piercings, or doing some other crazy shit. Hell, I can't pee in peace in those sketchy situations.

I also found out that the debate team meets during lunch and that a group of boys play basketball in the gym. There's a room in the library where students like to lounge, a classroom where black kids hang out and freestyle, and a group of students playing strange games in the computer lab. Band, orchestra, and choir students use the practice rooms on the second floor. Cross-country and track students practice outside. It seems like no one actually eats lunch during lunchtime. I know all of this may sound judgmental, but I spent my day walking around this whole building, observing, taking in all these new surroundings. This is where I'm gonna be for the next few years.

Am I ever gonna fit in?

January 7

This school is a joke.

Earlier today I got in trouble by some teacher. Apparently, I broke the dress code.

I was wearing a black tank top. The school thinks they're inappropriate.

So what happened was, this teacher came up and told me I needed to change or I'd be sent home. No one even told me there was a dress code in the first place. We argued for a couple of minutes. Luckily, Lucas had a hoodie on, so he let me borrow it for the day.

I doubt any males in this joint are gonna look at me and

think, "Damn, K9's got some fine-ass broad shoulders going on there."

This school is a joke.

January 8

Lucas and I are sitting on the bus when a girl who seems taller than six feet gets on.

She settles down in the seat that's reserved.

This chick's gotta be Joanie.

She's freaking tall. I swear her head hit the ceiling on the bus. All I could focus on were her huge, meaty hands that could knock me out with a single punch.

"Are you Joanie?" I have no clue why I just opened my mouth.

"Kalamiti, what are you…" Lucas starts.

Joanie cuts him off. "Yeah. What do you want?"

"Who gave you the right to reserve seats?"

The bus is moving, but clearly Joanie doesn't care. She makes her way down the aisle.

I'm screwed.

She picks up Lucas by the collar of his shirt and shoves him into another seat.

She picks me up like she picked up Lucas. "I can do whatever I want. You hear?" Spit flies out of her mouth.

I don't have anything to say.

"You better quit trying to get so much attention," she says. "You'll never fit in."

She lets me go and my head hits the window. Joanie's got a grip.

Lucas returns to our seat. "What are you thinking? Are you trying to get your ass kicked?"

"It's not fair that she's reserving seats. What if I wanted to sit back there?"

He tilts his head to the side. "Kalamiti. It's a public school bus. Who the hell cares? We can always take my car to school. You know, to show it off and all."

"No one wants to see your car."

He looks at me. "Take that back."

"No."

"I'm never giving you a ride again. And I'm never letting you drive my car again."

Judging by his arms crossed, he's pretty pissed.

I nudge him. "Are you mad at me?"

"What do you think?"

"I was just playing." I give him a really awkward hug.

He cracks a smile.

With my arms still around him, I say, "You know you can't stay mad at me."

"And you know you can't stop flirting with me."

I immediately let go of him and I sit back in my half of the seat. I don't know what just happened.

* * *

Second hour comes around. Mr. Knox is assigning everyone partners to work on an assignment together. He partners me with Betsy.

"That was brave, what you did," she says.

"What exactly did I do?" I ask.

"On the bus. No one has ever stood up to Joanie. Especially a new student. No one challenges her."

I shrug. "I was just trying to stand up for everyone."

We work on the assignment until the bell rings.

During lunchtime, Lucas and I sit at an empty table. Betsy approaches us.

"Can I sit with you two? My friend isn't here today," she says.

"Sure," I say.

She sits next to me. "So Lucas, I heard you have a nice car," she starts.

I look at her and right away I know that she overheard our conversation on the bus.

She smirks at me.

Lucas' eyes light up. "See, Kalamiti? Some people care about my ride."

I roll my eyes. He begins describing every single detail about his car. I don't think she actually cares.

"That's nice," she says.

Lucas grabs his tray and stands up. "I'm gonna head to class now. I'll see you ladies later."

As soon as he leaves, Betsy says, "Yeah, nobody cares about his car."

And just like that, we click.

January 9

The final bell rings.

I take a different path than usual. On the second floor, I approach a stairwell near the gym. I barge through the doors.

A group of four guys stand near the bottom of the stairwell.

As I'm about to head out the back door, one of them asks me, "Do you have a lighter?"

He's in my history class. I think his name is Turner? Really, though, I have no clue. He might be one of those people that goes by their last name.

"I do. But you'll need to let me take a few hits in return."

He shrugs. "Sure."

Together, we all exit through the back doors of the school and sit at one of the picnic tables.

I hand him my lighter.

In return, he passes me the blunt.

I inhale way too much, making me cough uncontrollably. My lungs.

No one says a word. This is rather awkward. We pass the blunt around for a second round.

The bus.

"Gotta go, thanks," I say to them.

Before they can respond, I dash to the bus loop. It's not like they were gonna say anything anyway.

The moment I step foot on the bus steps, the door slams shut and the bus pulls out of the loop.

I sit next to Lucas. He looks at me oddly. "Dude, did you just smoke?"

"What makes you think that?"

"You smell like weed and your eyes are bloodshot."

I open my eyes as wide as I can. "No way."

He grins. "You do know your grandma is gonna be home?"

"I thought she worked until five?"

"Yeah, but she took time off today. She's taking me to the dentist."

Oh snap. "Uh…"

Soon the bus drops us off at our stop.

Lucas unlocks the door and holds it open for me.

"How was school?" Nonna asks, while she walks from the kitchen to our side.

Lucas responds, but I'm out of it, so I stand there and stare off into space.

Nonna steps in front of me and puts her hands on my shoulders. "Kalamiti, are you high?"

She's staring at me. I stare back. "What are you talking about?"

Lucas laughs.

"I'm not stupid, Kalamiti. You smoked marijuana at school today, didn't you?"

"Sure, yeah, I did. So what?" All I want to do is take a nap.

"You're grounded."

"What does that mean?"

"Give me your phone."

This is rubbish. I guess I'll just sleep for the rest of the day.

January 10

Identity.

It's a tricky subject.

Some of the students here have asked me where I'm from. When I'm asked that, I'm never sure what to say. I'm Mexican and Italian, but I'm also American. I'm from California and Illinois. How much backstory should I give?

To make it more confusing, I inherited most of my looks

from my dad and his side of the family. Tan skin, dark hair and eyes. Nonna and my mom both have fairer skin. Because my dad passed so early on in my life, I never really got to learn about or experience the Mexican culture. I'm glad he would speak in Spanish to me. Thankfully, because of Lucas, I was able to retain my Spanish-speaking ability. Through his perspective, I also learned a bit about Argentine culture.

In a way, the student body here is segregated. It makes me wonder why. It's difficult for me because I don't feel Latina enough, but I also don't feel "white." Does that make sense?

The Crew was composed of all different appearances and personalities. It was great, and I miss it.

Society shouldn't put such an emphasis on people's skin color, gender, race and ethnicity, and the list goes on. Whoever I befriend at this school, I don't care who they are or what they look like. I only want genuine interactions with others. Is that too much to ask for?

January 11

"Do you want to go get coffee with me?" Lucas asks. "Let's celebrate the end of our first week of school."

I'm in the middle of doing homework, but I smile and say, "Sure."

We order our drinks. Sunlight peeks through the large storefront window. A small table next to it calls our names.

I take a sip of my macchiato.

Lucas crosses his arms and rests them on the table. "Can I ask you something?"

I nod my head.

"You've never really told me about your parents. Or your life before The Crew."

I stop looking out the window. That caught me off guard. "I don't really want to talk about my life before The Crew."

"Why?"

"It's ... dark."

"You can tell me anything."

I don't know if I'm ready to talk about the past. I don't even know if I ever want to completely reveal it to anyone. "Can we go somewhere else to talk about it? Someplace where it's just us two?"

"Yeah, I know the perfect place."

After driving back the way we came from, Lucas takes me to the park near Nonna's.

We sit down on the grass. Although there's sunshine, it's a bit chilly out.

He initiates the conversation. "So tell me."

The to-go cup's warmth heats up my hands. "Why do you even want to know?"

"Because there's so much I don't know, and I want to know about you."

I can't believe I'm doing this. "Well, my parents were dating in high school. Here in San Jose. They were both 16 when they had me."

"Really? I never knew that."

"My parents ended up dropping out of high school. They wanted to start a new life, so they eventually moved to Chicago after they had me. Some of Dad's family lived there."

I swallow. Talking about death is hard. "My dad died. He was hit by a drunk driver. I was only like four when it happened."

"I'm sorry."

"Life sucked after he was gone. My mom was a wreck. We were always moving from place to place. She couldn't hold down a job. We had no money because she did drugs."

Lucas places a hand on my shoulder.

"She ended up hooking up with this one guy. And so Alessandro was born. My mom didn't want him, so his dad has custody. It's a bad home, though."

"Wouldn't the government have intervened and taken him away?"

"That's what I would think, but they never did." I pause, then say, "In the end, my mom was tired of moving from place to place and not having enough money, so we returned to San Jose and stayed with Nonna. But that didn't last long."

Lucas takes a sip from his drink. "What happened?"

"I woke up one day and my mom was gone. She went missing. After staying with Nonna for a year or two, I stole some of her money and ran away to search for my mom in Chicago. I was so stupid, thinking I could find her in such a huge city."

"So is that how you ended up with a foster family?"

I nod. "Yeah. I was eventually found and placed with the Reeses. I hated them, Lucas. They gave me everything I didn't want. They bought me all these girly designer clothes and toys. They wanted me to be somebody I'm not. All I wanted was to be loved and accepted for once. It's not that I think my mom never loved me, she was just never around."

"I accept you. I wouldn't change a thing about you."

I manage to smile. "That's when we all started making plans and we ran away and formed The Crew."

"I didn't know you've been through so much."

I run my hand through the soft, green grass. "I don't understand why all of this had to happen to me."

"Everyone has bad experiences. It's a part of life. There's the good and the bad."

"Life keeps throwing lemons at me, and clearly I haven't figured out how to make lemonade that isn't too watery or too concentrated."

Lucas looks at me. "We're all still trying to figure out how to make lemonade."

I look at him, he looks at me. We end up laughing.

I guess "The Shitty Life of Kalamiti Sol" isn't so shitty after all.

January 13

Lunchtime. Betsy brought her friend Annabelle over to our table. Annabelle is in my chemistry class.

Lucas hasn't shown up.

I scan the cafeteria, only to find him sitting at another table not too far from ours. The entire table is packed with students laughing and talking amongst each other.

"I can see Lucas is with the populars now," says Betsy.

I turn back around in my seat. "Populars?" I question.

"Yeah. It's mostly juniors and seniors," Annabelle says.

"It looks like he's having a good time," I say.

They stare at me.

"Kalamiti, are you serious? Once he's with them, he's not going to come back," says Betsy.

"If that's what he wants, then it's cool," I reply.

They glance at each other and then they continue eating. I let my food sit in front of me.

This might sound a bit messed up, but I kind of hope Lucas leaves them and comes back to our table.

January 14

Our chemistry classroom reeks of chemical reactions from today's lab. Beakers of hydrochloric acid, test tubes, and goggles are scattered throughout the room.

Right before stepping out of the room to talk to another teacher, Mr. Oxford asks me to put away all of the test tubes from the lab we conducted.

I walk around the classroom with a cart, picking the test tubes up from the lab stations. I'm about to store them in the cabinet, when Joanie comes over and knocks a whole rack on the floor. She then crushes a test tube with her bare fist.

Mr. Oxford returns from the hallway and scowls at the floor. He yells at me and tells me to clean it up.

I take a broom from a closet and sweep up the shards of glass. When I'm finished, I return to my desk and there's a slip of paper on it.

A detention slip.

I get detention for breaking test tubes? No. I didn't even break them. It was Joanie.

"Why are you giving me detention?" I confront him.

"There's no way you could've broken that many test tubes on accident. What you did was clearly on purpose," he says.

I tilt my head to the side. "Well I'm sorry for breaking your precious test tubes."

"Sorry isn't going to fix them."

"It wasn't even me who broke them. It was Joanie."

"Class? Did you all see Joanie break the test tubes?"

No one says a word. Seriously?

"You see, Kalamiti? Blaming others isn't going to help you."

I glance over at Joanie, who's slouching in her seat with her arms folded across her chest. I walk over to her, lift her arm up, and point at her blood-covered fist. "How much more evidence do you need?"

He adjusts his glasses. "Why don't you march off to the principal's office?"

"But it wasn't me."

"Principal's office. Now."

I pick up my backpack. Before walking out, I open the cabinet doors and knock over every single rack of test tubes, beakers, and glass containers in sight. I'm already going to get in trouble for something I didn't do, so I might as well break some myself.

As I stand by the doorway, I point at one student. "Screw you," I say. I point at another student. "Screw you." I do the same to two more students, then I say, "Screw all of you guys." At least half of the class witnessed what happened and no one stood up for me.

"Kiss my ass, Mr. Oxford," I say. At this point everyone's staring at me. Some are laughing.

I storm out of the classroom and head to the office.

The principal, Mr. Cooke, calls in Mr. Oxford, Joanie, and a couple other students from our class.

I'm sentenced to a week of detention because of what

I said and did. I also need to pay for the test tubes I broke. There goes my allowance.

Mr. Cooke changes my schedule. Mrs. Ramos is my new chemistry teacher.

Good. If I had to keep dealing with Mr. Oxford, I'd be breaking test tubes every day.

January 15

The school called Nonna about my behavior. She's pissed.

"You need to respect your teachers and fellow classmates," she says to me.

"Mr. Oxford is probably racist. I'm the only tan person in that class."

Lucas, of course, is eavesdropping. His laugh booms through the living room. "Aw, man, the whole school's been talking about it!" He walks into the kitchen.

Nonna silences him with her stern look. "I don't need your input."

I slam my fist down on the counter. "None of the class stood up for me. No one took my side, Nonna."

"I understand that. These kinds of things will happen. But you need to be the bigger person."

There's no point arguing with her. "I'm sorry. It won't happen again."

I'm grounded for a week. Oh, well.

January 16

I'm starting to regret my actions from a couple days ago. I don't regret breaking the test tubes, but what I'm contemplating is what I said to Mr. Oxford and the students.

Instead of saying "screw you," I should've said something else. What's the point of swearing at people? What's the point of throwing out the middle finger at someone? Does that accomplish anything? No.

What I really should've said was, "Take a hike." Telling people to take a hike is a kind gesture. It's basically saying get lost, but in a good way.

Hikes are beneficial. Go to a park. Visit some mountains. Take a long walk on the beach. Climb Mount Everest. Jog around the neighborhood.

People can contemplate their actions while taking a hike. Go do some serious soul searching. Immerse themselves in nature, breathe in, and meditate or something.

Yeah. I'm gonna start telling people to take a hike. In fact, I should take one myself.

January 17

Lucas is sitting with the populars in the back of French class. They're the same people from his lunch table. I never knew they were popular until Betsy and Annabelle brought them up. I thought Betsy was popular, but in reality, she's just an average student.

Even though Betsy and Annabelle have joined me at my

table, many times I quickly eat and leave the cafeteria early. Something about the cafeteria environment really frustrates me. There are way too many people. Too many people results in too many voices.

When I leave the cafeteria, usually I walk around the halls or hang out in the piano classroom. I love that room. It only fits twelve keyboards, so it's a small class size. I always look forward to sixth hour.

The door to the piano classroom is before me. My hand is on the door handle, but I don't turn it. Beautiful piano music emanates from the room. That's a first. Usually I'm the only one in the classroom during lunchtime.

It can't hurt to go in. It's not like I'm gonna practice right now. I'm just here to have a place to sit and not be around so many people.

I turn the door handle and quietly walk in. There's a boy sitting at a keyboard in the back of the room. He continues playing as if I'm not even there. I take a seat at a keyboard on the opposite side of the room.

I've seen him before. He's one of Ms. Hayley's student assistants. He has visited my piano class once. The guy must take private lessons with her, because the stuff he's playing would probably take me a lifetime to learn.

He stops playing to check his phone.

"You're really good," I say out loud.

He looks up at me. "Thanks."

"How long have you been playing?"

"For about eight years now."

Eight years? No way. He's a pro. The dude wasn't even using sheet music. He played all that from memory. "I just started playing this year. I'm in Piano I."

"You're new here, aren't you?"

I nod. "Yeah."

"I'm Griffin."

"I'm Kalamiti."

"That's a cool name. Do you go by Kal?"

"Yeah, sometimes." Alessandro is the only one who's ever called me that.

He sets his phone down. "Junior?"

"No, sophomore."

"Oh, nice. I'm a junior."

Say something else, Kalamiti. "I really liked that piece you were playing."

He smiles. "Thanks, Kal."

The bell rings.

I put my backpack on and walk toward the door. "I should probably get going to class."

He takes a piece of paper and a pen out from his backpack. "Before you go, I can write down the name of the piece I was playing."

He quickly scribbles, then hands me the note. "I'll see you around."

As I walk to class, I unfold the piece of paper.

"Who You Are" by Jonny Southard
(209) XXX-XXXX
*Griffin

January 18

The other day I bought some pot cookies from Turner. I want to trick Nonna into eating them. I bet her reaction to it will be hilarious. I doubt she's ever touched anything with marijuana.

While Nonna is at the grocery store, I place them in a bowl mixed with regular cookies I baked.

Lucas walks into the kitchen.

"Wow. Those look amazing," he says.

"They're gonna taste amazing, too."

The sound of the garage door cuts through. Moments later, Nonna walks in, holding a couple of grocery bags.

Lucas takes a bite from a triple chocolate cookie.

She glances at the bowl. "You made cookies? Yum."

"I thought it would be a nice treat," I say.

"They're delicious," says Lucas. He's eaten half a cookie.

Shoot. That might be one with pot.

I help Nonna put the groceries away. Lucas devours the other half of the cookie.

Nonna takes a cookie in her hand. "These are edibles, aren't they?"

"Wait, what?" Lucas' face goes pale.

They both stare at me.

"Um ... some of them."

Nonna places her hands on her hips. "Why are you trying to get this whole household high?"

I let out a nervous laugh. "I was trying to trick you, Nonna. I thought it would be funny. You don't seem like someone who's ever tried it."

She laughs harder than I did. "You don't know anything about my youth, do you?"

Lucas and I stare at her. We then glance at each other.

"Back in the day, I used to be a major pothead. I would smoke all the time."

"You're kidding," I say.

She grins. "What did you think, that I'm old and strict and didn't go through life?"

I can't help smiling.

Nonna sets the cookie back in the bowl. "And what are you, Kalamiti, a one-hit-wonder?"

My mouth drops open. Lucas and Nonna laugh.

Nonna walks off.

"She roasted you," says Lucas.

I lean against the kitchen counter. "She's kind of right, though. I am a one-hit-wonder. I can't believe she didn't ground me."

He laughs. "Looks like I won't be waking up for the next few days."

Nonna sure is a wild card.

January 19

I've been texting Griffin. He's a nice guy. I don't know if I can call him a friend yet, but he feels like one now.

I've listened to all of his music recommendations. Piano music relaxes me. I lie in bed, headphones in, and escape to another dimension. Different melodies and chords paint various images in my mind. Even the most melancholic pieces bring me peace. It's a nice break from school and homework.

Griffin has offered to meet with me to practice piano. He said he can help me with reading sheet music and piano fundamentals. I can't wait for our meetings.

January 20

During French class, I tried talking to Summer. She sits right by me.

Big mistake. It was a one-sided conversation, as if I were talking to a wall. She clearly didn't want to talk to me.

This is why I don't have any friends. I'm too scared to talk to people first. If I do get the nerve, it ends horribly. My mind always ends up thinking that they're judging me, causing me to feel physically ill.

I'm the definition of anti-social. I'm the definition of awkward. I really wish it were easier for me to befriend people.

January 21

I'm with Betsy and Annabelle at our usual lunch table. Lucas is with the populars again.

"Do you guys know Griffin?" I ask.

"The soccer player?" Annabelle asks.

"Yeah," I say.

"Well, of course we know him," says Betsy.

"What about him?" asks Annabelle.

"He gave me his number. And we're sort of talking. I mean, not actually talking, you know?"

Annabelle nearly spits out her drink.

"No way," Betsy says, freaked out.

"What?" I ask.

"First of all, are we talking about the same guy? Griffin Phoenix, right?" asks Betsy.

"Yeah," I say.

"Do you have any idea how lucky you are?" asks Betsy.

"He's just like any other guy, isn't he?" I ask.

"No, Kalamiti. Get a clue. He's a soccer player. He's a piano player. He's a junior. And he's one of the hottest guys at this school," says Annabelle.

"You know, Kalamiti, your friend Lucas is pretty hot, too," says Betsy.

Hearing my friends call my best friend "hot" kind of sort of makes me want to throw up. It's weird. I guess I should play along with them. "Yeah, Lucas is pretty charming." I look around to make sure no one's listening. "I mean, I try to not like him since he'd probably never like me back. He could probably get any girl he wants. Take a look." I turn around. "He's got all those girls on his ass."

We all laugh.

Annabelle rests her head on her hands. "So you and Griffin—"

"We're just friends. I assure you there's nothing going on. Trust me."

"That's what they all say," says Annabelle.

I need to focus on myself right now. I'm not looking for a boyfriend. The truth is I've never even had one.

I'm pretty sure nothing's going to happen between us.

January 22

Geometry time.

I'm scrambling to finish yesterday's homework assignment before Mr. Johnson comes around to pick them up.

Phew. Just on time. As he collects our homework, he hands out stapled packets, fresh from the printer.

Mr. Johnson sets the stack of homework on his desk, then directs our attention to the screen. "Today we'll be starting our group project of the semester."

Hold up. Group project?

He continues, "Each group will be responsible for designing a home. You will make a blueprint on graph paper and include square footage and a scale." As he speaks, he changes the slides on the screen.

Gee, I didn't realize we're all qualified architects now.

I don't want to work with anyone. I don't know anyone in this class. You lost me at "group," dude.

"I will leave it up to you all to pick your groups. We will have seven groups of three and one group of four. Pick your groups now."

Everyone gets up from their desks and walks around. Everyone except me. I stay at my quiet little table in the back of the classroom.

Soon everyone is sitting with their groups.

"Kalamiti, do you have a group?" Mr. Johnson asks me in front of the whole class.

"No," I respond.

He approaches a group of three girls. "Can you three join Kalamiti?"

I interject. "What if I don't want to work in a group?"
"This is a required project. You have to work in a group."
"So I can't do the entire project on my own?"
"No."

The three girls take a seat at my table. My peaceful space has been invaded.

There's no way I'm working in a group.

At the end of the day, I email Mr. Johnson. He needs to know that I'm serious about not working with others.

Here's what I sent him:

> Dear Mr. Johnson,
>
> After hearing about this new project, I got excited. It sounded like a lot of fun.
>
> Here's the thing. I don't want to work on this with anyone. I work better alone. It's nothing against the three girls you assigned me with. Honestly, I don't talk to anyone in that class.
>
> Being able to sit at my own table in the back of the classroom was pretty dope. No one messed with me, people wouldn't stare, and I could get my stuff done.
>
> I don't like being put on blast in front of everyone, so asking me if I had a group was kind of embarrassing. If you really wanted me to be in a group, you could've talked to me privately after class. You're a cool teacher and all, but at the moment I'm a little pissed at you.
>
> All I ask is that I please, please, PLEASE get to work on this project on my own. I know it's a lot of work to do, but I'll do my best and I'm committed to getting it done.
>
> Thanks,
> Kalamiti Sol

January 23

The bell rings.

I pack up my stuff. I tend to take my time because I'm always one of the last students to leave the classroom.

As I'm finishing, Mr. Johnson approaches me.

"Kalamiti, let's talk."

There aren't any students left in the classroom. Good.

We're both standing by the doorway.

"I received your email," he starts. "I'm glad you emailed me."

"So can I work on the project on my own?"

"It's a lot of work. You'll have to design the home, make the slideshow, and present to the class. There's a reason I make this a group activity, since the work can be divided between students. Are you up for it?"

"Yes. I can do it. And if I don't manage to get it done, then you can give me an 'F.'"

"Okay. You can work on this independently. I'm also sorry for calling on you in front of everyone. I didn't mean to embarrass you."

"Apology accepted. I won't let you down, sir."

"Am I still a cool teacher, or are you still pissed at me?"

"What are you talking about? You've always been cool. I got my way, so I'm not pissed anymore."

We both laugh.

Mr. Johnson's cool.

January 24

"Who is Lucas talking to?" I ask Betsy and Annabelle, as I stare at the lunch table full of populars.

"That's Amelia," says Betsy.

Oh yeah, she's the girl who sits by Lucas in French class.

"Kalamiti, you need to go over there and get Lucas back," says Annabelle.

"He's just my friend. I can't really get him back," I say.

"Wait ... I know what it is," Betsy starts. "You like Griffin, don't you?"

"What? No, I don't. We already went over this," I say.

"Ooh, this is one of those love triangles. You like both of them, huh?" Annabelle asks.

"No. I don't know," I say. Sometimes I get annoyed because at times all they talk about is boys.

"Ready to go practice?" I turn around and Griffin's there.

As I walk off with him, Betsy and Annabelle giggle. I roll my eyes.

Lucas stares at us as we walk away.

Whatever. Two can play at that game.

January 25

Behind Nonna's house, land stretches beyond what my eyes can see. It's like a whole new world aching to be discovered.

Upon walking into the unfamiliar territory, I feel at peace. A beautiful willow tree overlooks a glimmering pond.

I gently push aside the willow tree's branches and become one with its embrace. As I sit, leaning against the trunk, I'm protected by the leaves and branches. The pond water ripples. Birds chirp from nearby telephone wires.

I tilt my head toward the top of the tree. The sky peeks through the branches. Layered clouds appear to move quickly in the distance, making me wish I could hop on and take a tour of the atmosphere. I could stare at them all day.

And then I have a flashback to Denver, when Lucas had me visualize a sunflower field.

That's it. That's what's missing here. Sunflowers.

January 26

Thirty minutes ago, Betsy called an emergency get-together at Annabelle's.

Code Red. I'm not sure what that means, but it sounds bad.

Annabelle is lying in her bed, sobbing. By the look of her puffy eyes and tear-streaked face, who knows how long she's been crying for.

"What's wrong?" I whisper to Betsy.

"Her boyfriend broke up with her."

For the record, I didn't know Annabelle had a boyfriend.

It's hard to know what to say or do in these kinds of situations. I want to be supportive, but how do you help someone who's feeling down? Do you solely listen? Should you give them advice or your opinion? What about saying sorry and giving them a hug? I can't tell what Annabelle needs at the moment. I wish I knew.

Annabelle sniffles. She hugs a square-shaped pillow against her chest.

I whisper to Betsy again. "How long were they together?"

"Three months. She'll get over it. This is not her first rodeo."

Three months? That's nothing. She's crying as if it's the end of the world.

Betsy and I take a seat next to Annabelle.

Annabelle says, "I miss Turner."

Wait, what? She was with Turner?

"Turner? The stoner? I once smoked weed with him after school," I say.

Annabelle gasps. "He does drugs?" She begins to cry more.

Betsy stares me down while she hugs Annabelle.

This was not the right time to give an anecdote. What have I done?

One day I'll figure out how to be a comforting and supportive person.

January 27

Today was my first time meeting up with Griffin after school. I was initially nervous about playing in front of him because I was worried about missing notes and screwing up simple rhythms. The practice session ended up going well.

I tried giving him some of my allowance, but he refused. I guess he just likes to help others.

After practice ended, I walked home.

As soon as I closed the front door behind me, Lucas asked, "Where were you?"

"Practicing piano with Griffin," I said.

"Griffin? The junior?"

"Yeah. Got a problem?"

He shrugs. "Just a little."

"Well, look who's talking. The guy who left my table to go sit with a bunch of popular girls at lunch. Here's a taste of your own medicine."

I can see the jealousy in his eyes. It's kicking in full time.

January 28

I stayed after school again for another practice session.

When I arrived home, Lucas looked at me, but he didn't say anything.

There's a lot more distance between us now. To be honest, it's killing me.

January 29

Today we had a test in Mr. Bold's class. Today was also one of the worst and most humiliating days of my high school career.

So something messed up my stomach. Bad. I'm not talking about a little stomach ache here. This is the kind of pain and rumbling that disrupts your entire day.

I was sitting at my desk, trying to focus on writing my

name and date at the top of the test. Pain started creeping into my abdomen. Then the rumbling started.

Oh, it was bad. When the entire classroom is silent except for the sounds of a clock ticking and pencil lead leaving its mark on paper, it's impossible to try to hide your stomach's unsanctioned remarks. Let me tell you, it was louder than the shot heard 'round the world. It was so loud that students in classrooms in Brazil could probably hear it.

Students in the rows in front of me were using their peripherals, searching for the rumble's epicenter. Sweat beaded up on my forehead.

Look out, Room 102, we've got a 9.0 earthquake coming through.

And that's when I knew.

My arm shot up in the air. Mr. Bold called on me.

I asked, "Can I go to the bathroom?"

He said, "What?"

Remember, he can hardly hear a thing.

I asked again, only to have him repeat, "What?"

I stumbled out of my chair. Clutching my stomach, I yelled, "I'm about to shit my pants!"

Before he could respond or before I knew if he even heard me, I sprinted out the door and straight to the nearest bathroom. I sprinted so fast the soles of my shoes burned rubber. I could've qualified for the Olympics.

Holy smokes, though, I made it to the throne just in time.

At least that time of the month didn't pay a visit simultaneously. Thank God and Mother Nature.

January 30

Right before leaving piano class, I check the bulletin board. Attached to it is a bright green piece of paper.

A talent show is coming up.

Ms. Hayley approaches me. "Are you interested in the talent show?"

"Uh, I don't know," I say.

"Here." She takes the piece of paper off of the board and hands it to me. "Take it. If you decide to audition, it'll have all the information you need."

I take it from her. "Thanks."

TALENT SHOW
MAY 1ST @ 7 P.M. IN THE AUDITORIUM
SIGN UP BY FEBRUARY 7TH
1ST, 2ND, AND 3RD PLACE AWARDED
MORE INFO – MS. HAYLEY

Should I do this?

January 31

The other day, I visited a local nursery. I only expected to be there for a few minutes. Instead, I was there for an hour. So many plants and seed packets lined the never-ending shelves. I didn't know there were so many kinds of sunflowers. I ended up buying a couple of different varieties.

I'm going to start a garden next to the pond and willow tree. I don't want anyone to know about any of this. Not Nonna, not Lucas, not my friends from school.

A small patch of dirt is next to the willow tree, slightly overrun with grass. Using a shovel I found in the garage, I try my best to remove the grass and break the compact dirt apart.

I rip the seed packets open and grab a few seeds from each. I scatter them and loosely cover them with the dirt. I take my water bottle out of my backpack and water them.

Seeds have been sown. Let's hope they'll sprout and grow.

February 1

Every Saturday for an hour, Ms. Hayley leaves the piano room unlocked for students who want extra practice.

Griffin wasn't busy with soccer or his other hobbies, so we agreed to meet up.

After practicing scales, he asked, "Do you want to try out for the talent show with me?"

I bit my lip. "What would you want to do for the show?"

"I've been composing a duet for two pianos."

"I'm not that good."

"What are you talking about? You're great. You learn fast. I can play all the complex stuff and your part can be simple. I think it'll be fun. What do you say?"

Hey, why not? Ms. Hayley had given me the form, so this all must be a sign. "Sure, I'm in."

It can't hurt to do something different and out of my comfort zone. Maybe if we win, it'll change things. I could make more friends. People around here would respect me. Maybe. Just maybe.

February 3

Progress reports. Didn't know there was such a thing as them until today.

My only A is in piano. I have Bs in geometry, English, and history. Cs in chemistry and French.

Compared to Lucas, my grades are trash. He has all As and Bs. I'm slightly jealous. Nonna is gonna be proud of him, but mad at me.

I want to burn my progress report, but Lucas is probably gonna gloat about his, so Nonna's gonna be expecting mine. There's no hiding it.

This blows.

February 4

Wanna know something crazy?

Amelia's here.

The reason Amelia came over is because she and Lucas are studying for their history class. They have almost all the same classes, which explains why they've become so close.

That's one thing that sucks about high school. Having different schedules than your friends makes it difficult to actually see them during the school day. I share one class with Betsy, two classes with Annabelle, one class with Lucas, and no classes with Griffin.

I'm in my room, sitting on the carpet, leaning against the wall. Even though my bedroom door is shut, I can hear them. They're getting their work done, but it also sounds like they're laughing too much. Come on, history isn't that funny.

Her personality is the opposite of mine. We're nothing alike. Why does Lucas like her so much?

Time to go disturb the peace.

I approach Lucas' open bedroom door and knock.

They're sitting at the edge of his bed.

"What's up?" he asks.

"Could I borrow a pencil? I can't seem to find mine."

"Sure."

I walk over to the desk.

As I search for a pencil, Amelia talks. "So there's this new Italian restaurant that just opened. I was wondering if you'd like to go. How about Thursday night?"

Hold up. No. Say no, Lucas.

"Yeah, I can pick you up."

Son of a gun.

I'm holding the pencil in between both hands. Next thing you know, I snap it in half.

"Are you good?" asks Lucas.

My hands are still shaking. "Yup, I don't know how that happened, but I'll get a new one." I chuck the broken pencil into the trash can, with as much force as possible.

Lucas goes back to writing in his notebook. Amelia continues to stare at me, her gaze cutting through the voluminous, light brown hair that shields part of her face. I grab a new pencil and return to my room.

So much for getting my homework done.

February 5

Betsy and I are at Annabelle's house. We're hanging out.

I need to tell them about Lucas and Amelia.

"So, Amelia came over the other day. She was studying with Lucas. She asked him to go to some restaurant tomorrow night, and Lucas said yes."

Betsy says, "I don't know what Lucas sees in her. Did you know she lost her virginity in an airplane lavatory her freshman year?"

I didn't need to know that. That's probably the nastiest thing I've heard in a while. "So do you think it's like a date or something?" I ask.

What even is a date? Is that a more sophisticated way of saying "hang out?" What do people do, spoon feed each other? Reach across the table and hold the other person's hand? Kiss them half-way through to seal the deal? What's the point of the date if you're just gonna watch a movie where you can't even talk to the person you're interested in? And how do you know they aren't using you to get free food or drinks? Sounds like a date is just an excuse to dress up in non-school clothes and gaze into someone else's eyes while sitting across the booth from them, trying not to say anything stupid, and hoping cilantro doesn't get stuck in between your two front teeth. So cringey and complicated.

I don't have the guts to ask Betsy or Annabelle what exactly a date is and what it entails because I don't want them to think I'm uneducated.

Annabelle joins in the conversation. "It sounds like a date to me. It's obvious she's into him. And as for Lucas, he didn't turn her down."

I sigh. "I just don't think he likes her like that. He's a nice guy. He wouldn't say no to her." I don't know why I'm so annoyed about this, but it's been bugging me.

"There's only one way to figure out what's going on between them," says Betsy.

I hesitate.

"No. No way," adds Annabelle.

They're looking at each other, exchanging glances. I'm completely clueless. I have no idea what Betsy has in mind.

"What's going on?" I question.

"We can go spy on them at the restaurant!" says Betsy.

"What? How? They'll see us," I say.

"We'll come up with something," says Annabelle.

I smirk. "You guys are crazy. But it sounds kind of fun. I'm in."

Hell, yeah.

February 6

Annabelle, Betsy, and I wait in the jam-packed restaurant parking lot. Betsy's mom let us borrow her car.

I wonder if this Italian place is better than Nonna's cooking. Doubt it.

Annabelle brought two walkie-talkies and binoculars. We're prepared.

From this part of the parking lot, we can't see anything.

Betsy says, "I think we're gonna have to get out. We could all go to different sides of the restaurant and hide."

My friends go to one side of the restaurant, while I go to the other. I hide behind a bush by a large window.

The moment I peer through the window, I spot Lucas and Amelia. But they're not alone. They're with two other populars, Lauren and Jeremiah.

This could possibly be a double date.

So far, there's nothing interesting to observe. Lucas and Amelia are sitting in a booth across from each other. No action, no moves, no nothing. I wish I could at least hear what they're talking about.

Even though they're with others, it bothers me that they're spending time together. I don't want to see him with Amelia. He's been spending more time with her than with me. Back in Chicago, Lucas and I used to always hang out. Getting fast food late at night. Sitting at the top of the boxcars and talking for hours. I miss that.

My eyes meet Lucas'.

I press a button on the walkie talkie. "Abort. Meet me back in the parking lot." I make a run for it.

We meet each other in the lot, hop in the car, and lock the doors.

As Betsy drives down the road, I say, "I made eye contact with Lucas. Now he's gonna know we were spying."

"Who cares? It didn't really look like a date," Betsy says.

The first thing I do when I get home is lie down in my bed and stare at the glow-in-the-dark stars on the ceiling.

Going there was a stupid idea. Everyone at the restaurant probably noticed me and wondered why I had a walkie-talkie and binoculars. Amelia and the other populars are going to tell everyone at school about how much of a weirdo I am. I should've never agreed to spy on them. I should've stayed home.

My bedroom door swings open. Lucas walks in and lies down next to me.

"I saw you and your friends. Why were you guys spying on me?" he asks.

"I honestly don't know. I guess I have nothing better to do with my life?" I turn away from him and face the wall.

He sighs. "We're just friends."

"I never mentioned anything about me wondering if you and Amelia had a thing going on."

He pauses. "I just made that assumption. I mean, why else would you guys be spying? And why would you break a pencil right when she asked me to go with her? Someone's clearly jealous."

"Get out, Lucas." I throw a pillow at him.

"We need to talk about this."

"I don't want to talk right now." I sit up.

As I'm about to crawl out of my bed, he says, "Listen to me. Please."

"You have ten seconds."

Once again, we're laying side by side.

"I didn't ditch you for Amelia. I have other friends, too."

"I don't care if she's your friend."

"Oh, really? It's evident there's something bothering you."

I bury my head under my pillow.

The door swings open. "Kalamiti, what is all that racket?" Nonna gasps. "What are you two doing?"

Lucas quickly gets out of my bed. "It's not what it looks like."

"You guys know the rules," she says. "It's late."

"I'm sorry. I was just about to leave." He meets Nonna at the doorway. "Goodnight, Ms. DiAngelo."

She closes the door. "What is going on here? I heard you two arguing and yelling at each other." She sits down on the side of my bed.

Head still buried under my pillow, I say, "I wasn't going to do shit with Lucas, if that's what you were thinking."

"Kalamiti, you know I don't appreciate the use of that language."

"Sorry."

She sighs. "I think Lucas has feelings for you, sweetie."

I take the pillow off of my head. "Then why does he only hang out with the popular kids? Why does he act like I don't exist around everyone at school?"

"Perhaps he's trying to get a response out of you. If you have feelings for him, you need to show him. Have you noticed the way he looks at you?"

"I don't know. I don't know anything right now."

Nonna smiles. "Why do you think he moved here?"

I sit up in my bed.

"Do you really think he moved here because he 'needed a change?'" She inserts air quotes, then laughs. "He moved here because of you."

"What?"

"You'll see it eventually. Goodnight, Kalamiti."

I'm kind of mind blown right now. I can tell it's going to be another sleepless night.

February 7

The final bell rings. As everyone leaves the classroom, Ms. Hayley organizes sheet music. I walk up to her, talent show application in hand.

"Here's my application." I hand it to her.

She gives it a quick glance. "You and Griffin are doing a piano duet? That's wonderful."

I nod my head. She starts walking to her office.

"Ms. Hayley?"

She stops and turns around. "Yes?"

"Why aren't you touring the world? Why are you teaching instead of playing piano?" I've been dying to ask her that.

"Well, Kalamiti, I sort of gave up on that dream. I didn't think I was good enough. I actually really enjoy teaching. I love helping others learn how to play and read music. Even though teaching is my primary job, I still have a lot of opportunities to continue playing."

"Oh, that's great." I don't really know what to say.

"You should always follow your dreams, Kalamiti. Don't let anything get in the way."

I hesitate. "I don't think I have any dreams."

"What? You don't have any goals you want to accomplish?"

Ms. Hayley doesn't know anything about my past. I'm not some spoiled kid with rich parents who can send me to college. I'm not some girl who wants to be something when I grow up. I've never been encouraged to dream big. Growing up, the only thing on my mind was surviving and having enough food to eat. Half the time I don't even know who I really am.

I reply, "I just want to be the best I can be."

She studies my face for a second, then smiles. "That's fantastic, Kalamiti. So I guess there is no deadline for that goal. It's something you'll always keep working on. It's something everyone will always keep working on."

I nod. "I'm not doing so well right now, but I'll get better."

"If you ever need someone to talk to, I'm here."

"Thanks."

I'm thankful for Ms. Hayley. She's one of the few teachers I like at this school.

February 8

It's been a week since I planted my sunflower seeds. I should check their progress.

When I'm sure that Lucas and Nonna are asleep, I walk out the back door.

No sign of growth, at least not from the surface. Some of the seeds are peeking through the soil. I'm not sure if that's how it should be.

They're going to need time to germinate. Patience, K9.

February 10

Ms. Hayley is going to post the talent show contestant list at the end of the school day.

I need to become familiar with my competition. Like that old saying goes, keep your friends close, but your enemies closer.

Sixth hour is finally over. While students are packing up and heading out the door, Ms. Hayley heads to her office. I bet she's fetching the list.

I continue sitting by my keyboard. A crowd of students have gathered by the door.

Ms. Hayley opens the door, moves past the students, and tapes the list to the wall.

Time to face the mob.

I get up from my desk, go through the doorway, and stand at the back of the crowd. I'll just wait for everyone to move.

Next thing you know, I'm pushed aside by some girl who's fighting her way to the front. Rude. She didn't have to push me. I wasn't even in the way.

The crowd has finally dispersed, so I take a look at the list. All twenty slots are filled with people's names and the category that their act fits in. Griffin and I are right in the middle at number ten. Perfect. I was afraid about being one of the first performances. I also didn't want to be at the end because I'm impatient, and I'll be anxious leading up to it.

I'm surprised to see Betsy and Annabelle at number seventeen. Next to their names is the word "dance." I guess they're being low-key about this because they didn't tell me they were entering. I don't know if I should be mad or upset about that.

Other than them, I don't recognize any of the other names on the list. Some sound familiar. I probably share classes with a few.

I'm a little nervous about the show. Most of the contestants are doing music-related acts. There are a lot of singers. It's gonna be hard to stand out amongst all the musicians, but at least Griffin and I are the only pianists competing.

February 11

Betsy and Annabelle are using lunchtime to practice their dance routine for the talent show, so I'm sitting alone at the lunch table.

The table in front of mine is filled with girls. Icy green eyes are fixed on me, which belong to a girl from my English class. I'm 100 percent sure she's the same girl who shoved by me to see the talent show list.

A "psst" comes from her direction.

"Are you gonna shit your pants today?" asks icy green-eyed girl.

The rest of the girls at her table laugh. My face heats up. Because she said it so loud, nearby tables are staring at me. I need to get out of here.

Right as I'm gathering my things, the girl leaves her table and takes a seat next to me. "You're Kalamiti, aren't you?"

I hesitate. "Yeah."

This chick has "bitch" written all over her face. She has this obnoxious platinum blonde hair with red-brown ends. She's wearing burgundy lipstick that's way too dark for her pale complexion. I don't know shit about makeup, but aren't you supposed to blend foundation from your face to your neck?

"So I saw you're doing the talent show with Griffin."

Why does she care? I reply, "Yeah, got a problem with that?"

"Are you sure about doing the show with him?"

Instead of answering her question, I ask her the same

thing. "The better question is, are *you* sure about doing the show?"

I throw my backpack over one shoulder. As I'm about to make my way down the cafeteria aisle, she gets up and stops me in my tracks.

"Griffin is mine. You better stop hanging out with him," she says.

I've never seen her talk to Griffin. "I don't care. I don't even know you."

"I'm Mindy." She picks up a chocolate milk carton from a nearby table and dumps the milk on my head.

From the corner of my eye, Lucas is standing up from the populars table. He comes to my defense, holding a tray of spaghetti. He takes a handful and throws it at her.

Holy hell.

Mindy reaches for a tray from the table. Before she's able to do anything with it, I take my own tray of uneaten lunch and smash it into her face, like a pie.

Mindy's friends haven't joined in. Are they really true friends if they haven't taken her side?

Lucas grabs a ketchup bottle from a cart and shoots ketchup all over her. I add mustard.

A bag of chips being popped open echoes across the cafeteria.

The Mayfield High Food Fight is now in full swing.

Mindy flings a frisbee tray straight at us. Lucas catches it and uses it as a shield.

Something mushy hits the back of my head.

We're gonna need more ammo.

Food's flying from all directions. It's impossible to dodge it. The floor is a sticky and slippery mess. At a certain point, it turns into us aiming and shooting in whichever direction we can.

The principal and two security guards walk through the battlefield and drag me out, along with Lucas and Mindy.

Straight to his office.

After a long meeting, the three of us get sentenced to in-school suspension for the rest of the week. We're also required to clean the cafeteria.

I wipe the tables while Lucas sweeps the floor. Mindy is sitting on a chair in the corner. Her face is glued to her cell phone screen.

"Are you going to help?" I confront her.

She ignores me.

I continue to clean.

Our clothes are wet and gross. Too bad I can't ditch suspension to go take a shower. Hair soaked in milk is disgusting.

Lucas stands the broom up straight and rests his hands at the top. He whispers to me, "She has to help. This isn't fair."

"I know. But we can't really do anything about it," I whisper back.

Lucas and I finish cleaning. After getting a change of clothes from the nurse's office, we all walk down to Room 145.

We're gonna be stuck here for a few days. At least Lucas is with me.

February 12

It's after school. Griffin and I practice piano.

I need to tell him about Mindy and what she said to me. "So you know about the food fight, right?"

"Yeah. What about it?"

"That girl who started it, Mindy, she seems to have a problem with me. A problem with us."

"Oh, gosh," he starts. "What did she say to you?"

"She said that we shouldn't do the talent show. I think she's into you because she said, 'Griffin's mine.'" I insert air quotes.

"Of course."

"Do you know her? Are you friends with her?"

He laughs. "No. She's had a crush on me for a while now, but I'm not into her. She seems so superficial. She threatened you because she's jealous that we're doing the show together."

"Is she popular?"

"No, but she and her friends try to be. I don't get why everyone wants to be popular around here."

"Aren't you popular?"

He shakes his head. "I don't consider myself popular. I think there's a difference between being popular and being friendly and well-rounded, like someone who gets along with a lot of people."

"Yeah. I see what you mean."

"That group that Lucas sits with at lunch? They're definitely popular. I occasionally talk to them, but I get along better with my teammates."

I nod. "Lucas seems to love them. Especially Amelia."

He pauses. "I actually dated Amelia for a couple months. I guess it doesn't really count. She was just using me for attention."

"Do you think she'd use Lucas?"

He sits there, grazing his hands over the keys on the piano. "I'm not sure," he pauses. "This was a few years ago. So maybe she's changed since then."

I pack up my sheet music in my backpack. All I can think about is when Amelia studied with Lucas. What if she's just using him to cheat off his homework so she can get good grades?

Griffin interrupts my thoughts. "Anyway, don't listen to Mindy. Don't listen to anybody. We're doing the show whether they like it or not."

I smile.

February 14

It's Valentine's Day. Bleh.

Metallic balloons, teddy bears larger than me, and billions of bouquets fill the hallways. Red, pink, and white glitter garnishes the floors. These high school couples are acting as if they're never going to see their sweetheart again. This is high school, not a world war. You know they're gonna go out tonight and see each other again first thing in the morning.

As Lucas and I approach the suspension room, Griffin's standing by the doorway, holding a rose with a yellow ribbon tied around it. Griffin's a saint. I doubt he got in-school suspension.

"What are you doing here?" I ask him.

"This is for you." He hands me the rose.

Lucas walks around us and enters the room.

I can feel my face turning slightly red. "Thanks."

I wasn't expecting to get a rose, much less anything. I don't care for Valentine's Day, but it was a nice surprise.

Griffin looks up at the clock in the classroom. "I gotta get going to first hour. I'll text you about practice."

He hugs me, then leaves.

I take a seat next to Lucas. I set the rose on the corner of my desk. Time for a long day, stuck in this dreadful classroom.

* * *

The final bell rings. Lucas and I part ways. He said he needed to return a library book, but that he'd meet me outside.

A card is attached to my locker door.

Happy Valentine's Day!
You're amazing, never forget that.
Lucas Santiago

Inside, a small golden vase with sunflowers sits on one of the shelves. It's an assortment of burgundy, beige, and yellow.

As I approach the bus loop, Lucas calls out my name.

He catches up to me. "I'm walking home today. Wanna join me?" he asks.

"Sure."

As we walk, he asks me, "Did you like the flowers?"

"Yeah."

"Better than the rose?"

I laugh. "I like both of them."

"Why would Griffin give you a rose? What was the point of that?"

I smirk. "Why would you give me sunflowers?"

"Because you're my friend and I thought it would be a nice gesture."

"That might be the same reason why he gave me it."

Footsteps fill the pause. Lucas then asks, "Do you like Griffin?"

Jealous. He's jealous, for sure. "Only as a friend."

He doesn't respond.

When we reach home, we slowly climb the porch steps.

Lucas stops me from going inside. "Wait," he starts. We stand across from each other. Sun rays shine right on us, highlighting the different shades of brown in his eyes.

I don't know why, but I really want him to kiss me.

No, Kalamiti, you don't like him, remember?

Lucas takes a step closer to me. Just then, Nonna opens the door.

"What in the world?" She looks back and forth at us. "I don't even want to know." She storms back inside, leaving the door wide open.

Lucas rolls his head back and then he runs inside.

I'm left on the porch by myself, flowers still in my hands.

I'm crushed.

February 15

Last night I called an emergency get-together for this morning.

We gather at Betsy's.

I tell them my story. "So I think he was going to kiss me. He took a step closer, but Nonna opened the door to get the mail and interrupted."

Betsy and Annabelle remind me of moviegoers, scarfing down popcorn in the middle of an intense scene.

"No way! He definitely likes you," says Betsy.

"How do you know for sure? Maybe he was just being friendly," I say.

They look at each other and burst out laughing.

Betsy says, "Really, Kalamiti? Just being friendly? Most friends don't kiss each other for no reason."

I turn red.

Betsy continues. "It seems like there have been multiple occasions where he's tried to kiss you. Why don't you take the reins? Just go up to him and kiss him right on the lips."

I shake my head. "I don't know about that. What if he thinks I'm gross?"

Betsy does a face palm. "Those are some of the stupidest words I've ever heard come out of your mouth. Usually you're hilarious and say some pretty brilliant stuff. Stop being so hard on yourself."

Annabelle nods in agreement, then adds, "You two have known each other for years. Why would he even think that?"

I shrug. "To be honest, I have no experience with any of this, so yeah."

Betsy gasps. "You've never kissed a boy? Or had a boyfriend?"

I shake my head.

"Awws" come out from them.

Annabelle asks, "Did you want him to kiss you?"

"There's a voice in my head that kind of wanted it to happen, but I tried to ignore it."

Betsy smiles. "I think you like him, Kalamiti, you're just

forcing yourself to not let it happen for whatever reason in your subconscious."

I sigh. "I don't know. I guess I need to think about it. I don't want to ruin our friendship."

This is too complicated. I'm gonna pretend like yesterday never happened. Lucas only gave me sunflowers, that's all.

February 17

Finally. I'm free from in-school suspension. I'm so glad I don't have to sit in the same room the whole day anymore. I kind of missed regular school.

I also checked my garden earlier, and some of the sunflowers have finally sprouted! They're so tiny. I heard they can grow over six feet tall. It's crazy to think that a seed can blossom into something so magnificent. It's surreal and truly out of this world.

Today feels like one of those days when I used to dance in the rain. When I let out all the bad things and I soaked in all the good things.

Yeah, that's how it felt.

February 18

I learned a lot on the piano today.

Thanks to Griffin's help, I can already play a handful of simple songs. I can read music better. Learning hasn't been too hard because I've read some music books from the library back home. Ms. Hayley says I'm making a lot of progress.

I'm hoping to get my own piano or keyboard soon. That way, I'll be able to practice at home. I'll need to save up my allowance for it.

February 19

As I'm walking back to class after lunch, someone slams me against the lockers.

It's Joanie.

"What do you want?" I ask.

"The school's having a talent show. Can I show everyone how hard I can slam my fist into your face?" She slams my head against the lockers. "I heard you're doing the show with Griffin."

"I am."

"I bet that pretty white boy is just gonna embarrass you in front of the whole school. Think about it. Why would he talk to an outcast? Why would he try out with you?"

I want to punch her, but I know that wouldn't end so well.

Now her face is an inch away from mine. "This is a warning, Sol. Don't do the show. You're only going to hurt yourself." She says it in a low voice. My head slams against the lockers a final time, hard. She lets me go and walks off.

She has a point. Why is Griffin so interested in me? I'm some deadbeat teenager who grew up on the streets while he's a boy who can play soccer and piano and is going places. I don't even have the motivation to tie my own shoelaces, yet he composes music and has real goals.

But why am I going to listen to Joanie? I'm not that stupid.

The bell rings. Dang it, I'm late to class.

"Do you have a pass?" asks Mrs. Ramos.

"No."

Joanie made me late, does that count as an excused tardy?

I sit down at my desk. I can't wait to go home.

February 20

Last night's chemistry homework was easy. When I first started school, the subject sounded intimidating.

As soon as I take a seat at my desk, a classmate who sits behind me taps my shoulder.

"Hey, did you do the homework?" she asks me.

"Yeah."

"Can I see it real quick?"

Reluctant, I hand over my assignment. She quickly copies down the answers and passes it back to me.

I wish I wouldn't have let her cheat. She has never tried talking to me, hasn't tried being a friend, and now she just used me for answers.

What a fake.

February 21

It's Friday. No school. The teachers have a professional development day. I'm not complaining.

Since Nonna is on a business trip and Lucas went to go hang out with some of the popular guys, I decided to meet up with Betsy and Annabelle.

We spent a couple of hours at a coffee shop and then went back to Annabelle's, where we had dinner.

It's late. I wonder if Lucas is home. He hasn't texted me all day.

Betsy drives me and Annabelle home.

As we pull into Nonna's neighborhood, a line of cars parked outside of the house captures our attention.

What in the world?

Loud music rumbles the car. All the lights are on inside.

"He throws a party at your grandma's house without you? That's messed up," says Betsy.

"What's more messed up is the fact that he didn't even ask my grandma if he could throw a party," I say.

Betsy stops the car in the middle of the road.

"That boy's gonna get his ass whooped when your grandma returns from her trip," says Annabelle.

I shake my head. "I'm gonna go find him. I'll see you guys later."

This is definitely a populars party. Everyone's lounging in the living room, huddled up in small groups. Bottles of booze and red cups are on the coffee table.

Lucas is in the corner of the living room, talking to the guys.

He walks up to me. "Hey, you made it."

I made it? Dude, what the heck. You didn't even tell me about this.

"We need to talk." I lead him to his room.

He closes the door behind him.

"What were you thinking? Why would you throw a party?" I question.

"This isn't a party. Only a few friends came over," he says.

"Did you even ask Nonna for permission?"

"No, but I think she'll be cool with it."

"I don't think she'll be okay with the mess or the alcohol."

"I swear that wasn't my idea. Everyone brought it. I haven't had a single drop." Lucas lies down on his bed.

I sit down on the edge of his bed, not facing him.

He continues, "If you get to know everyone here, they're all pretty cool people. Join us in the living room."

"You need to understand that I'm not you. I'm not as friendly or outgoing as you. We don't have the same friends. I don't fit in with them and I never will."

"Kalamiti—" he starts.

"I'm not as attractive as you, Lucas."

He bursts out laughing. "What?"

I finally look at him. "You're hot and I'm not. And people care a lot about looks."

"That's not true."

"Yes, it is."

I stand up and make my way to the door.

"You're beautiful, Kalamiti."

I stop in my tracks. Hearing those words come out of his mouth takes me aback.

I turn around.

Focus, K9. "Doesn't beauty have to do with looks? That's exactly what I'm talking about."

He gets up from his bed and walks toward me. "You're beautiful inside and out."

"Stop lying, Lucas. You're just saying that because you feel bad for me."

He puts a hand on my shoulder. "I'm telling the truth. I hope you realize it someday."

Our eyes meet. He's so close to me that I can smell that familiar scent of his. My eyes wander to his lips.

His hand travels down my arm and interlocks with my hand. "I'm just trying to help you."

I let go of his hand. "Well, maybe you should stop. Stop trying to improve my life and stop trying to change who I am."

As I leave his room and ditch the house through my bedroom window, I scroll through the short list of contacts in my phone.

Griffin. I haven't seen him in a while.

I call him and ask if he can pick me up. He says yes.

I'm not surprised that Lucas didn't invite him to the party. It's obvious he doesn't like him.

A black Dodge Charger pulls up to the house. Griffin rolls down the passenger window. "I guess I wasn't invited."

I shut the door and buckle up. "You didn't miss much."

While we drive to his place, we listen to classical music.

We arrive at his house and go upstairs to his room. I explain everything to him.

"You can spend the night here," he tells me.

"Are your parents okay with me being here?" I ask.

"They're out of town. No one will know."

He shows me to the guest room.

At the doorway, he says, "I'm sorry about Lucas."

I shrug. "It seems like we're two completely different people now."

"Sometimes it takes a lifetime to realize someone's true colors. It happened with me and a friend I used to have."

Deep thoughts and questions start swirling in my mind. "Why do you talk to me?"

He wrinkles his nose. "What?"

"Why did you give me a chance? Out of everyone at school, I never thought we'd become friends."

"Look, I'm not shallow or judgmental like a lot of other people. You're different than the other girls at school. I like that."

I scrunch my eyebrows. "What do you mean, I'm different?"

"You're not afraid to be yourself. You stand up for what you believe in."

"You don't care about my past?"

"Everyone has a past, Kalamiti. I'm not proud of who I was in middle school. For a while, I got involved with the wrong crowd. But I've changed."

"I didn't know that about you."

"Change is possible. I believe in you, Kal."

"Thanks."

He hugs me. "Sweet dreams."

February 22

The smell of coffee brewing downstairs jolts me out of deep sleep.

"Morning, Kal. I made breakfast."

Griffin is standing by the stove, spatula in one hand. He's wide awake and dressed in nice clothes. Compared to him, I look like trash.

A stack of pancakes, maple syrup, a bowl of fruit, orange juice, and a pot of coffee sit on the table, waiting to be consumed.

"Wow. This must've taken a while to get ready. When did you wake up?" I ask.

"I got up around 7 a.m. I went for a jog, showered, got dressed, then made us some breakfast."

Griffin has his stuff together. "You didn't have to do all this. I could've just gone home and eaten breakfast there."

"You're a guest. Take a seat, Kal."

I do what I'm told. I take a seat and serve myself. Griffin joins me.

Everything is delicious. As we're eating, I say to him, "I feel like I owe you so much. How can I ever repay you?"

"You don't owe me anything. Your company is enough."

I take a sip of coffee. "You have like a perfect life and have everything together. You have good grades and all these hobbies. I wish I could be like that."

He runs his hands through his light brown hair. "I'm definitely not perfect. My parents put a lot of pressure on me so that I can get scholarships to college."

"Well, you're doing so much better than I am."

His eyes are fixed on his glass of orange juice. "Whose fault is that? That's on you, Kalamiti."

Before I can respond, he stands up from his chair, opens the cabinet, and grabs a plate. Porcelain meets the floor and shatters into a million pieces.

He stares at the ground, his hands in his hair again.

I stand up from my chair and take a couple of steps back. "I think I'm gonna walk home."

"Don't go," he pauses. "I need to talk to you about something."

We both sit down at the table again.

He takes a deep breath. "My parents have been arguing a lot. I think they're gonna get divorced."

"I'm sorry. That must be rough."

"My sister is in college. My dad moved out a couple of weeks ago. It's just me and my mom here now."

I shift around in my chair. "Why didn't you ever tell me any of this?"

"I don't like to talk about this kind of stuff with anyone. I keep it all inside. At first, I thought I was fine, but now it's been bothering me."

"I'm sorry. I shouldn't have said what I said."

"That's why I play piano and do soccer. It's a way to take out my anger without breaking things. Doing things I love distracts me from the negative things going on in my life. It's an escape."

I lean over and hug him.

As he pulls away, he says, "I'm sorry for what I said. But you really need to stop being so hard on yourself. You see all the good in others, but you fail to realize all you have to offer the world."

"I know. I'm working on that." I manage to smile. "By the way, you can always talk to me about anything. I know what it's like to be going through tough times with family."

Together, we sweep the floor and clean the kitchen. Then, he drives me home.

Before opening the passenger door, I ask, "You're not mad at me, are you?"

"Not at all. Thanks for listening."

I make my way to the front door and unlock it.

As I close the door, Nonna approaches me. "Where have you been?"

I turn around. Lucas is standing right behind her.

I say, "I slept over at a friend's house."

"Which friend?"

"Betsy."

"I called both Betsy's and Annabelle's moms. You were at neither of their homes."

"Well, Lucas threw a party."

"I know."

"Aren't you gonna yell at him or something?"

"Yes. But we are talking about you right now."

"I'll go to my room." I close the door behind me and search for my phone charger.

Seconds later, Nonna walks in.

"Where were you?" she asks with a firmer tone.

"At a friend's house, where I could actually get some sleep."

"Which friend?"

"Griffin."

"You slept over at a boy's house?"

"What's wrong with that? I always sleep under the same roof as Lucas."

She doesn't reply.

I kick my shoes off of my feet. "So am I gonna get in trouble? I didn't do anything wrong."

"No. I trust you, Kalamiti."

She leaves my room.

Waves of hostility are flowing between everyone under this roof. I'm not liking it.

February 23

"There's going to be a bad thunderstorm near the end of the week," says Nonna.

I'm starting to worry. Too much water for my flowers isn't good.

"Ninety-five percent chance," she adds.

I glance at the TV.

I'm trying to focus on homework, but the weather isn't a good sign.

I'll need to check my garden's progress. I hope the storm doesn't uproot my plants.

February 24

It's 11 p.m.

As I open the back door, I hear a noise. I turn around, but there isn't anything there.

It's chilly. I should've grabbed a sweater.

My plants have grown a little more.

I'm sure my sunflowers can survive the upcoming storm. I'm sure the weather won't be as bad as the meteorologist claims it will be.

Bring on the storm. This means war.

February 25

French class is the one class I can't ever pay attention in. It's not like I'm ever gonna need to use this language. I'm never going to be able to afford to travel to France or some other French-speaking place.

My eyes are drawn to Lucas, who's sitting on the other side of the room, talking to the usual group of populars. As always, they're loud as hell, which is one of the reasons why I can't pay attention in this class. Ms. Adler doesn't ever say anything to them because they're her favorite students.

Lucas never bothers looking in my direction. In this class, I don't exist to him. I can't help observing the behavior and actions of the populars. They act completely different than I do, so I'm not sure how they reeled Lucas in.

I'm sick of Ms. Adler picking favorites and letting them do whatever they please. She low-key bullies the quiet kids, too.

That's it.

Like the populars, I begin to laugh as loud as I can. I stomp my feet and bang my fists on the desk. I say, "That's hilarious! Good one, Summer!"

Summer turns around and glares at me. Soon, everyone's staring. At least I got the populars to stop their ruckus.

Ms. Adler says, "Kalamiti."

My chorus of laughing, stomping, and banging continues. Clapping and knee slapping are added into the mix. The five sounds fall into a looping pattern.

Ms. Adler stands up from her desk and yells, "Kalamiti, stop it!"

I stop and freeze. I've never heard her yell that loud.

The usually suspiciously happy and upbeat Ms. Adler is now standing before us, both hands formed into fists, red-faced with nostrils flaring.

"What was all that for?" She folds her arms across her chest.

"I'm proving a point. Those guys over there were practically doing the same thing. They're always loud and distracting. You never say or do anything about it, yet you tear into me?"

The class is silent. She stares me down. "Excuse me?"

"I said what I said. You have favorites and you don't treat all your students equally."

She sits back down at her desk, writes on a yellow slip of paper, and delivers it to me.

Lunch detention.

I say, "I just proved my point again."

She avoids eye contact with me. Everyone goes back to what they're doing.

She knows I'm right, but denies it.

Instead of the usual noise level, the class is quieter while we work on our vocabulary worksheets. One of the quiet girls named Penelope, who sits to the right of me, extends her fist out. We exchange a fist bump.

The bell rings. At the doorway, Lucas takes me by the arm and pulls me to the side of the hallway.

He says, "When are you going to stop embarrassing yourself?"

All I can do is look at him and wonder what's happened to him. Like Betsy and Annabelle had warned me, he's one of them now.

He walks away.

The end of the school day comes around.

I climb the narrow bus steps. As soon as Lucas sees me, he starts calling out my name from the back. I quickly sit in one of the front seats.

What does he want? I don't want to talk to him. He was rude to me.

The bus comes to a stop. After being the first one off of the bus, I run home.

"Kalamiti!" Lucas yells.

I throw my heavy backpack in the front yard and I continue to run away. He does the same and follows me.

Out of breath, I stop at the park.

"Kalamiti!" He stops right next to me. "I'm sorry." He's out of breath just like I am.

Through heavy breathing, I say, "I don't want to talk to you."

His eyes peer around the park. "Follow me."

We take a seat at a stone fountain's edge, whose coat of paint is chipping. An abundance of coins rests at the bottom.

"You know, I threw a coin in here once," Lucas starts. "I made a wish."

"What was it?" I ask.

"I can't tell you. It hasn't come true."

Tranquil sounds of trickling water play in the background.

He speaks. "I'm sorry for what I said. You're not embarrassing yourself, because you were right. Ms. Adler lets our group do whatever we want."

"Then why did you say that to me?"

"Because people in class were talking about you and making fun of what you did. It made me mad." He sighs. "I wish I didn't care so much about what others say or think."

"I know what you mean. It's hard to not let things get to us, huh?"

He nods.

"You don't always have to protect me, Lucas."

"I know. It's instinct."

I smile.

"Ms. Adler's face was hilarious. She knew. She knew you were right, that's why she didn't have anything to say. You called her out on her bullshit."

I laugh. "I guess I could have brought it to her attention in a less childish way, but I acted in the moment."

He laughs. "By the way, why are you always staring at me in class?"

"I'm not always staring at you."

"Yeah, you are."

I tilt my head to the side. "Well if you know that I'm staring at you, then that means that you're staring at me, too."

He smirks. "I dare you to get into the fountain."

I dip my hand into the water. Cold water meets my skin, sending a shiver through my spine. I twist my body, dip my feet into the fountain, and stand up.

"You have to completely submerge yourself."

I roll my eyes. I sit crisscross on the floor, hold my nose, and lay back. After being submerged for a few seconds, I return to the surface.

He laughs. "I should've known you were gonna do it."

I splash him.

"That's cold!" He splashes me back.

As we laugh, I take his hands and bring him into the fountain with me.

Like water benders from *Avatar: The Last Airbender*, we continue to splash each other.

Lucas is the first to crawl out of the fountain. He helps me out and we once again sit on the edge. Our bodies shiver in unison.

Despite being cold and soaked, I can't help smiling. "That reminded me of the stream near The Hideout, when The Crew used to swim together."

Lucas runs his hands through his hair, which is sticking up at all different angles. "Those were some good times."

I giggle. "Here, let me help you." Using my hands, I brush his hair back in place.

As I do that, he does the same to me. With care, he gently untangles my hair between his fingers. I move my hands back by my side.

When he finishes, our eyes meet. Kind, empathetic eyes study my face. My breathing stops. I can visualize us kissing in this very moment. Sparks ignite in my belly.

For the first time, I see what Nonna meant when she said she could "see it in his eyes." Has he always looked at me like this?

Maybe I should show him I care. Maybe I should respond to him in the same way, like Nonna told me to do.

I kiss his cheek.

Shades of red and pink mingle with his tan face. "What the hell is wrong with you?"

I can't help laughing. "Nothing's wrong with me. Let's go home." I smile.

"I was an asshole to you earlier and now *this* happened?"

I take his hand and pull him up. He's still in some sort of daze.

As we walk home, Lucas says, "I don't understand you, Kalamiti."

"I don't understand myself, either. We'll figure it out later."

February 26

Remember that huge geometry project and presentation I had to do? Our presentations were last week. I was nervous, but it went well overall.

The projects have been graded. Everyone's design is now hanging on the wall outside of the classroom. It's cool to see my blueprint, which I spent hours on, displayed for the whole school to view.

As Mr. Johnson walks around the room with the stack of graded rubrics, my heart races. I'm scared to see what I got on it.

He makes his way to my table in the back of the classroom and sets my rubric in front of me, facedown.

When he walks away, I briskly turn it over to reveal a "92 A" written in red ink. Attached is a sticky note:

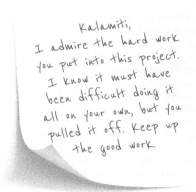

Kalamiti,
I admire the hard work you put into this project. I know it must have been difficult doing it all on your own, but you pulled it off. Keep up the good work.

February 27

The thunder is killing me. All of the sunshine is leaving me.

Lucas tunes into the Weather Channel. "There's a flood warning in the area," he says.

I thought it was only supposed to be a thunderstorm. If there's a flood, my sunflowers aren't going to survive.

A noise comes from the garage. Nonna is back from the store. "I bought flashlights and first aid kits," she says.

"You're acting like the world's about to end," I joke.

"I needed to update our emergency supplies. You never know, we might have to evacuate the place. It's always good to be prepared."

I want to laugh, but I don't. "I doubt it's gonna flood. There's probably only like a centimeter of water."

Lucas adds to the conversation. "Have you even looked outside?"

I join him at the window.

"It's rising fast," he says.

Without thinking twice, I grab a raincoat from the coat closet and open the back door.

"Where do you think you're going?" Nonna interjects.

I slam the door behind me and I run out to my garden. On my way there, I slip and fall into the mucky water and grass.

I kneel next to the willow tree. The pond water has risen, and the soil has absorbed way too much water. It's too dark, so I can't see my sunflowers.

Where's the sunshine when I need it?

There's nothing I actually can do to save my sunflowers. I guess I just have to give up my fight.

I get up from the ground. I take my time walking back.

I knock on the back door.

"Kalamiti!" Nonna yells. "What were you doing?" Lucas is standing next to her.

"I was putting my bike away. I didn't want it to rust in the rain."

"Sweetie, you don't have a bike."

Whoops. "Yeah, I do."

"Did you steal that, too?" Lucas laughs.

I push him aside.

Nonna says, "Get inside before you get sick."

I really hope the sunshine returns.

February 28

It's midnight.

The grass is still wet. With every step, my feet sink into the ground. Water splashes around my ankles.

My sunflowers have been washed away.

It's all trial and error. I just need to plant new seeds.

"So this is your dirty little secret."

I get up from kneeling on the ground and I turn around. "Lucas? What are you doing here?"

"I could see you from my window," he starts. "Why did you decide to keep this a secret?"

I shrug. "I don't know."

"Look, K9, I know you're afraid to admit things."

"I know I am."

"Why?"

"I just feel like people won't accept me."

"Why do you think I talk to you? What about The Crew? Your friends at school? We like you for who you are, and you shouldn't be afraid to show it."

"I know," I pause. "I wanted this to be a place of my own. A place all to myself."

He puts a hand on my shoulder. "And that's okay."

We stand in silence, our eyes gazing into the distance.

"Kalamiti. I need to tell you something."

I hesitate. "What is it?"

He's pacing back and forth with his hands on his hips, something he doesn't usually do. He's making me nervous.

He exhales. "I'm moving back to Chicago soon."

I was not expecting him to deliver bad news. "So when are we leaving?"

He looks at me in a flustered way. "We? No. I'm going alone."

"What? Why? Why are you going back? And why can't I go with you?"

He's staring down at the ground, as if he's collecting the right words to say to me. "June asked me to go back. And you have your grandma now. You need to stay with her."

"Why did June ask you?"

"I'm not sure."

He's hiding the truth from me. "You didn't even ask me if I wanted to go with you."

"Because that's not a choice."

"I'm going with you, whether you like it or not."

"No, Kalamiti," he starts, with a harsh tone. "Your grandma needs you, and you need her. Focus on school."

I shake my head. "You're not my dad, Lucas."

I storm off.

"Kalamiti! K9! Wait!" He chases after me.

I shut my bedroom door, lock it, and lie down on my bed.

This can't be happening. Lucas can't leave me. He can't leave without me.

If June asked him to return, that means The Crew is in danger. Who knows how long he's been hiding this from me?

I don't want to talk to him anymore.

February 29

Lucas left this morning, without saying goodbye.

Leap Day only happens every four years. I wonder what it would be like to be born on that day. Not gonna lie, it would be pretty rad to be a leapling. When it's not a leap year, you could celebrate your birthday on multiple days.

Since this day doesn't occur every year, I keep thinking that I've woken up in some sort of alternate timeline. It's gotta be a coincidence.

Tomorrow, I'll wake up, and Lucas will be here again, right?

March 1

I couldn't sleep last night. The first thing I did this morning was go to Lucas' bedroom. When I opened the door, his bed was empty, and his belongings were gone. He really did leave.

"Why would Lucas leave?" Nonna asks me, while she makes breakfast.

"Because June asked him. That's all I know," I reply.

"Maybe I made him mad when I punished him for throwing a party."

I can't believe she thinks it's her fault. "No, Nonna, I promise it has nothing to do with you."

She pours me a cup of coffee. "Did you guys get into a fight?"

Our friendship has been a rocky road, but I don't think it had to do with him leaving. "Like I said, it's because of our friends back in Chicago."

"This must be hard on you. I'm sorry, Kalamiti." She sets a plate of pancakes in front of me. "I just have a bad feeling those kids aren't safe out there. Maybe they're in some sort of danger."

I slam my mug down, causing coffee to spill onto my hand and table. The burn doesn't hurt as much as Lucas leaving. "Can we not talk about this? Don't you realize they're my family? I've been worried sick about them since the day I moved here. And you saying you have a bad feeling isn't helping me."

She stands there, looking at me. I shouldn't have raised my voice.

She leaves the kitchen.

I really need to learn how to talk to people.

March 2

Today was the longest day ever.

School was completely different without Lucas. It was odd not sitting next to him on the bus. We didn't get to walk down the halls together. We didn't open our lockers at the same time. French class was lonely without his presence on the other side of the classroom. Although he usually sat with the populars, it was comforting seeing him across the cafeteria.

I don't want to do my homework. I don't want to go to school anymore.

I want to be back with The Crew. I miss June, Blake, Jay, Maci, and especially Lucas.

I want my life back.

March 3

Griffin invited me to come watch his soccer practice.

The back of his grey jersey displays "Phoenix" and "27" in large green font. He plays forward.

Griffin's a natural. I heard our soccer team is one of the best in this area.

Practice ends. After some announcements from the coach, Griffin waves at me from the other side of the chain link fence.

I go up to him.

"What did you think?" he asks.

"You're really good," I say.

"You should come to my soccer game this Saturday."

I smile. "I'll be there."

He flashes one of those signature smiles of his.

March 5

Lately, I've been skipping some classes. I don't have any motivation to do my work.

Sometimes I'll skip French by sitting in the office lobby. I'll pretend I'm waiting to meet with a principal or counselor. Most of the time no one questions why I'm there. I haven't been counted absent at all because I either email Ms. Adler that I'm "in the office," or the secretary emails her saying that I'm waiting to meet with someone. I can't believe they haven't realized I've repeatedly been doing this. It's like I'm invisible.

Isn't that ironic? I cut class by sitting in the office.

This school is a joke. I could probably get away with murder. But you know, I wouldn't actually do that.

March 6

I'm skipping history. I'm trying to get to the practice rooms in the music hall, so I can practice piano and possibly take a nap.

I open the door to one of the rooms. There's a dude in there.

"Oh. Sorry," I say.

"It's all good. You're the new girl, aren't you?"

I don't really consider myself new anymore. "Yeah, I guess so."

"Come in." He beckons me inside.

I don't know this guy. An uncomfortable feeling builds in my stomach.

He begins unzipping his backpack. "Want a drink? I've got beer." He pulls two glass bottles out.

There are very few people at this school who have tried talking to me. It can't hurt to chat for a second.

I set my backpack down and take a seat across from him.

He opens a bottle and hands it to me. "I'm Sedgwick. Sedgwick Myers. You can call me Sedg."

Huh. The kid's got an odd name like me. "I'm Kalamiti. Kalamiti Sol. You can call me K9."

He takes a sip. "Two of my friends will be here soon."

"Do you guys usually meet in here and drink?"

"Yeah. There aren't any cameras or anything. Security never comes over here."

We sip beer and talk for a bit. I finally made another friend.

March 7

Game day.

The Mayfield Bears are competing against the Sunnyvale Lions.

Both sides of the bleachers are hyped up. It's perfect weather for a soccer game.

Griffin has already scored two goals.

We're down to the last few minutes.

We win!

I leave the bleachers and wait for Griffin by the sidelines. He approaches me, drenched in sweat. I congratulate him.

With the back of his hand, he wipes the sweat from his forehead. "You. Me. Movies tonight. I'll pick you up. What do you say?" he asks.

"I'm down."

Is this a date, or are we just hanging out? Other than the one time I slept over at his house and had breakfast with him, I've never really hung out with Griffin outside of piano practice sessions. I wonder how things will go.

When I get home, I ask Nonna for permission to go to the movies.

"Who is this friend?" she questions.

"Griffin. The pianist," I say.

Nonna has only heard about him, but she's never met

him. "So that's the boy whose house you slept over at that one time," she starts. "Is he your boyfriend?"

Heat rushes to my face. "No."

She takes a couple of seconds to respond. "You can go, but I'd like to meet him."

Later that day, Griffin rings the doorbell.

I open the door. "Griffin, this is Nonna. Nonna, this is Griffin."

They shake hands. Nonna asks him a couple of questions and states rules, like bringing me home by 10 p.m.

"Ready?" he asks me.

"Yeah."

After the action movie ends, we hop back in his car.

Griffin says, "I need to play some tracks for you. I found this new playlist that's phenomenal." He connects his phone to the audio in the car.

Classical music is soon produced from the speakers.

Griffin talks about the pieces, using musical terms I'm not familiar with. He knows what he's talking about, and it shows. He's passionate about all of it. I wish I understood more.

As one song ends and another begins, I speak. "I think I like the simplest of piano music. There's something beautiful about simplicity."

He smiles. "I agree. Sometimes the simplest tracks are the most beautiful. It shows that you don't need a complex formula to create something that resonates with people."

Time zooms by. The playlist ends, which is followed by a CD.

I lean my head back against the headrest and close my eyes. I could listen all day.

"Thanks for inviting me. This was fun," I say.

"We should do this more often." His eyes are fixed on the steering wheel. "I'm glad you like the same music as me. It's hard to find people who appreciate certain things."

Griffin starts the car. We drive around town for fun, luminous piano music still playing in the background.

What a great night.

March 8

Nonna is mad at me.

A couple of days ago, I received another progress report from school. My grades have dropped. She doesn't understand how that's happened, because I had finally gotten them up a couple of weeks ago. The thing is, it's probably all of the skipping I've been doing. Assignments have been getting harder, too.

She wants me to bring them back up or else she's going to stop giving me an allowance.

Waking up and getting out of bed at 6 a.m. is difficult enough.

March 9

I never get to see Betsy and Annabelle anymore. They're always practicing for the talent show. Because I'm not always in class, I don't see them much during the school day.

What's crazy is that neither of them has texted or called me. Maybe they forgot about me.

I miss my friends.

March 10

Lately I've been hanging out with Sedg's group. The other two people I've befriended are Chad Cunningham and Nina Flores, one of the few Hispanics at school. Chad and Nina are boyfriend and girlfriend.

Sometimes we'll hang out in the practice rooms. Other times, Sedg will drive all of us to his place and we'll drink there.

I'm hardly ever in class anymore.

March 11

A big assignment was due yesterday for history class.

This is one of my easier classes. But since my progress report grades were poor, I paperclipped a five-dollar bill to my assignment.

Mr. Knox hasn't mentioned anything about it. He probably accepted my bribe.

The bell rings.

"Ms. Sol," says Mr. Knox.

It's hard to read his poker face.

While the class exits the room, I saunter over to his desk.

"Explain this." He brings out the assignment with the bill attached to it.

Is he angry, or is he curious why I attached money?

I swallow. "I thought it would help my grade."

"So you really think you can bribe a teacher for a better grade?"

"Think of it as a tip." I'm not kissing up. This is one of the more decent classes, and he does teach well.

He places a hand on his forehead. "I don't know if you're trying to be funny or not, but this isn't necessary."

My heart races. "Nonna, I mean my grandma, wasn't happy with my progress report. I was worried I didn't do well on that assignment."

"In my fifteen years of teaching, I've never had a student do that. Before Mayfield, were you homeschooled?"

I hesitate. "Sixth grade was the last time I was enrolled in school. It was in Illinois."

He looks away. For the first time, I can read what his face is saying. He's trying to figure out what to say to me.

"In school, bribing isn't necessary. In fact, you could probably get in a lot of trouble for it. The best advice I can give you is to have good attendance, study, and make an effort to turn assignments in. It's better to get some credit instead of a zero." He unclips the bill and hands it back to me.

"I'm sorry—"

He holds a hand up. "No, don't apologize," he starts. "You didn't even need to pull that trick. You got an 'A' on this assignment."

"I did?"

"Yes. Put in the effort, that's all you need."

That backfired.

March 12

Everyone's walking down the hallways to their next class. As I turn a corner, I catch a glimpse of Joanie in the distance.

"Hey, new girl!" she calls out.

New girl. That's me. I turn around and walk in the direction I came from. She catches up, takes a hold of my backpack, and pulls me into the nearest bathroom.

I'm expecting her to throw some punches at me, but she doesn't. Instead, she looks frantic. She peers through the stalls, as if to make sure there's no one else around.

"What do you want?" I question.

"I've noticed you've been hanging around Sedg and his clan," she pauses. "You need to be careful around those punks."

I scrunch my eyebrows. "Why should I listen to you? You're a punk and bully yourself. I finally made more friends and I'm not gonna let you ruin that."

"I warned you, Sol." She walks off.

She's always getting up in my face. I wish she would mind her own business.

March 13

Nina wanted me to accompany her to the bathroom because she doesn't like going alone.

She stands by one of the sinks, staring at herself in the dirty mirror. She pulls a tube of mauve lipstick out of her purse and reapplies it.

Here's the thing about Nina. She's obsessed with her looks. Nina's the kind of girl who always has a full face of makeup, and her outfits tend to match with her purses and shoes. Her long brown hair is always perfectly flat ironed at a temperature way higher than your typical 350° oven, which is why it's insanely damaged from heat. If any strand of it starts acting up, or if a tiny pimple pops up on her face, it's the end of the world.

I will say, her makeup and outfits are always poppin'.

She tucks her hair behind her ear. "My hair looks awful today."

I say, "I think it looks fine. You're overreacting."

The bell rings. We're both late to sixth hour.

She stops looking in the mirror. Instead, she cocks her head to one side and looks at me. "Why don't you do something to your hair, Kalamiti? Why don't you wear makeup?"

As she takes a strand of my hair in her hands, I glance at the ground. No one has ever asked me that before. "Because I'm fine with the way I look. I don't really like makeup."

She grabs my jaw in her hand and studies my face, making me uncomfortable. "You could always fix your eyebrows. Do something different. How about a makeover?"

"I'm good," I start. "I need to get to class."

Honestly, that was pretty rude of her to say stuff like that to me. It's almost as if she wants to change the way I look. Now it's making me wonder if there truly is something wrong with my appearance.

I'm kind of hurt. Just because I'm a girl, it doesn't mean I'm required to look a certain way. No one goes around asking boys why they don't wear makeup. It's strange.

All I was trying to do was reassure Nina that she looked

fine. Maybe my comment made her mad, so she took it out on me.

I'm not going to dwell on this and let it ruin my day. It's whatever.

March 14

It's a Saturday.

Griffin and I agreed to meet up so we could practice. Our focus is on our talent show piece. We've been making a lot of progress.

We sit next to each other on the bench.

"Thanks for helping me. I really appreciate it," I tell him.

"No problem, Kal."

I gaze at the keys on the keyboard. "I'm scared to perform in front of so many people. I've never done anything like this."

He rests his hand on top of mine. "It's normal to feel that way. I've been playing for years, but I still get nervous when I perform in front of people. You're brave for doing this."

I smile. "Sometimes I like to take risks."

He smiles. "That's awesome. You're not afraid to be yourself and you seem to not care what others think about you."

"I do care, though. My mind sometimes wonders why some people don't want to talk to me and why some people have a problem with me when I haven't done anything to them."

"They probably wish they could be like you. You have something they don't."

He might be right. Maybe girls like Mindy hate me for

reasons that aren't about me, but about them. "Yeah. Maybe that's the case."

I stop staring at the keys and look into Griffin's eyes. He puts one hand in my hair and he kisses me. Instead of pulling away, I accept his kiss.

After what seems like an eternity, he pulls away.

"I like you, Kal," he says.

I'm not sure what to say. I like Griffin, but do I like him like that? How am I supposed to know when I like a boy? I wonder if I'm supposed to experience a physical sensation running through me, like a jolt of electricity. Or maybe it's an emotional feeling within the brain, like a high. It's probably a combination of the two, but there's definitely more to it.

Without thinking, I respond, "I like you, too."

He smiles. "I want to take you out sometime. We could get dinner and listen to more music together in my car."

I nod. "Yeah. I'd like that."

We part ways. As I walk home, my mind replays the scene.

When he kissed me, it didn't feel right. It's not that I didn't enjoy it, but something about it gave me an odd sensation in my stomach.

Love is complicated. People seem to throw out "I love you" so frequently that it starts to seem insincere. It's like the whole "How are you?" small talk. I don't think I've ever been in love. I don't even know what love is.

I also don't understand how some people at this school jump from one person to the next. One week they're with one person, then they're with someone else the following week.

It's like someone trying on different outfits before going to school, hoping to find the perfect one. How do they move on that quickly? Did they truly love the previous person, or were they just attracted to their looks? You would think people need time to heal, but maybe some people can't stand the idea of being alone.

March 15

Griffin has been calling and texting me all day, asking me what day I'm free to go out with him.

I haven't responded to any of his calls or texts. I don't know what to say. I'm scared. A part of me is ecstatic that a guy like him is into me, but another part of me has a feeling that it's not right.

I need time to think. I hope our friendship won't be ruined.

March 16

It's Spring Break.
Days are going by so slow.
I haven't heard from Lucas. No updates about The Crew.
I know it's only been a few months since I've been away, but it feels like forever.

March 18

Nonna and I are redecorating the living room. We're going to rearrange furniture and add some decorations.

Nonna brings out a box filled with new candles, coasters, and picture frames.

I begin taking the items out and placing them on the coffee table. As I pick up one of the frames, I notice it's holding a photo of me, Nonna, and Lucas.

She joins my side. "That's the first photo the three of us took together when we came home from Colorado."

I didn't know Nonna had printed these out. I completely forgot we even took this photo.

"I miss him," I say.

She leans over the box and reveals another picture frame. She hands it to me. "Here's one of you and Lucas. A photo can't replace him, but he'll always be with you."

I look at both photos. How thoughtful. "Thank you, Nonna."

We finish. Together, we break down the cardboard boxes.

"Nonna?"

"Yes?"

"I made some new friends at school. Is it okay if they come over tomorrow?"

"What are their names?"

"Nina, Sedg, and Chad."

"Yes. They can come over. I would love to meet them."

To be honest, I didn't want to invite them over. I don't like having people at my house, especially ones I just met. In the past, we've hung out at their places, so I feel obligated to invite them over for once.

We'll see how it goes.

March 19

Today's the day. I'm scared about Nonna meeting my friends.

The doorbell rings.

I welcome them in and introduce them to Nonna. After offering us something to drink, she departs to her room.

We lounge in the living room.

Sedg and Nina complain about their classes. How there's too much work, their teachers are boring, and they have no friends in their classes.

They complain a lot. They talk so much trash, they'd be millionaires if they got paid for it.

Chad sits and listens. He doesn't say much. That's his usual way. Sometimes, he reminds me of myself. There's probably a lot going on in his mind.

Sedg proceeds to light a cigarette.

"Dude. Don't do that in here," I say.

If Nonna saw, she'd kick him out of here and ground me.

He rolls his eyes, then steps out the back door.

Can they go home already? I'm bored, I'm not interested in their conversations, and my social battery is on low.

Nina's phone goes off. She answers it.

Sedg comes back inside, smelling like an ashtray.

Nina hangs up. "We gotta go. My mom wants me home."

About time.

They make their way to the front door. Right as they're stepping out, Nina turns around and says, "I'll be buying alcohol the next time we get together."

I close and lock the front door.

Nonna joins me by the entrance. She puts her hands on her hips. "I don't like those kids. You need to get rid of them."

Nonna doesn't realize how hard it is for me to make friends. Shouldn't she be happy that for once I was having friends over?

She interrupts my thoughts. "Whatever happened to Betsy and Annabelle? What about Griffin? Those are good friends."

"They're busy. Betsy and Annabelle are doing the talent show together, so they're always practicing. Griffin does piano and soccer. They don't have time for me."

"Real friends make time for each other. I suggest you reach out to them."

I still don't know what to say to Griffin, so I haven't responded to him. Nonna has no clue about everything that's happened between us. I don't want to tell her.

Yesterday I finally heard from Betsy and Annabelle. They had asked me to hang out over Spring Break, but I didn't respond because I knew Sedg, Chad, and Nina were coming over. I was initially mad at them because they hadn't texted or called me in a while.

I doubt they're gonna want to hear from me now and listen to my excuses.

March 20

I lied to Nonna. I told her I was going to practice piano with Griffin, but I actually went to go smoke with Turner. This is my second time smoking with him in the last few weeks.

His car is parked in the back of the school's parking lot.

These smoke sessions are quite awkward. Neither of us talks. Straight to business, I guess.

The car quickly fills up with smoke. We crack the windows open.

I can't stop coughing. My heart rate accelerates. From the sideview mirror, my eyes are halfway shut and red.

All I want to do is sleep. I need to escape reality. This allows me that escape, even though it's only temporary.

March 21

Trial #2. I planted some new sunflower seeds. I want a bright and beautiful garden, with tall sunflowers looming over me, just like the willow tree.

Hopefully they'll grow this time. I need some serious sunshine in my life.

March 22

"Come to church with me," says Nonna.

Without looking up from my book, I say, "Uh, no thanks."

Nonna is super religious. She knows like every single prayer, prays the rosary daily, and goes to mass more than once a week. She has never tried making me or Lucas go to church before.

"Church will help you. You'll make better choices."

For a while, she's been saying that I need Jesus and all that bologna.

"I think I'd rather finish this book first," I say.

Portraits of Jesus and the Virgin Mary are hung all over her home. There are a couple of wood crosses, too. Sometimes she makes me kiss Jesus' feet on the cross. I think it's kind of dumb, honestly. Isn't Jesus everywhere? They say he's always watching us, and that he's always around. If so, then why does he need to be represented by some wood cross?

"We need to go. Mass starts in ten minutes."

My eyes are glued to my book's pages. "I'll go some other time."

"You are just filled with the devil! You need to ward off all that evilness!" She raises her voice.

I'm no devil. How dare she call me evil? "You know what? The devil can kiss my—"

Before I can say it, she takes her sandal off and smacks me with it. After giving me a good whooping, she yanks my ear and pushes me into the bathroom.

"You are staying in there until you apologize! That is unacceptable!" she yells.

I sit on the cold white tiles.

I can feel her presence on the other side of the door. She's still waiting for my apology. I need to stop giving her a hard time.

"I'm sorry."

A couple of seconds pass. She then opens the door. "Will you go to mass with me now? We're going to be a little late, but it'll be okay."

"Yeah. I'll go."

We arrive at a beautiful, brown, brick building with an array of stained-glass windows. A little garden adorns the entrance.

We take a seat on a wood bench near the center.

It's hard to pay attention. Crying babies distract me as well as annoying kids who think they're whispering. The row in front of me is filled with all these people who are miles taller than me.

The priest reads something from a book and then he talks about it.

People in rows in front of us begin to line up for communion. I want to follow Nonna to get some wine, but she says I'm not allowed.

Mass ends, and Nonna kneels. "Kneel down and pray with me, Kalamiti."

As I kneel and put my hands together, I ask, "How do I pray?"

"Close your eyes and thank God for everything you have and tell him about your needs. He is always listening."

Am I supposed to feel something? Are angels going to swoop in and take me to heaven for a few seconds? Will I see God standing before me? Am I going to witness bright white light and see visions? Or will it be like some sort of psychedelic experience?

I don't feel anything. It's just the voice in my head. All I hear is shuffling feet and murmuring coming from the other side of the church. Rose-scented incense lingers in the air.

Coming to church with Nonna wasn't too bad. After everything I've put her through, it's the least I can do for her. It's a way to spend time together.

They do say that with the power of God, anything is possible. Maybe He'll guide me toward a brighter path and help me make better choices.

March 23

Just got home from school. Since it was the first day back from Spring Break, I wanted to start off on a high note, so I actually showed up to all of my classes today.

One of the dudes in my English class pissed me off, though. Asher's his name. As soon as I walked in, he said, "You finally decided to show up to class?"

I was pretty close to committing a violent act. But then I realized I would've probably gotten in a lot of legal trouble. You see, Asher is one of those dudes who wears polos, colorful shorts, and boat shoes. He drives a $35,000 truck that his parents bought him as a Christmas gift. I found out that his dad is a lawyer, which is why a lot of people don't mess with him. So yeah. I sure as hell am not in the mood to end up in delinquent camp again.

Screw that.

March 24

The calls and texts from Betsy, Annabelle, and Griffin have finally stopped.

The guilt was eating me up. I felt bad for not responding, but I didn't know what to say. And a part of me was still angry at Betsy and Annabelle because they were so focused on the talent show.

At this point, I'm not even sure if any of us are friends anymore.

March 25

Sedg is driving me, Nina, and Chad to the mall.

For the record, I didn't want to go to the mall. I asked them about hiking somewhere, but none of them wanted to do that. They hate the outdoors. It sucks because I like to be out in nature.

After taking an eternity to find the closest parking space to the entrance, Sedg finally parks his car with one of the worst parking jobs I've witnessed. I open the passenger door and I barely squeeze through without hitting the car next to me.

Once inside the mall, we part ways. Nina and I go in one direction, while Chad and Sedg go in another.

Nina leads me to a department store at the end of the mall. Clearance racks fill the second floor of the store.

After browsing for a bit, we hit the fitting rooms.

I don't have any money on me, so I'm not planning on buying anything. I didn't want to be bored waiting for Nina, which is why I decided to try on a pair of jeans and some shirts.

I finish trying on my things first, so I wait for Nina. I sit in a chair in front of the trifold mirror, holding the clothes that I have just tried on.

Her fitting room door creaks open. "Kalamiti."

I stop looking in the mirror and make eye contact with her.

"Throw these in your backpack for me. I'm out of room in my purse." She holds out a dress and blouse.

She wants me to shoplift. I don't want to go down that path again. I can't remember the last time I've stolen anything.

She's my friend now. Friends do favors for each other. This is something I can do to prove my loyalty.

I take the items from her and stash them in my backpack.

"Did any of your things fit?" she asks me.

I hesitate. "Um, yeah, this pair of jeans." I toss them in my backpack. "I need to put these shirts back."

We return some clothes to the racks and we leave the store.

I don't know why I did it. This is the first time I've felt guilty about stealing. These are cheap clothes anyway. The jeans I threw in my backpack are thinner than bedsheets.

Next time, I'm not agreeing to shopping with them. I can't keep doing this. If Nonna found out, she would be so disappointed in me.

March 26

Just my luck.

Griffin was assisting Ms. Hayley in piano class.

He walked around the classroom, helping students with chords and rhythms. He avoided my area.

I placed my headphones over my ears and pretended I

was focusing hard on the short piece I'm doing for a quiz next week.

He didn't wave at me. He didn't smile. He didn't even greet me. Nothing.

I guess our friendship is over.

March 27

Mr. Johnson emailed me the other day. He asked where I've been and why I haven't been attending class. He even said that class isn't the same without my presence at the table in the back of the classroom.

I'm shocked he bothered emailing me. I didn't think he'd care. I didn't think any teacher cared that much about their students.

March 28

Sedg is throwing a party tonight at his place. Apparently, a lot of people from our high school are gonna be there. I've never really been to a real party, so I'm curious to see what they're like.

I knew Nonna was gonna say no if I asked, so I snuck out and walked to school, where Sedg picked me up.

We pull into his neighborhood. His block is packed with cars lined up on both sides of the street.

Scanning the living room, I don't know anyone. They're

probably from other schools. I recognize some from Mayfield, but I don't vibe with any of them.

Who knows where Sedg went. As soon as we walked into the place, he ditched me.

I wander to the kitchen and grab a drink. The smell of weed fills the house. I feel underdressed. I'm wearing jeans, gym shoes, and a baggy, long-sleeved shirt.

People continue to walk through the front door. My eyes are peeled, begging for a familiar face to stroll through.

Who knows how much time has passed. The occupancy has doubled. It's crowded.

I step outside to the fenced backyard. I thought there would be less people, but it seems more packed than inside.

The loud music, shaking my entire being, is making it hard to concentrate. Hanging lights and torches are the only light sources.

People are lounging in furniture on the deck. The pool is filled with people tossing a beach ball around. Couples are holding hands. No one is alone. Everyone is within a small or large group of friends. Everyone except me.

A part of me wishes that someone will come up to me and invite me into their circle. No one bothers to even look in my direction. It's almost as if I'm a ghost, haunting the party.

I continue to walk around the perimeter, trying to see if I recognize anyone. I wish Griffin, Annabelle, and Betsy would show up. I can't even find Chad or Nina.

I feel like a loser. I probably look like one, too, because all I've been doing is walking around on my own, clueless as can be. There's this sick feeling in the pit of my stomach. I don't like it.

Everyone around me is having a great time. People are

dancing, smoking, drinking, and swimming. Conversations are being exchanged. Laughter. I'm not a part of any of it.

I walk back around to the front. I sit down on the curb, next to the mailbox.

I don't know why I bothered coming. None of my friends are here. I don't belong. I'm an outsider. I feel like I was born in the wrong generation. I don't even have a desire to party. I am nothing like these people, nor will I ever be like them. I'm never going to be some social butterfly who gets along with everyone. I feel so sick.

I want to go home.

"K9," a voice calls out.

It's Sedg.

"You good?" He sits down next to me.

"Yeah. I think I'm just tired. Can you take me home?"

"Sure."

Sedg starts the car and then lights a cigarette. The car ride seems like forever.

At last we're at Nonna's house.

"You sure you're good?" he asks again.

I shrug. "I didn't really know anyone there."

"Who needs them when you've got me?" He leans closer to me and presses his lips into my neck. One of his hands reaches for my thigh.

"What are you doing?" I question.

"Let's just lie in the back of my car together. Just for tonight," he whispers in my ear.

I pull away from him as far as I can. "You're just my friend."

A different expression takes over his face. "You really think we've been friends this whole time?"

All I can do is look at him.

He continues. "Look, you've got a nice body, but that's all you've got going for you."

I clench my teeth. "Excuse me?"

"It's whatever, Kalamiti. You're weird anyway."

You've been fooled, K9. "I don't need you. I don't need any friends." I unbuckle my seatbelt and open the car door. I look back at him. "This whole time I've just been using you for alcohol."

Not true. Not true at all. I really thought we were friends. But he hurt me, so I'm going to hurt him back.

"You have a shit personality," he says to me.

"I may have a shit personality, but at least I don't smell like cheap cologne, cigarettes, and nastiness!" I step out of the car and slam the door.

Really, Kalamiti? Nastiness? You couldn't come up with a better word?

He rolls down the window. "No one at school even likes you. You're a nobody."

My trembling hand is still clutching the red cup of alcohol from the party. I throw it at him through the window. "Screw you, Sedgwick, or should I say Sedg-dick!"

"Go to hell, bitch!" he yells at me, then speeds off.

I can't believe I thought he was a friend. I'm so stupid. Joanie was right. Nonna was right. I'm mad at myself. This is exactly why I don't trust people, because they always end up screwing me over.

Bastard.

I don't know how to explain how I feel. I was used. He didn't deserve my friendship in the first place.

Why is it so hard for me to make friends and keep them? Maybe it's me. Maybe there's something wrong with me, something that steers people away. I'm not a likable person.

My mind won't shut off. One depressing thought spirals after another. It's a domino effect. I want to pretend like today never happened. I want to pretend like I never met Sedg, Chad, or Nina.

I want to sleep and forget everything.

March 29

I haven't been able to contact The Crew. I've tried all different forms of communication. Not even Lucas or June have replied to me.

At this point it's safe to assume that something horrible has happened, Lucas wasn't able to help them in time, and The Crew has disbanded.

If only I could've gone with Lucas. If only I could've done something. If only.

March 30

For the first time in a while, I'm attending all of my classes. If I focus on my schoolwork, I can forget about everything else going on.

Lunchtime comes around. I'm dying to meet up and practice with Griffin, but at this point we're most likely not doing the talent show anymore.

I'm not hungry, so I walk around the halls of the school. I want to avoid as many people as possible. I'm not in the mood to talk.

I enter the bathroom that's near my locker area. I peer into the mirror and gaze at the face of a girl I don't even recognize anymore. My soul has been sucked out of me.

The bathroom door swings open and in walk three girls. Out of the corner of my eye, I realize one of them is Nina.

She walks right up to me. "You've been sleeping with Chad?" she questions.

"What? No, I haven't. Who said that?"

"Sedg."

Now he's spreading rumors about me just because I refused to have sex with him. Great. "He doesn't know what he's talking about. I hardly even talk to Chad."

"You were with Chad at the party. He wasn't with me."

"I wasn't with him. Maybe he was with another girl."

And boom. I'm on the ground. I probably shouldn't have said that to her.

One of the girls guards the door while Nina and the other girl kick me and pull my hair back.

Nina brings out a pair of scissors from her purse. She proceeds to cut my hair. I twist and turn, trying to get both of them off me, but I'm pinned to the floor. "I didn't do anything! Stop!" I yell at them. Strands of my long wavy hair are now scattered all over the floor.

I manage to grab the scissors out of Nina's hand. After I quickly get up from the ground, I push Nina's friend into one of the stalls. I then throw a solid punch at Nina. "You messed with the wrong person," I say.

I fling the scissors at the girl guarding the door, like a dart at a bullseye. As she collects herself, I run out of the bathroom.

Lunchtime is almost over. I need to get out before the halls get crowded.

I make my escape through one of the side doors of the school.

I'm running, running toward home. Nonna shouldn't see me yet. I can't imagine what my hair or face look like right now.

I'm home. I run straight to the backyard and to the pond. The willow tree welcomes me in.

I'm safe.

* * *

I open my eyes. I'm sitting against the willow tree.

The first thing I do is glance at my hair. It's long again, untouched. The pain all over my body has vanished. My hand is no longer swollen.

The sky is bright blue, the most beautiful hue of blue I've ever seen. The sun is shining brightly in the distance. It's hard keeping my eyes open. The air is completely still.

There's a shadow on the ground. It isn't mine. My gaze wanders to the origin.

It belongs to my mother, who is sitting a couple of feet away from me. Her eyes are fixed on the pond.

I scrunch my eyebrows. "Mom. What are you doing here? Where have you been?"

She doesn't respond.

She looks exactly how I remember her. Fair skin. Long, dark hair. Tired, lifeless eyes.

"Say something. Anything," I plead.

No response. She's still in the same exact position. The only movement is from her eyes blinking.

The pond is stagnant. There's nothing interesting to observe, yet her gaze is still fixed upon it.

"Mom. Please."

Finally, she tilts her head. Our eyes meet.

* * *

I open my eyes. I'm in the same exact position against the willow tree. Once again, my hair is disheveled. The pain throughout my body has returned. My hand is swollen, shades of red and purple mixing with my tan skin.

The sun is beginning to set. A gentle breeze has made its comeback.

I must've fallen asleep. It was all a dream.

I don't think I've ever dreamt about my mom like that. It felt so real.

Nonna. I need to see her. I need to get inside.

I take my time walking home. Once I reach the back door, I knock.

"Kalamiti! Where have you been?" Nonna hugs me.

"I fell asleep outside. In the backyard. I'm okay."

"What happened to your hair?" She runs her hands through it.

I feel weak. I feel defeated. "People at school are mean to me." There's no other way to put it. I haven't done anything wrong to Nina or her friends.

"We need to report this to the principal and counselor."

My eyes begin to water. "No. They're not going to care. Nothing's going to be done."

"Who exactly did this to you?"

"It was Nina and two other girls," I say, then pause. "You were right all along. They weren't real friends. I should've listened to you." Tears are now streaming down my face.

Nonna takes me into her arms. "This is a part of life, a part of growing up. You will realize who is there for you, and who isn't. You will realize who is true, and who is using you. It's going to be okay. I'm so sorry this happened to you, but I'm glad you're done with them."

I'm so happy to have Nonna. I don't know what I would do without her.

March 31

Nonna took the day off. I'm not going to school today.

We go to the hair salon. I haven't looked in a mirror and I'm scared to do so. So far, the hair stylists have been kind to me.

It's my turn. At last, I look in the mirror. My face looks pretty beat up. My hair is all different lengths. It's messy. I miss my long hair.

"You have beautiful hair," the stylist tells me. "I'm sorry those girls had to ruin it. It'll still look beautiful afterward."

The stylist's name is Kayla. She takes her time. She washes and conditions my hair, then brushes and untangles it. She even styles it. She asks me questions about myself.

Although it was choppy, she's able to save most of my hair, so it's shoulder length.

I thank her. Nonna and I leave her a good tip. At least there are still good humans out there.

April 1

It's a new day and I'm getting revenge.

The first thing I do when I arrive at school is head to a storage room in the gym. I grab a metal baseball bat and make my way to the student parking lot.

Three egg cartons are in my backpack. I throw two of the cartons at Mindy's convertible. Sucks for her, she left the top down, so now there are eggs smeared all over the interior. That's payback from the day she didn't help clean the cafeteria after the food fight.

I throw the last carton at Sedg's car. Without thinking twice, I swing the bat and smash the driver's side window.

Too bad Nina's car isn't parked in the lot, or else I would've done the same to hers.

I walk back home. No way will I step foot in that building today.

Revenge is sweet.

April 2

This is my first day back at school in a while.

No one knows I vandalized Sedg's and Mindy's cars. I

don't care if I get caught. The school doesn't even care, so if I were to get caught, I probably wouldn't be punished.

The moment I enter the building, students stare at me. My new haircut must be bringing in a lot of attention.

I grab my books from my locker and head to first hour.

A single voice cuts through the hallway noise. "What you did to Nina was messed up."

It's Summer from French class.

"What?" I ask.

"You slept with her boyfriend. And you broke her nose."

"I barely even talk to Chad. And I broke her nose because I was defending myself."

She shakes her head and walks off.

Now she's so interested in my business? What a joke. I defend myself and I'm suddenly the villain.

If she's heard the rumor, then the whole school has heard it. I'm screwed. My reputation is even worse now. I'll always be known as the outsider who sleeps around and fights "innocent" students.

I'm standing in the middle of the hallway. Time is at a standstill. People continue to walk around me. Through the crowd of students, I spot Betsy and Annabelle talking to Griffin. I make eye contact with them, something I haven't done in a while.

They begin to walk toward me, so I flee. I can't face them. What if they think the rumors are true? What if they're judging me and questioning why they even became friends with me in the first place?

I wish I could turn back time. I wish I could go to a different school. I could start off fresh, with a new name, something simple like Ashley Smith. I could be a straight-A student and be liked by the majority of the student body. I could make up a whole life, one that seems ordinary. I could be happy.

There's no turning back now. It is what it is. Things will never be the same.

April 3

I thought things would be better at school today, but they're not. People continue to talk negatively about me in the hallways and give me dirty looks. I wish the rumors would die down already.

I need to get to a staircase so I can sit and be alone. There's no way I'm sitting in the cafeteria, surrounded by all those students.

Joanie beat me to my spot.

"You were right," I start.

She sets her milk carton down. "I heard the rumor about you and Chad. I knew immediately that it wasn't true."

I take a seat next to her. "I should've listened to you."

She speaks. "Last year I used to hang out with Sedg and a couple other students from his circle. I was a new student here. They took advantage of me and screwed me over. They got the whole school to make fun of me for being overweight and bi."

"I'm sorry."

"He made up a rumor about me. Something about me strangling a student. Everyone ended up scared of me. And then he made up another rumor about me being a drug dealer. My locker was being searched weekly."

"Sedg is an awful person."

She shrugs. "I don't care anymore. It just makes me mad that he continues to target new students and girls."

I hesitate and scrunch my eyebrows. "I don't understand why you bully others, especially after the way you just said you were treated. Why did you mess with me?"

"I need to get revenge. Everyone hates me for no reason."

"You're just fueling the fire. Nothing's ever going to change if you keep acting like you're the bad guy."

She looks away. "I guess you're right, Sol. Actually, you were one of the only students who confronted me. You weren't scared of me on the bus. You haven't been mean to me at all."

"There was no reason for me to be that kind of person with you."

A different expression takes over her face, one that I've never seen. I've learned a lot about her today. She isn't so bad after all.

April 4

I can't stop thinking about everything that's happened within the last few days and weeks.

I keep closing my eyes and expecting things to be different when I open them. Lucas would be here. The Crew would be here. Betsy, Annabelle, and Griffin would still be friends with me. Dad would be alive. I would have good grades. My hair would be long again. I would have clear skin. The rumors would have never existed.

And Mom. Mom would be here, too.

Every time I lay in bed, negative thoughts take over. My brain won't shut off. I need to do something to get my mind off things.

Nonna opens my bedroom door. "You've been lying there all day."

I pull the covers up to my neck. "I haven't been getting enough sleep."

She takes a while to respond. "Sweetie, I've noticed a change. You're not doing well in school. You can't even get out of bed. Something's wrong."

"I'm fine."

"You aren't, Kalamiti. This isn't normal behavior."

I sit up in my bed. "Then what is normal?"

She hesitates. "Doing your homework. Being motivated. Playing piano. Spending time with me. Being happy."

I lie back down and hide under the covers. "Leave me alone. Please."

She stands there for a couple more seconds, then leaves.

Why can't there be a shortcut? Why can't I pass through this stage of life and get this part over with?

April 5

"We need to talk about your grades and attendance."

It's Nonna, her voice booming through the living room.

I shut off the TV. "What now?"

"Some of your teachers have called me. You're still failing classes, and not much effort has been put into raising your grades."

"So? Why do grades matter so much? That's all adults care about. Our lives shouldn't revolve around getting good grades and being a perfect student."

She folds her arms across her chest. "Your grades affect your future. Having a good education is what you need to succeed in this world."

I get up from the couch.

As I attempt to escape to my room, Nonna says, "Running off again?"

I stop in my tracks. "Who do you think I got that from?" I pause. "You. Every time I argue, or you feel uncomfortable, you walk away. When have you ever stopped to consider what I'm saying? Why can't you stand your ground?"

She raises her voice. "I do not walk away all the time."

"Yes, you do. Mom was the same way. It's intergenerational. She's a failure, so let's face it, I'm going to be one, too." My voice softens. "You should just give up on me."

Her eyes fill with tears, something I don't usually see.

Instead of escaping to my room, I take the back door.

The pond, willow tree, and sunflowers can't respond and won't argue. They listen. And sometimes, that's all I need.

April 6

I'm home from school. I haven't eaten all day. Let's see if Nonna will order a pizza.

I walk down the hallway.

"…I'm thinking about sending her to boarding school. Or possibly homeschooling her."

I stop outside of her bedroom door. She's on the phone with someone.

"She's had a difficult life. She ran away from me, her mother abandoned her, she grew up on the streets, and she's done drugs and alcohol. Spending time at a detention center didn't help. She was making progress, but now she's failing classes and skipping school. She's not getting along with other students and she seems to have depression. I don't know what else to do."

Wait. My mom abandoned me? I thought she went missing…

And now it all makes sense. She never wanted me in the first place. I was always neglected as a child.

I crumble to the ground. I can't believe it. I guess my mom saw Nonna as an opportunity to finally get rid of me, but then I ran away trying to find her because I thought this whole time she was missing.

I'm so stupid.

Her bedroom door opens.

Through watery eyes, I try my best to put on a brave face. I stand up and confront her. "My mom abandoned me?"

She's standing there, a horrified look spread across her face.

I continue. "Why didn't you ever tell me? Why did you lie to me?"

"She didn't really abandon you, sweetie."

"Then why isn't she here? Where is she?"

"I don't know where she is. All I know is that she left you with me. She wanted to get her life together."

"She didn't want me, huh?"

"No, Kalamiti, that's not true. I'm pretty sure she's in

rehab. She wanted you to be in good hands. She knew she wouldn't be able to provide for you."

"Then why hasn't she contacted us?"

"I don't know. I don't know exactly where she is or what she's doing."

"First Alessandro, and now me."

"Who?"

"Oh, she didn't tell you? She had a son with another man. But she abandoned him, too!"

I storm off, lock myself in my room, and hide under the covers.

I wish this were just a dream, but unfortunately, it isn't.

April 8

I haven't talked to Nonna. I've been avoiding her.

I haven't even been sleeping at her place. I've been camping out on a park bench. All I have with me is my backpack and a thin blanket.

Before I left home, I went to Lucas' room. He left a couple of things behind, including a sweater. It still smells like him. I'm wearing it right now, and I also use it as an extra blanket at night.

I've been showing up to school because I have nowhere else to be during the day. Lucas' sweater shields and protects me. I pull the hood over my head and tuck the sleeves under my hands. I don't want anyone to notice me or look at my body. I don't want anybody to grimace at my unwashed hair, the breakouts on my face, and the bags under my eyes that worsen with each passing day.

Part of me wishes I would've never found out about my mom abandoning me. Some things really are better left unsaid. Some things are better left unknown.

April 9

I feel lifeless. I feel like I have no soul. I have no friends, I have no family, The Crew has vanished, and I don't know what to do anymore.

I want to run away again, but I'm scared of what I'll find at The Hideout if I go looking for The Crew.

One of our English assignments was to write a poem, so this is what I turned in.

<u>The Girl with No Sol</u>
by Kalamiti Sol

Pouring rain
crashes down my windowpane.
The sunshine is gone,
the dark is here.

The shadows are taking over,
but I'm stuck.
It's hard to know right from wrong
when you're filled with fear.

These endless days go back and forth.
I've been to many places,
but my sunshine hasn't returned.
I'm losing all hope.

I'm troubled between two sides,
and my brighter path can't be found.
I guess it's because I'm Kalamiti Sol,
the girl with no sol.

April 10

<u>The Girl with No Sol (Part 2)</u>
By Kalamiti Sol

Days fly by,
like the arms on a clock telling time.
A few months
seem like forever.

Grey clouds move forward in the distance,
swallowing the sun.
They are coming toward me.
There is no escaping.

Part 2 of my poem was for extra credit. Mr. Bold complimented my writing style. He wrote an "A" in red ink at the top. These poems are the only good grades I've received recently.

After class, Mr. Bold talked to me privately. He suggested therapy. He said that I've looked down. I'm surprised he's bothered paying attention to me.

I don't need therapy. I don't need rehab. What I need are emotional pain relievers. I'd take some of those. If my mind could shut off, that would make things so much easier.

The things I truly need aren't with me. They're humans, human beings I wish would come back.

I don't think I'll ever get them back.

April 11

I still haven't completely returned home. I've lost track of the number of days that I haven't slept in my bed. During the day, sometimes I return home to grab food, take a shower, and change into new clothes, that way I won't run into Nonna.

I don't want to see her, talk to her, or have anything to do with her. She betrayed me.

April 12

Death.

What's the point of living if you're just going through the motions, barely making it through a 24-hour day? What's the point of living if you have nothing to live for? No one who cares for you? No one who would be sad to see you go?

I want to end it all. I want it all to stop. The noise in my head. It's self-sabotage.

I contemplate death, but I don't think I could actually take my own life. I can't visualize myself holding a rope between both hands. Pills. Who knows if that'll do the trick. A gunshot to the head. I have yet to pull a trigger in my lifetime. Slitting my wrists. I don't want to experience pain during my last few breaths.

Maybe some deadly disease will strike me and take my life quickly. Maybe my organs will give out on me and I'll die instantly.

What even happens the moment you die? What happens to all your blood and tissue, the brain that holds your every thought? Do you physically feel your soul fade away? Does everything go black?

If I die, here are a few things I'd like to leave behind in this memory book:

Nonna. I'll miss you. You always wanted the best for me, but I'll never be a perfect granddaughter. I wish we could just be honest with each other. Trust is all we need.

Lucas. I've missed you since the day you left California without saying goodbye to me. You were always looking out for me. You'll always be my best friend. Will I ever see you again?

June. Though we haven't been in touch, you were my first best friend. I miss seeing you read books in the boxcar. I miss trips to the library with you. Sometimes I wonder if you still remember me.

The Crew. You all will always be family, no matter where we are or how far apart we are from one another.

Griffin. You always believed in me. Your positive and encouraging words were a bright light, even through all of my negative self-talk.

Betsy and Annabelle. I wouldn't have survived Mayfield High without the two of you. You two made me feel included.

I'm glad we were able to talk to each other and have emergency get-togethers.

Mom. Wherever you are, you have a lot of explaining to do. Maybe I'll see you in the afterlife.

April 13

I'm comforted by the piano in one of the practice rooms, playing away to songs I've learned this semester.

As I finish playing a short piece from my workbook, my fingers are called to the initial notes from the talent show piece. Although I haven't played it in weeks, it's like it's ingrained in my memory. I'm amazed my brain remembers it without looking at the sheet music.

I close my eyes and picture myself on stage with Griffin. I run through it without looking at the keys.

For the first time in forever, I feel less sad. What would I do without this beautiful instrument?

April 14

Piano class. The only class I truly enjoy and look forward to anymore. It's the one class I don't want to miss.

Ms. Hayley is a great teacher. Every lesson is interactive and fun. She always tells me I'm making progress, but I can't tell if she actually means it or is obligated to compliment her students.

The final bell rings. As I grab my backpack from the floor, Ms. Hayley approaches me.

"Kalamiti, could I talk to you?"

I nod. My hood slips off the back of my head.

The remaining students pack their things. As soon as the last student leaves, she says, "Are you doing okay?"

I wasn't expecting those words from her. I assumed she wanted to talk about piano. "Yeah, why?"

"Your attendance has been spotty for your other classes, but I've noticed you're in this class most of the time."

"This is my favorite class. I really like to play the piano, even though I'm still new at it."

She smiles. "I'm glad to hear it. We've been worried about you."

I shift the weight of my backpack to my other shoulder. "We?"

"Griffin. He's been asking about you. Did something happen between the two of you?"

Where do I start? Should I tell her about the time I spent the night at his place and how we got into an argument? Should I mention the numerous text messages and calls he's sent to me that I haven't responded to? What about the time he kissed me in this very classroom?

I look away. "No. Nothing happened."

She leans against the wall. "You guys were such good friends. You two were frequently practicing for the talent show. Now I don't even see the two of you in the classroom together. He's concerned about you, Kalamiti. He wanted me to check on you."

"Tell him I'm fine. He doesn't need to worry about me." I pause. "I needed a break from rehearsals, but I'm still practicing my part."

A worried look spreads across her face. "I'll let him know."

As she departs to her office, I call out, "Ms. Hayley?"

She stops in her tracks. "Yes?"

"We should have drinks together sometime."

There's no way I said that to a teacher.

She chuckles. "What are you, 21?"

I can't help grinning. I can feel my face heating up, turning redder with every second passing. "I didn't mean to say it like that."

She grins. "I'd love to have you over sometime."

Man, I'm so awkward.

April 15

I'm about to smoke all the weed in the world, so maybe I can overdose and die. Just kidding. Well kind of.

Turner's got a new girlfriend named Sofia. She's sitting in the passenger seat, so I have the whole back seat of the car to myself.

We've already passed the pipe around a few times. I'm starting to get drowsy.

"Where have you been?"

I'm not sure if I actually heard a voice. Maybe this weed is laced with something and I'm tripping. No one ever talks during these smoke sessions. All we listen to is rock tunes playing softly in the background and the sound of our lungs gasping for air. I've gotten used to that.

He repeats himself. Turner. He spoke. He actually spoke.

I squint at him, my eyes halfway shut. "Uh, what do you mean?"

"You're hardly in class anymore. When you are there, you just hide behind that sweater. How are you even passing?" he asks.

I blow out some smoke and cough. "So?"

He takes the pipe and lighter from my hand. "Class is different without you. It's not fun anymore."

Sofia laughs and joins in the conversation. "Yeah! Like that one time you yelled out you were gonna shit your pants and Mr. Bold didn't hear you!"

Turner nods in agreement.

They think that was funny? That was embarrassing to me. Mindy made fun of me for it.

Sofia adds, "And French. You're never there anymore to confront Ms. Adler."

I totally forgot she was in that class.

I shift around in the back seat. "So you guys actually miss me?"

They look at each other.

Turner says, "Well, duh. You're mellow. If I didn't like you, why the fuck would I share my weed with you?"

Sofia pulls a tube of mascara out of her backpack and reapplies it. "You're one of the few girls I can tolerate."

I stare out the windshield. "I didn't think anyone ever noticed me. All people seem to care about are the rumors."

"And? So what? Ten years from now, no one will care or remember," Sofia says.

She's got a point. I let a couple of things that aren't true affect me.

I want to hug them, but that would be weird.

In a way, they've saved my life, and they don't even know it.

April 16

I'll be "having drinks" with Ms. Hayley after school.

This morning, I tried to wash my marijuana-reeking hair in the bathroom sink. I can't remember the last time I showered. My hair was starting to annoy me, and I didn't want Ms. Hayley to think that I stink or assume that I'm homeless.

After dismissal, I wait for a rideshare. There was no way I was going to ask Nonna for a ride, and at this point, there's no one else I could ask.

A silver sedan pulls into the car loop.

Classical music plays in the car, which reminds me of Griffin.

After a long drive, we arrive at Ms. Hayley's apartment complex. I thank the driver and give him a cash tip.

I climb the flight of stairs to the fourth floor. What a workout. I try to breathe normally and not look out of shape.

I ring the doorbell. Ms. Hayley opens it and welcomes me in.

Talk about apartment goals. The decorations catch my attention. I don't know if I should sit, so I stand and look around in awe.

She says, "Have a seat. What type of tea would you like?"

"I'm okay—"

"I insist."

"Do you have Earl Grey?"

"Yes, I'll bring it right out."

I take a seat on the couch in the living room.

She hands me the coolest teacup I've ever seen. It's the shape of an owl, showcasing an earthy palette of colors. "Do you invite a lot of students over?"

Ms. Hayley sits across from me in a recliner. "Of course. I teach piano lessons from home."

The Earl Grey's aroma is mesmerizing. I'm tempted to take a sip, but it's still too hot. "I like the decorations."

"Thanks. I like to buy interesting things from the thrift store."

"Are you married, or do you live alone?"

She takes a sip of her tea. "No. I never got married or had kids."

"You're like what, 25?"

She laughs. "I'm 37. But I guess that means I still look young."

I laugh. I don't know what else to talk about. I'm a bad conversationalist.

"How are you liking Mayfield?" she asks.

I guess it's my turn to answer the questions. "It's good."

She sets her teacup down on the coffee table, crosses one leg over the other, and interlocks her hands together on her knee. "Is it really?"

Maybe this woman can read minds like she can read music. She knows something's up. "No. I actually hate it."

"Would you like to talk about it?"

Ms. Hayley isn't just patient and kind when teaching music, but as a person. She actually seems to want to hear what I have to say. A force in the back of my head nudges me to speak. "I don't feel like I belong there."

"How come?"

"I hardly have any friends. I don't feel motivated to go to classes because no one wants to talk to me, and I hate being surrounded by so many people. Most teachers seem to only like the extroverts and popular kids."

"I'm sorry, Kalamiti. Starting at a new school is tough. I moved around a lot as a kid."

I nod. "Yeah. It's difficult."

"It'll get easier. Growing up, we were poor. My mom was on her own handling me and my two older brothers. I'm a first-generation college graduate. I even got a master's degree. Music saved my life. Because of it, I'm the person I am today. Plus I get to do the best job in the world—teach."

I take a sip of my tea. "That's inspiring, Ms. Hayley. I didn't know that about you."

"I have a feeling you have a similar upbringing. The past doesn't define you, and I'm sure your life story will be a good one."

I manage to smile. I needed to hear that. Her words made my week. "Do you ever feel weird being one of the only black teachers at the high school?"

She looks at her teacup. "I don't necessarily feel weird, but I would like more diversity amongst our staff. Whenever you talked about feeling like you don't belong, I understood where you were coming from." She pauses. "When I teach, I try to push aside those feelings of not belonging. My hope is to always encourage my students to achieve whatever they desire."

"Well, so far you've inspired me. So I guess you're doing a good job."

She smiles. "What happened to that boy who started going to Mayfield at the same time as you? I haven't seen him at the school."

"Lucas? He moved back to Chicago."

Ms. Hayley's eyes shimmer with empathy. "I'm sure you miss him."

I nod. "Lucas has been there for me all these years. If it weren't for him, I would've had a rough start at school."

My eyes are fixed on my teacup, hoping she won't notice them beginning to water.

"It's okay to cry."

I can't. My body won't let me at the moment. I can hardly blink. "I feel like I've let down all my friends. They probably don't want to talk to me anymore."

"Your friends will be there for you when you're ready. Have you thought about writing or making music about how you feel? It could help you express yourself."

"No. I'll have to try that out sometime."

Ms. Hayley walks over to the piano and opens the lid, revealing gently worn keys. "Would you like to play your talent show piece for me?"

I smile, join her by the piano, and take a seat. My hands meet the keys. "Good thing I have it memorized."

April 17

My hands press down minor and diminished chords, with the occasional half-diminished chord thrown into the mix. These are newer chords to me, ones that I recently learned in piano class.

My fingers are drawn to notes that create dissonance. As I play, the music crescendos with every note.

I'm trying to express myself through music, like Ms. Hayley suggested, but I feel bad taking it out on this poor keyboard that doesn't deserve it. Guilt floods through me as I slam down on the keys.

Griffin is somehow able to compose pieces. I've yet to learn. It'll take me some time to get inspired and to think of an idea.

Writing. I need to try that out, too. Maybe I can write down exactly how I feel.

As I sit with a felt pen in hand, I get a sudden urge to write about Lucas.

Lucas. The guy with dark hair, kind eyes. Mystifying smile. The guy that every girl at school thinks is charming and handsome. He's good at everything he does, whether it's schoolwork, helping fix things, snowboarding, or giving me life advice. The one stable person in my life, the one who has been there for me through thick and thin. We have gone through similar experiences. He has saved me countless times. When I look into his eyes, or when he touches my shoulder, I feel safe.

Now that he has gone back to The Crew, it's almost as if a part of me is missing. I don't know how I can continue on at Mayfield High. I don't know how I can live life without him by my side. No matter how far apart we are, Lucas will always be my closest friend. I would do anything to be able to see him again.

My eyes have filled with tears. I set my pen down on the keyboard, and before I know it, a single teardrop lands on the page.

* * *

I managed to close my journal before any other tears smeared the ink. This is the most I've cried in months. I haven't cried about Lucas leaving.

I never realized how much he meant to me. I think I'm in love with him, and I'm just now realizing it.

April 18

It's nighttime. I'm by my garden. A couple of sunflowers are growing, but they haven't made flowers yet.

The other night, cops were patrolling the park, so I escaped.

This is where I'll be sleeping tonight. It's safer than the park bench.

Raindrops begin to fall from the sky. I'm lying down, with outstretched arms, almost motionless, under the safety of the willow tree. Lukewarm water droplets hit my face. The only thing truly alive is my steady heartbeat.

I'm at peace.

April 19

A warm breeze brushes my hair into my face. As I sit up against the willow tree, I push it back and tuck it behind my ears.

It's as if I've been transported into a sepia photograph. Everything around me is a reddish-brown color.

"Dad?" I ask.

He sits near the pond, a couple of feet away from me.

"Kalamiti. How have you been?"

He's talking. He's really talking to me.

I swallow. I can hardly speak. "Not too good."

"And why is that?"

"Everything is going wrong."

Dad studies me. "It may feel like that, but there's still hope burning inside you. You're a Sol."

My eyes fill with tears, distorting my view of him. "Why did you have to die?"

He looks at the sky. "It was my time. My soul's purpose."

I shake my head. "If you were still here, Mom would've never changed. She would've never abandoned me. She would've been okay. We all could've been a family."

"Why ponder the whys and what ifs?"

I'm not sure what to say to him. My mind is always filled with endless questions and theories.

He continues. "Even if I were still alive, your mom would've chosen the same path. It's written in her life path. She refused to accept help and didn't acknowledge her actions."

I turn away from him and hug my knees to my chest.

"I don't want the same to happen to you, Kalamiti. You need to be there for Nonna."

I clench my teeth. "She lied to me. I don't want to talk to her anymore."

"Allow her to enter your sacred space. Hear her out. She's got a lot to tell you and it's nothing but the truth."

Sacred space. That's the perfect name for this place.

I face him again.

A flood of sadness ensues. "I miss you, Dad. I wish you were still around."

He gestures toward my neck. "Look at the necklace I gave you."

I gently grasp the gold sun between my thumb and index finger. "I wear it every day."

"I'm always with you."

* * *

"Kalamiti."

I'm at the foot of the willow tree. My head is resting on the thin, folded-up blanket. Lucas' sweater is pulled up to my neck. I sit up and rub my eyes.

It's Nonna.

She takes a seat next to me. "I'm so glad you're safe."

I shrug. "I can take care of myself."

She smiles. "I'm so sorry, Kalamiti. For everything. The reason I kept the truth from you was because I was trying to protect you, but it ended up causing more damage."

Instead of making eye contact, I keep my eyes on the pond. "My whole life I believed she was missing, so my initial thought was that she would be in Chicago. That's the reason I ran away from here and created a life of my own over there."

"I didn't think you would run off."

"Chicago was my home. It was the place I grew up, which was one of the reasons I wanted to go back. You don't know anything about me." I fold my arms across my chest.

"We've missed out on so many years together. I want to get to know you more and cultivate a better relationship between us."

"What about Mom? Doesn't she want a relationship with me? How could she have abandoned us?"

She places her hand on my shoulder. "Oh, Kalamiti, your mom was troubled, even more than you. She faced many challenges in school and had you when she wasn't ready to have a baby. Your mom rebelled, didn't care about her future, and was suicidal. I tried to help. I tried to be there for her, but no matter what I did, it was never enough. I don't want you to go down the same road."

I finally make eye contact with her. "It's not your fault, Nonna. Ultimately, she was the one who made her decisions. After Dad's death, it scared me how drastically she changed. Drugs and alcohol became the center of her life. Her body grew thinner and thinner. Her face was lifeless and lacked expression. She stopped caring about me and focused on random men. Even though I was only a kid, I could tell something was wrong with her, and she would take things out on me. It wasn't until I was older that I realized everything."

Nonna shakes her head and wipes her tears away. "You didn't deserve any of that. I should've done more to protect you."

I lean my head against her shoulder. "You did the best you could. That's all that matters. Wherever she is, I hope she's getting help. When she's ready, she'll come back to us, don't you think?"

"Yes. I truly believe so."

I readjust Lucas' sweater over my body. "What was my dad like?"

"He was the kindest man. Always respectful and treated your mom well. Because of him, your mom became a better person. But we need to remind ourselves that it isn't the job of someone else to fix and heal you. All of that needs to come from within you."

I can't help smiling. "I don't remember much about him, but I do remember that he would always speak in Spanish to me. He wanted me to learn, and it was hilarious because Mom didn't know the language."

Nonna smiles.

"I just had a dream about him. He was here with me. I've had multiple dreams about Mom and Dad under the willow tree. Dad's side of the family is like a mystery. I don't know much about them and their culture."

"His immediate family was lovely. As for the extended family, I believe they're near Chicago, so I guess you weren't too far from them. Perhaps one day we'll be able to be in touch."

I smile. "I'd like that."

Nonna takes a hold of my hands. "Please come home, Kalamiti. I don't want to see you sleeping in the streets anymore. I don't want to hide anything from you anymore. I need to do better."

I nod my head. "I'll come home. This is just my sacred space, a place where I come to recharge and be alone."

She hugs me and pats my back. "By the way, Annabelle and Griffin came looking for you the other day. Betsy wasn't with them, so she probably wasn't able to join them."

I hesitate. "I thought they wouldn't want to be friends with me anymore."

"If they didn't want to be friends with you, they wouldn't have bothered coming all the way to the house. You should reach out to them."

Nonna extends a hand and helps me up.

I know what to do now.

April 20

Progress.

I'm slowly chasing the sun, striving for change and a better outlook on life.

The first step I've taken is showing up to school today. I'm not only attending my favorite classes, I'll be attending all of them.

I need to reconnect with Betsy, Annabelle, and Griffin. Even though Nonna said they were looking for me, I'm worried about how those conversations will go.

It's like I've just woken up from a coma. Everything is kind of a blur. Puzzle pieces are being brought together, and I'm trying to make sense of it all.

Betsy wasn't in school today. Her desk was vacant during second hour. I wanted to talk to Annabelle, but she was sitting with some other girls at the usual lunch table, so it didn't seem like the right moment.

Lunchtime is going to end soon. Griffin wasn't in the cafeteria at all.

My legs lead me to the piano classroom. The sound of a keyboard fills the music hall.

I recognize the opening line of "Who You Are," the very same piece Griffin had played the day we first met.

My hand meets the door handle. Right before turning it, I close my eyes and take a deep breath.

After walking in, I take a seat by a keyboard in the back of the room.

He stops playing, but he doesn't look at me. His eyes are frozen on the keys.

"Ms. Hayley said you've been worried about me. My grandma said you were looking for me the other day," I start.

His head slowly tilts up and we make eye contact. He nods. "Yeah, I was."

I stand and walk up to him. "I'm sorry for ignoring you and for not showing up to rehearsals."

He sighs and runs his hands through his hair. "I shouldn't have kissed you. Did I scare you? Did I do something wrong?"

"No. You didn't do anything wrong. I needed time to think."

"It's Lucas, isn't it?"

I slowly nod. "I like you as a friend, Griffin. I didn't know how to tell you, so I ran away. I wasn't sure if you would even want to hear all my excuses for not responding to you."

"I knew something was up," he starts. "What happened? Are you okay?"

He scoots over on the bench. I sit down next to him.

"Too much has happened. Lucas left. I tried being friends with Sedg and his group, but that ended bad. My grandma hid the truth from me. It turns out my mom isn't actually missing."

"I'm sorry. That's a lot to process. I don't blame you for disappearing from school for some time and for taking a break."

"I didn't know how to handle it all. I was angry. Sad.

Confused. Shocked. Some of these emotions are still here, but Nonna and I are on good terms again and I returned home."

"I'm happy you're back. I had no one to talk about music with."

I smile. "So do you still want to be friends? Things won't be weird between us, right?"

He smiles. "They don't have to be."

I hug him.

I'm relieved.

April 21

Mrs. Ramos is the best.

She had all of my make-up work organized and ready for me. She said I could use lunchtime to make up a lab I missed, and if I needed more help, she could stay after school to help me. A couple of extra credit opportunities were paperclipped to the stack, too.

I have a lot of work to do for all of my classes. I'm sure I'll be able to get caught up.

April 22

Betsy still hasn't been at school.

Annabelle continues sitting with some other girls during lunch. There's even a guy who sits at her table, too.

I can't help but wonder if they aren't friends anymore. Or what if Betsy moved?

I might have missed my chance to reunite with them.

April 23

Still no sign of Betsy. She's never missed a day of school since I started going here. I haven't been able to talk to Annabelle either. The ideal setting to apologize is with both of them present.

School days have been quite boring without them, but at least I can focus on my schoolwork and get my grades up.

Because of a meeting with Mr. Johnson, I'm late to sixth hour. I speed walk through the halls, almost tripping over my own two feet.

As I turn a corner, someone's arm wraps around my waist. Simultaneously, a hand covers my mouth and I'm dragged into the nearest girls' bathroom.

The hand moves away from my mouth. Before I can say anything, a sharp pocketknife meets my neck. The cold blade is pressed against my skin.

The mysterious person drags me from the entrance of the bathroom to the front of a mirror.

Sedg.

He initiates the conversation. "You destroyed my car."

"Why do you think it was me?" I ask.

"Who else would've done it?"

The mirror holds a reflection of his face, one I don't want to look at. "I'm sorry."

I really am sorry. I regret what I did.

The bathroom door swings open, revealing Annabelle. Her already pale face turns whiter. She screams.

I mouth the word "help," and she sprints out the door.

Sedg says, "You're gonna pay."

"I can pay for the damage, I just don't have any money on me. I need to get my allowance from home."

"I don't want your money." His grip on the knife tightens.

"Let me go!"

His hand is turning red and shaking. "No."

"I shouldn't have done what I did. I'm sorry. I was angry and I didn't know how to react."

He tries to push me into a stall, but I resist.

He puts the knife away. One of his hands reaches for my shirt and attempts to pull it off. Half of my abdomen is now exposed. His cold and calloused fingers inch up my body.

Before he can touch me anymore, I elbow him in the stomach. "Don't touch me!"

The cold and perilous look in his eyes scares me. "You're gonna do whatever I say and want, or you're dead."

He pushes me to the ground. His face is now inches from mine. His hands wrap around my neck.

"All you did was take advantage of me and treat me like shit. I'm ashamed that I once called you a friend," I say.

He laughs. "I'm never going to change. This is who I am."

That's the worst mindset to have. In a way, I feel sorry for him.

The door once again swings open. Two security officers walk in and arrest Sedg. I'm free, unharmed, although I might end up with a few bruises from how tight he was holding onto me.

Upon walking out of the bathroom door, Annabelle is leaning against the wall. She greets me with a hug.

"Are you okay?" she asks. Tears run down her freckled face.

"Yeah. I'm fine."

"Do you want to visit the nurse or counselor?"

I shake my head. "No, I think I'm good." I pause. "I do need to talk to you, though."

We sit down against the wall.

I start. "I'm sorry for being a bad friend."

"I'm sorry, too. I should've checked on you more often."

"There was so much going on. I didn't want to bring you and Betsy down. You two were busy practicing for the talent show and I didn't want to bother you guys."

"We should've made more time for you, though."

"It's okay. For a while, I was scared to approach you two. I didn't think you all would want to be friends with me anymore because of the rumors."

"Are you kidding? We knew they weren't true. Sedg Myers is trouble. I hate what he did to you."

"If you wouldn't have walked into the bathroom, who knows what would've happened to me."

She hugs me again.

"Where has Betsy been? I've been wanting to talk to her, too, but I haven't seen her at school."

"Her family went out of state for vacation. On their way home they got into a car accident. She's been resting at home, but she should be back at school on Monday."

"I need to go visit her."

"We can go together."

I've missed Annabelle. I'm happy she's back in my life.

April 24

After everything that went down yesterday, Sedg has been expelled from school.

Aside from threatening me with a weapon and sexually assaulting me, the security guards found drugs in his locker. He's probably going to serve time at a detention center.

Good riddance. Take a hike, Sedg.

April 25

Annabelle and I picked wildflowers for Betsy from random fields on the side of the road.

When we arrive at Betsy's house, we find her lying in bed. A large bandage covers part of her forehead. Her wrist is wrapped up.

Doctors told her she was lucky. Their car may be totaled, but her family escaped with minor injuries.

"Thanks for visiting me," she says to us.

I say, "I'm sorry. For everything. I promise you two I'll try to be a better friend."

Betsy says, "We'll try to be better, too."

Annabelle nods her head in agreement. "We became so focused on the talent show that we forgot about everything else."

I look at Betsy's wrist. "Are you two still going to be able to compete?"

Betsy says, "We're planning on it. I just won't be able to do certain moves."

Annabelle adds, "We haven't been able to practice, but luckily we practiced a lot at the beginning. What about you and Griffin?"

"We missed out on a lot of practice, too. But we're still competing."

We all hug each other. I'm glad I was able to reconnect with them.

April 26

Griffin and I have been using every bit of our free time to prepare for the talent show.

Since I've been practicing on my own, I haven't fallen too far behind. Griffin is impressed that I have my part memorized.

I can't believe the show is this week.

April 27

After reconnecting with my friends, it's dawned on me how much I've missed from their lives, and how much they've missed from mine. Betsy and Annabelle's talent show rehearsals. Griffin's soccer games. Betsy's family vacation and car accident. Annabelle's new boyfriend, Derick. Griffin becoming friends with Betsy and Annabelle. Not to mention everything that happened to me.

Life is so precious and fragile. So little time passed, yet so much happened. Time flies by quickly. You better enjoy it and make the most of it.

April 28

Mayfield High has been advertising prom, just like people advertise their lives away on social media, all for some pyramid scheme. People really spend months planning for this night?

In the front office, there's a decorated cardboard box with a slot at the top to submit prom theme ideas. Annabelle told me it's a Mayfield High tradition. Students make submissions and a panel of teachers vote on the theme. Although submissions are open to all students, the panel prioritizes submissions from upperclassmen.

You won't believe it, but yesterday I submitted an idea. As I stared at the submission box, I had a flashback to when I was a kid. Back in Chicago, my mom and I were planning my birthday party. I was so excited to invite the whole class over to my house. I knew exactly what colors, decorations, and food I wanted. The day of the party, Mom was passed out on the couch and nothing got set up, so it didn't end up happening. Although it was so long ago, I still remember that day so clearly.

I picked up a submission form and the idea for a sunshine dance popped into my head. It was almost exactly like what I had in mind for that birthday party. Bright shades of yellow, orange, and red flashed before my eyes. Tables full of lemon bars, key lime pie, and different flavors of lemonade. A giant decoration of a sun in the center, like a disco ball. The vision was so vivid that I had to write it down and submit.

This will be the most I participate in this school's events.

April 30

We finally came up with a name for Griffin's composition. For the longest time, "Untitled" claimed the top of the sheet music. Now it's called "The Journey."

Griffin described the title's meaning so perfectly. Life is a journey. Each of our piano parts is different and represents paths you can take. His part is complicated and implements a variety of chords and rhythms, while mine is simple and uses limited notes. There is no right or wrong path. Both parts come together at the end, which is the destination. The piece concludes with a Picardy third.

Our dress rehearsal went well.

I'm nervous, but excited at the same time. Our piece is gonna be amazing.

May 1

The talent show is tonight.

I make my way down the halls, trying to get to the auditorium.

I can't take the stares.

I stand out. A lot.

Girls are wearing dresses made for parties, pounds of makeup, and their hair is curled up like curly fries.

And me? I'm standing in the crowd of contestants, wearing a black V-neck, black pants, and faded kicks with flowers printed on them. I'm as normal as can be.

Griffin's wearing a plain black T-shirt, black pants, and

Converse. We dressed up like this on purpose. We wanted to be simple, like our piece. Which is ironic, because "The Journey" is about life, which isn't so simple after all.

Backstage directors corral all of the contestants to the holding area in the music hall. We're able to view everything going on onstage from the TV in the room.

The dark green velvet curtain opens, revealing the audience.

Ms. Hayley begins the announcements. "Welcome to the Talent Show!"

After a round of applause, the first act takes the stage.

Time is moving so slow, yet so fast. Waiting is hard.

Two students who performed a magic show return backstage, which means Mindy is next.

As she walks by me and my friends, she gives us a dirty look.

She sings a ballad. Most of the other singers have done upbeat songs, so it's a nice mix.

I have to admit, she wasn't that bad.

"Kalamiti, Griffin, you're up next," says a backstage director.

"You're gonna do great," says Griffin, as he grabs my hand and squeezes it. Maybe he can sense I'm a little nervous. I've never performed in front of a crowd before.

We step onto the stage.

The immense crowd is finally before us.

This is it, K9, there's no turning back. You've got this.

I take a seat at my piano. Griffin takes a seat at his. I scan the crowd and spot Nonna, sitting near the front of the audience. She smiles at me and I smile back.

Griffin starts us off. Sometimes he plays by himself,

sometimes I play by myself, and sometimes we play together. He can write some pretty incredible harmonies.

Occasionally, I look over at him. I can't help but smile as we play. He's so immersed in what he's doing, it's as if he's breathing the music.

We play the final chords. Applause echoes through the auditorium. We stand from our piano benches and take a bow.

The feeling I experienced onstage is indescribable. It's a good feeling. It's something I want to experience over and over again.

We return to the holding area. Betsy and Annabelle come up to us and we all hug one another.

Other contestants perform. Soon it's Betsy and Annabelle's turn.

Their dance routine is amazing. They've worked hard on their performance.

Once the remaining acts perform, everyone in the holding area is directed to stand in a line on stage.

Any minute now, the winners will be announced.

Ms. Hayley stands at the podium. "The judges have decided the winners."

The auditorium goes silent.

"In third place, Griffin Phoenix and Kalamiti Sol!"

Oh, yeah.

Ms. Hayley walks up to us and places the medals around our necks. She hugs and congratulates us.

"In second place, Annabelle Hastings and Betsy Paulson!"

Well deserved. They persevered, even with Betsy's wrist situation.

"And in first place," Ms. Hayley pauses, "The Saxophone Quartet!"

Their performance was incredible. I'm glad they won.

Mindy didn't place. She's standing on the other side of the stage. Her face is beet red.

A backstage director distributes participation ribbons to everyone.

Balloons and confetti fall from the ceiling. The audience gives us a standing ovation. The applause is louder than ever. Contestants go around and congratulate each other.

After leaving the stage, I search for Nonna in the lobby. She gives me a hug. "I got you these."

I take the bouquet of flowers from her. "Thank you."

She puts her hands on my shoulders and looks me in the eyes. "I'm so proud of you."

I can't stop smiling, the kind of smile that hurts your cheeks and corners of your mouth. I don't think I've ever smiled this much.

No one has ever told me they're proud of me. Hearing those words come from Nonna was an honor. I never thought she'd ever say anything like that to me.

* * *

We're home. I lie in bed, still in my black clothes. I can't stop staring at the medal around my neck.

I wish Lucas was here, so I could hug him and tell him all about the exhilarating and nerve-wracking sensation of being on stage.

Upon unlocking my cell phone, two missed calls and a voicemail from a random number are displayed on the main screen.

I hold my phone up to my ear and listen to the voicemail. It's Lucas, going on and on about how he misses me and how nothing is the same. His words are slurred as if he's drunk. Based on his tone, he sounds so depressed and defeated.

I run straight to Nonna's room. "Nonna."

"Yes?"

"Something's wrong with Lucas. I need a plane ticket to Chicago."

She stares at me. Her eyes haze over. "You're going to leave me again, aren't you?" A sad look spreads across her face.

"No, I'm not going to run away again. I need to see if Lucas is okay. Buy me a round trip ticket. Two days. That's all I need."

She studies my face. It wouldn't surprise me if she doesn't trust me.

I pull my phone out of my pocket. As the voicemail plays, her expression turns more and more concerned.

"I would accompany you, but this isn't a good time to request off work," she says. "I'm buying you a one-way ticket. You decide when you're ready to return. I'm giving you freedom and you know where home is."

I hug her. "Thank you."

I head to my room, grab a backpack, and pack some belongings. I'll be leaving tomorrow morning.

May 2

It's around 1 p.m. My flight has landed in Chicago.

Nonna gave me $200 to use while I'm away. I need to get a cab.

The woman driving the yellow taxi approaches a fast-food joint near The Hideout. "You can drop me off here," I tell her.

She stops the car. I hand her some money and thank her.

After walking down the streets and through the forest, I spot my home. It's as perfect as can be.

I'm so close.

The boxcar door is slightly ajar, so I walk right in.

There's hardly any stuff. Lucas' car isn't parked outside, either.

I check out the caboose. Again, most of the supplies are gone. There are a few cases of beer. I can't imagine the kids—like Jay and Maci—drinking.

I make my way through the forest.

A shirtless silhouette is hunched over near the stream.

I cautiously approach him. He looks in my direction.

"Kalamiti," he says.

Before I can respond, he comes up to me and hugs me.

"I'm home, Lucas."

"It really is you. I thought I would never see you again," he whispers.

I then pull away and scan the forest around us. "Where's the rest of The Crew?"

His dark eyes fill with sorrow. "I'm sorry, K9."

"What happened to them?"

"I don't know. When I came back from California, they were all gone."

My family. Gone. Who knows if I'll ever see them again. "What?"

"I'm really sorry, Kalamiti."

"I came home to see everyone, not to find almost all of them missing." With that, I run off, far into the forest.

This is not what I wanted to come home to.

I continue to run through the forest, which fades into a neighborhood.

I pass by the library, the same one The Crew used to visit. The library was June's favorite place. I can't believe she's gone. I can't believe they're all gone. Something awful must've happened.

In a flash, the same energy that I had when I wanted to find my mom has taken over my body. I'm longing to go search for my friends, but I don't know where to begin.

Walking. That's all I can do to clear my mind.

I walk through a neighborhood, observing dandelions and other weeds growing from cracks in the sidewalk.

Now that I think about it, I didn't listen to Lucas. I didn't give him the opportunity to speak. He's not okay. I didn't ask him about himself, or the voicemail he left, because I ran away. I'm so insensitive.

When am I finally gonna stop screwing things up?

As I make my way back to The Hideout, the sun begins to set, its last visible rays shining through the foliage.

I return to the spot where I found Lucas earlier, and there he is, as if he's waiting for me.

He skips a stone into the stream. "You always run off. You know that, right?"

I take a seat next to him. "Yeah, Nonna does it too. It runs in the family."

He chuckles. "I see what you did there." His expression

turns serious again. "I'm sorry about The Crew. There isn't much we can do about it at the moment."

Our eyes are set on the stream.

I hesitate. "I'm sorry for running off." I pause. "You left a voicemail. That's why I came here. I needed to see if you were okay."

He blushes and turns his head away. "I apologize. I was totally drunk. Nothing has been going my way. When I first showed up, everyone was gone. I looked everywhere. I waited days, but there was no sign of them. I messaged June on social media, and she said she gave up. She's back in foster care. And it turns out Maci had a biological family this whole time, so she's back with them. I have no clue where Blake and Jay are."

"We were only gone for a couple of months. All of that happened in such a short time frame."

He skips another stone. "I woke up one morning and my car was gone. I've been alone this whole time."

"I'm sorry, Lucas. I know what it's like to be alone."

A heaviness initiates from my heart and rapidly spreads throughout the rest of my body. It's as if I can feel Lucas' pain. I inch closer to the stream and stare into my reflection.

I don't say anything. He doesn't say anything either. As I continue staring at my reflection, my eyes begin to water. I'm trying not to cry. I don't think I've ever cried in front of Lucas or The Crew. I'm their leader, I'm supposed to be strong and fearless.

I can't help sobbing. Seconds later, his hand meets my shoulder. I tilt my head to look at him. It's the first time we've made eye contact during our conversation. His worried eyes are fixed on me. He's probably surprised to see me in this state. I feel so fragile, so vulnerable.

And then he does something I don't expect him to do. He extends his arms out, and I accept his invitation. I cry in his arms, a river of tears running down his bare back. He strokes my hair and holds me tight.

Neither of us says a single word.

Silence is a beautiful thing.

May 3

Ever since I broke down crying, Lucas and I haven't said much to each other. I guess he doesn't know what to say to me, and I don't know what to say to him.

This can't go on much longer. We can't be silent toward each other for the rest of our lives. Besides, I need to know if he knows anything about Alessandro.

I knock on the boxcar door and walk in. Lucas is lying inside in his sleeping bag.

"Have you heard anything from Alessandro?" I ask.

"I haven't seen him," he says.

"Let's go find him."

We head to the alley, a place that Alessandro used to walk through.

We wait around for a couple of hours, but there's no sign of him.

The park where I'd meet up with him is empty.

Last stop. His neighborhood.

A red and white "For Sale" sign is planted in the front yard of his house.

"They're moving?" I ask out loud.

As I stare at the sign, Lucas walks around the perimeter of

the home and peers through the windows. "K9, they already moved. The house is empty."

"Do you think he went with them?"

"Most likely."

"I can't think of any other place he could be." This is it. I might never see my brother again.

We begin making the walk back to The Hideout. Once we reach the forest, we step onto the railroad tracks.

As we walk side by side, Lucas says, "I've missed you so much, Kalamiti. It's nice to have you around to keep me company."

"I've missed you, too. I'm glad I was able to make it out here."

"I'm sorry about leaving California without saying goodbye to you or your grandma. I shouldn't have done that."

I sigh. "That was hard on me. But I get it. Sometimes we need to take a step away. I've left a lot of people without saying goodbye."

He puts his hands in his pockets. "I'm also sorry for how I was at school. I hope you don't think I ditched you."

"Why are you bringing this up now?"

"I could tell it was bothering you. I never got the chance to apologize."

Now I'm annoyed, thinking about things I don't want to think about. "I didn't exist to you at school. You only cared about impressing girls and hanging out with the populars."

He stops walking. "What? That's how you've felt this whole time?"

I shrug. "Yeah. Kind of."

"I'm sorry. That was never my intention. I was just trying to fit in and belong."

"Don't we all want to fit in?"

He nods. "I'm sorry. I screwed up."

"What's gotten into you?" I start. "Why are you suddenly so apologetic?"

"I have a lot of regrets, and now that you're here, I can try to fix things."

He's acting different. This is not like him, and it's freaking me out. "This is not like you. What's up with the change?"

He runs his hands through his hair. "Kalamiti, I've always been this way."

We face each other.

Lucas breaks the silence. "I've always been in love with you."

May 4

So I kind of ran off after what Lucas said. By ran off, I mean hid in the caboose, so I could be by myself.

I need to process all of this. Hearing those words come out of Lucas' mouth was hard to believe.

I'm currently in the midst of an existential crisis. I thought he only liked me as a friend. I thought we were just partners in crime. You know, ride or die.

It took me forever to realize what I felt for Lucas. This whole time, I've tried to push aside what I felt, and numb it in a way. The further away he got from me, the more I realized how much he meant to me.

Fear is still taking me over. That's part of the reason I ran off. Although he said those words, I was scared to admit that I love him too. How do I even admit it? Should I say it, or do something about it?

May 5

It's been a whole day since Lucas and I have interacted with each other. Things have been rather quiet. Still no sign of The Crew or Alessandro. I wish there were clues or leads to follow.

A gentle knock on the caboose door interrupts my thoughts.

"Kalamiti," Lucas starts, "I'm moving back in with my brother."

"What?"

He looks at the ground. "There's no point in being here anymore. The Crew is gone. We can't do anything about it. Someday we can all be in touch again."

"We can't give up so easily." I know I eventually need to go back with Nonna, but I don't want to completely abandon this place yet.

After a long pause, he says, "It's best if we both go home. We won't have to steal anymore, and we won't have to worry about the things we had to worry about here. We'll be living normal lives."

"Don't you want to go back to California with me?"

He doesn't reply.

How could I forget about The Crew? About Lucas? About The Hideout? What about the adventures and memories? Not every moment was positive, but it all shaped me into who I am today.

"My brother lives a few cities away. I can take a bus. Get your plane ticket. Your grandmother needs you."

A lump in my throat forms, leaving me unable to respond.

He hugs me. "Bye, Kalamiti."

I follow him to the door. He begins to walk down the railroad tracks.

I'm frozen in place. I can't move. Every step he takes down the track is like another tug at my heart and soul, unraveling it ever so slowly.

As he walks down the tracks, little moments between us flash through my mind.

Lucas has always been protecting me. I've known him almost my entire life. He's always been there for me, just like I've always been there for him. I've already lost Alessandro and The Crew. I can't lose Lucas. I can't let him go.

Nonna was right all along. I did need to show him how I felt.

He's walked so far now that I can barely see him on the track.

It's not too late. It's now or never, Kalamiti Sol.

I run after him, not caring about whether I come close to tripping over the railroad tracks. "Wait!" I yell out.

He doesn't turn around.

When I finally catch up to him, I touch his arm. He stops and turns around. I take him by his shirt collar and kiss him. My hands relax and reach upwards, uniting around his neck. He wraps his arms around my waist and pulls me closer.

Nothing else matters.

And then I pull away.

"Damn," he says.

I smile. "I love you, Lucas." He takes both of my hands. "I didn't realize it until after you left California. I wasn't sure how to tell you the other day. Please don't leave. Things might be hard right now, but we can overcome this together."

He stands there, looking into my eyes. A smile slowly forms. "I love you too, Kalamiti." He hugs me. I bury my head in his chest. We hold on for the longest time ever.

Yup, that's probably the longest hug in the history of hugs.

* * *

Nighttime has arrived. Lucas and I lay down, side by side, at the top of the boxcar, admiring the few stars in the sky.

Out of the blue, Lucas laughs.

"What?" I ask.

"I've lost track of the number of times I tried to show you how I felt. You couldn't take a hint."

I smile. "Yeah, I was clueless."

"That's why I decided to finally say it. Sorry if it freaked you out. I mean, you did run off without saying a word."

My face turns red. "I was shocked."

"Your reaction was adorable. And funny. I won't ever forget it."

"I always figured you'd never see me in that way. I thought you just saw me as a friend. As The Crew's leader. As an ordinary girl."

"You're not some ordinary girl."

"But you were surrounded by all those popular girls at school."

"They were just friends."

"Even Amelia?"

He sighs. "She was into me, but I didn't like her like that. She wanted to hang out more often, but I told her I wasn't interested."

"All those girls were better looking than me. They were cool while I was a nobody."

He abruptly sits up and says, "I can't believe all of that just came out of your mouth. None of that is true. Did someone at school say something to you?"

Sedg. Mindy. Nina.

I sit up and hug my knees to my chest as an array of bad memories flash before my eyes.

He touches my back. "What happened while I was gone?"

I take a deep breath and explain everything to him, ranging from school events, to Nonna, to my mom.

"I'm so sorry, Kalamiti. I wish I had been there. I wish I wouldn't have left." He wraps his arm around me.

"They were lessons learned. I had to learn to ask for and accept help. I had to learn to stop running from difficult situations." I pause, then say, "Not everything was bad, though. Something good that happened was that Griffin and I won third place in the talent show."

He smiles. "Congratulations. You've worked hard for it," he pauses. "Speaking of Griffin, I've been so jealous of him. You two were spending a lot of time together."

"He's just a friend. We bonded because we both like the same music."

He looks into my eyes. "I didn't want to intervene because I saw how much you liked playing the piano."

"And I didn't want to get in between you and your new friends. I didn't want to separate you from them and seem like I just wanted you to myself."

He holds my hand. "Let's put all of this behind us."

I tilt my head up toward the sky. "Every time something

good or bad happened to me, I wanted to talk to you about it, but you weren't physically there. It's like a part of me was missing. This grey storm cloud was hovering over me, and no matter what I did, I couldn't get rid of it." I look him in the eyes. "Before Nonna, you were the only stable person in my life. I could always trust you and relate to you."

His hand meets my cheek and caresses it. "That's exactly how I feel about you, too."

He kisses me. "I know you initiated the kiss earlier, but you don't know how long I've been wanting to do that."

We smile.

I ask, "Do you want to sleep up here tonight?"

"I'll go get the sleeping bags."

As he's about to climb down the ladder, he says, "Let's go back to California tomorrow."

I smile. "Deal."

May 6

The plane made it safely to the airport.

Amongst the crowd of people in the arrivals lobby, Nonna stood next to the elevator.

"Kalamiti, Lucas!"

We shared a huge bear hug.

"I promised I'd come back," I said.

She smiled. "I'm very happy you did. And welcome back, Lucas."

The first thing I did when we made it home was go straight to my bed.

I'll miss The Hideout, but this is my home now.

May 7

We went back to school today.

As we walked into the building, Lucas held my hand and made it clear that we're together. The look on Amelia's face was priceless.

Although he reunited with the populars, he sat with me and my friends during lunch. I even saw Lucas having a conversation with Griffin.

We both have make-up work to do. He has a lot more than I do.

May 9

Lucas and I are going to pull an all-nighter. Nonna doesn't want us in the same room after 9 p.m., so she doesn't know about this. Hopefully we aren't too loud.

Midnight is upon us. We're in his room watching a movie. We have a pepperoni pizza, popcorn, pop, and a few other snacks.

"Hey, K9?"

"Yeah?"

"Have you ever wondered what's in the attic?"

That's random. I haven't really thought about it. "I totally forgot there was an attic here."

He pauses the movie. "Let's go explore."

The entrance to the attic is located on the ceiling in the hallway. Lucas pulls on the rope. The door opens, revealing a small wooden ladder. I'm kind of scared to go up there. What if it's a black hole filled with rodents, bats, and other things, and once we go in, there's no way out?

On the other hand, Lucas has an excited expression on his face. He can lead the way.

With our only light source coming from two flashlights we found, we climb up into the attic.

"Whoa," says Lucas.

We're taken aback by the room, composed of yellow walls and wood floors, unlike a typical attic. Cardboard boxes fill the small space. All it needs is a bed, nightstand, bookshelf, and dresser, and it could be another bedroom.

We search for a light switch, but there isn't one. I wish there was a ceiling fan. I'm burning up.

Curiosity gets the best of us. We shine our flashlights into the cardboard boxes to see what they contain.

Lucas has his eye on the cardboard box holding photo albums. It's the same one Nonna showed me when I first arrived.

Nonna is a hoarder. One box holds some of my old clothes, the ones I'd wear when Mom used to be around. Another box holds more old clothes. It's gotta be my mom's, because I doubt Nonna would have ever worn these kinds of garments in her lifetime. Oversized, baggy T-shirts. Camo pants and ripped up jeans. Brightly colored gym shoes. Acid wash everything.

We stumble across the last two cardboard boxes, covered in a thin layer of dust. While Lucas opens one, I open the other.

Paintings. Canvases fill both boxes.

"Is your grandma an artist?" Lucas asks.

"No." I shine my flashlight on a canvas, revealing the initials "VR" on the bottom right-hand corner.

"What about your mom?"

I shake my head. "No. She's never been artistic."

I pick up another canvas which features a dead rose painted with lots of thorns. "VR" is printed on it, too. Looking through the boxes, most of the art features grey, black, and brown shades, things that are dead and dull.

"Kalamiti. Look at this." Lucas holds up a painting of a graveyard with a shadow in the center.

"What does all of this mean?" I ask him.

"I don't know. It's pretty interesting. Art can be interpreted in so many different ways." He puts the painting back in the box.

At the bottom of one of the boxes lies an old sketchbook with a light brown leather cover. As I open the cover, blue handwriting catches my eye. Immediately, I shut the sketchbook. It's not my place to read other people's personal letters and information.

Lucas holds up a sketch of a sunflower. What's weird is that the sunflower is dead and all around it is filled with color. It's one of the few pieces displaying color.

"Did you notice the initials on the artwork?" he asks.

"Yeah. I wonder if these are my grandpa's. The one time I asked about him, Nonna didn't want to talk about it."

"It wouldn't hurt to ask her about the paintings. She might be open to talking about it now."

In one hand I hold the flashlight and in the other I hold a canvas. "Are you kidding? If we ask her about this, she'll know we were snooping around."

Footsteps creak on the stairsteps. With every step, my heart races faster. Nonna appears in a light pink nightgown, hair down to her waist. One hand holds a candle. She looks like she came straight from the 1800s.

"I see you've found some of my personal belongings," she says.

Neither Lucas nor I say a word.

She tilts her head in my direction. "What were you wanting to ask me about?" she asks.

Lucas nudges me.

"Who painted these?" I ask.

She sets the candle down on the small table next to her. "Your grandfather was an artist. Painting was his hobby."

"Did he make these for you?" Lucas asks.

"Yes. I have kept them all these years. I couldn't get rid of them."

"Where is he now?" I ask.

Nonna stares into the candle's flame. "He's gone."

I hesitate. "What do you mean?"

Nonna sits down on the stool next to the table. "Take a seat."

Lucas and I sit on the floor.

She sighs. "His name was Valerio Renzetti. During my last semester of college, I studied abroad in Italy. It was one of the most magical moments of my life. I met him at a restaurant, and we fell in love. We were perfect for each other." Nonna clears her throat. "The semester was coming to a close, and it was then that I realized we couldn't be together. I had to return home."

"Wait, what? He could have moved over here, or you could have stayed over there," I interject.

Nonna smiles. "Life is not so simple, Kalamiti. I knew he wouldn't want to move over here. I was just a college student, about to graduate, and I had a job lined up."

Lucas asks, "So what happened? Did you keep in touch?"

"It was the last week of my trip. I told him I was soon going to return home and that I probably wouldn't see him again. He gave me one of his sketchbooks and a couple of his paintings to bring home with me." Nonna crosses one leg over the other. "A couple of weeks after returning home, I found out I was pregnant. I never told him."

My mouth drops open. "What? Why?"

"At the time I didn't think I needed to tell him. It's not like he would have moved to the states to be here with us."

Lucas asks, "Did you ever end up telling him?"

The candle flame reflects in her eyes. "No. I used to write letters to him in the sketchbook, but I never sent them. He mailed me more paintings, too. Eventually he stopped sending them."

Things aren't adding up. "I thought he left you? You said he was dead to you, and you never wanted to talk about it."

She sighs. "I didn't want to tell you what really happened. I was ashamed."

I glance at Lucas. Neither of us knows what to say.

I stretch out my hand and lay it on top of hers. "Thanks for telling us. That was brave."

She manages to smile. "I couldn't keep the truth from you forever."

I smile. "Didn't you grow up in Italy? Why didn't you just move back so you and my mom could be with him?"

"I grew up in Milan. I was a teenager when my parents decided to emigrate here. At first it was difficult to adjust and learn English, but I eventually loved it here. As much as I miss my home country, I couldn't imagine leaving now."

We all smile.

Her eyes sparkle. "Oh, I have so many lovely stories and

memories from my time in Italy. Perhaps I will share more with you two soon." She stands up from the stool and picks up the candle. "I need to get to bed. I want both of you in your own rooms now. It's late."

After the sound of her footsteps dissipates, Lucas asks, "How do you feel after all of that?"

"I feel bad for Nonna. I wish she could reconnect with him. I'm sure he'd want to know he has a daughter and granddaughter. Even if he couldn't live over here, we could still stay connected, couldn't we?"

"Maybe in the future we'll be able to meet him."

We leave the attic how we found it, return to his room, and continue our all-nighter.

May 10

I wake up in Lucas' bed. The TV is still on, at a volume that's much too high for this early in the morning. My eyes feel heavy.

Where *is* Lucas?

I get up to go turn off the TV when I almost step on him.

He's face down on the carpet. Popcorn and other snacks are scattered all over him. Pop is spilled on the carpet.

If Nonna saw this, she would flip out.

"Dude," I say.

"Huh?" He slowly lifts his head up.

You know when you take a nap and wake up with marks and indentations all over you? The carpet decided to leave its mark on half of Lucas' face. Pretty hilarious, if you ask me.

"Get up and look around you," I tell him.

"…too tired. Maybe later."

A door slams shut. I jump into the bed and pretend to be asleep.

Nonna's footsteps slow to a halt. She knocks on the door.

Before I can hide, the door swings open. "Why are you in Lucas' bed?" She then looks at the floor. "What in the world happened here?"

I sit up. "We kind of pulled an all-nighter."

"This room better be spotless by the time I finish making breakfast." She closes the door behind her.

Now that I think about it, how did the room get this messy? I guess we didn't successfully pull an all-nighter because we both crashed at some point in the middle of the night.

Lucas starts to stir.

"K9, did you pull a prank on me?"

"I swear I didn't do anything."

He sits up. "What happened to my room?"

"I was wondering the same thing."

After spending about an hour scrubbing the carpet, vacuuming, throwing out everything, and washing a few dishes, we finish.

Lucas says, "I don't know about you, but I'm going back to sleep." He grabs a blanket and pillow from his bed and throws them down on the carpet.

"I'm with you." I jump back into his bed.

May 11

As I walk with Lucas to French class, I stop in my tracks. Posters advertising prom deck the hallways.

My theme. They picked it. We're having a Sunshine Dance after all.

PROM: THE SUNSHINE DANCE
FOR ALL JUNIORS AND SENIORS
MAY 23RD AT 7 P.M.
WEAR BRIGHT COLORS TO CELEBRATE A GREAT YEAR!

"This is a great theme, huh?" Lucas asks.

I smile. "Totally."

He doesn't know it's my theme. I haven't told him I submitted an idea. Now isn't the best time to tell him because a lot of students are near us. Some of them are pointing at the posters, wondering who came up with the theme.

The school's receptionist, Mrs. Yoon, approaches us. "Kalamiti? We need to see you in the office."

Lucas glances at me, confused. We part ways.

She takes me into one of the offices.

"Congratulations! The panel picked your theme for prom. It was one of the most descriptive submissions we've ever received. You might've already noticed the posters in the halls."

I smile. "Yeah, they look great."

"We're going to be announcing it on today's morning announcements. We wanted you to say a speech."

My blood runs cold. "What? What do I say? How long does it have to be?"

"You can say whatever you'd like. It can be as short or as long as you want. We'll be live in eight minutes."

My friends weren't playing. Mayfield High takes this stuff way too seriously.

She beckons me to the intercom. I take a seat.

Where do I even begin? There's so much on my mind.

Eventually, a voice in the office next door says, "We're live."

From another room, Mrs. Yoon makes the announcements. Then, she announces my theme and name.

Go time. "Hey, everybody. First of all, thank you. A lot of you probably don't know who I am. The idea came to me because it was a theme I had always wanted for a birthday party. But I never ended up having a proper birthday party, filled with cake, and presents, and friends and family."

The words flow so naturally, like a river. As I speak into the intercom, I visualize an audience before me.

"I was homeless for most of my childhood years. Many of you look at me as if I'm a nobody, judging me based on my facial expressions and my physical appearance. From all the times I've wandered the hallways alone, or sat by myself in the cafeteria, or lounged in the back of a classroom on my own, I can't help but wonder if anyone ever noticed me. Why doesn't anyone make an effort to talk to me? And why do I feel like I can't approach others? Why is it so hard to make a genuine connection? I'm not the only one who's been in this situation. This is for anyone who has ever felt alone, for anyone who feels like their ideas and voices aren't heard. It means a lot to me that the Sunshine Dance theme was picked. After so much darkness, we could all use some light in our lives. Let's end the year on a bright note."

Mrs. Yoon opens the door to the office, teary-eyed, holding a tissue.

"That was beautiful," she says as she hugs me.

Who knows where that speech came from. It was so effortless. "Thank you," I say.

She takes me by the shoulders and looks me in the eyes. "I've noticed you, Kalamiti. Sometimes it's the quiet ones who have the most to say."

I smile.

The rest of the school day goes by in a similar fashion. As soon as I walked out of the front office, it was a different energy, as if a light switch had been flipped. I wasn't expecting all of the attention. I also don't want people to pity me. I was just sharing whatever came to my mind.

Penelope from French class fist bumped me after class. Lucas told me he's proud of me for being brave. Betsy, Annabelle, and Griffin hugged me and congratulated me, too. I ran into Turner and Sofia in the stairwell, where they made me laugh after calling me "the shit." Ms. Hayley praised me for placing in the talent show and now this. She said I should continue to speak up.

Some students, complete strangers, smiled and congratulated me. Other girls, like Mindy, still gave me dirty looks. You can't please everyone in this world.

I'm making a difference here, one step at a time.

May 12

School's out for the day.

I'm heading to the bus with Lucas, when Nina approaches us. She's crying, with one hand covering her mouth.

We stop in our tracks. She hugs me.

"I'm so sorry, Kalamiti," she says. "I was so mean to you."

I hesitate. "I'm sorry, too. For breaking your nose."

She wipes tears mixed with mascara from her face. "I didn't know you used to be homeless. I didn't know you went through all of that."

I swallow.

She continues. "I shouldn't have made you shoplift. I'm sorry for everything I said and did to hurt you."

"I forgive you," I say. "How are you and Chad?"

"We're doing good. You were right. He wasn't at the party. Sedg made everything up."

"You were my friend. I would have never hurt you like that."

She smiles. "Are we cool?"

I nod. "Yeah."

She hugs me again.

As she walks off, I call out her name.

She turns around.

I say, "Why are you and Chad even friends with Sedg?"

"Chad and Sedg have been friends since elementary school. But they're both different now. I don't think we're going to hang out with him anymore."

I manage to smile. She waves goodbye.

After everything that's happened between us, I'm glad we were able to straighten things out. I don't think Nina and I could ever be best friends, but it's nice knowing I have another familiar face to smile at or wave to at school.

May 13

Lately, I've been observing Joanie. In the past, I've always avoided her. After our last conversation, I'm curious to know why she's the way she is.

Based on my observations, she doesn't seem to have any friends. She's always alone, whether it's at the back of the bus, during lunchtime, or outside after dismissal. Her light brown hair is typically pulled back in a ponytail. Blue headphones usually cover her ears. She tends to wear simple clothes. Plain shirts. Worn, solid white shoes. Her checkered backpack is faded and torn. I don't know anything about her home life.

She's sitting on the staircase, eating lunch.

She could use a friend.

"Hey, Joanie," I say.

She pulls her headphones off and lets them rest around her neck. "Hi."

"Can I eat lunch with you?"

A bewildered expression is on her face. "I guess."

I sit across from her and set my lunch tray on my lap.

I need to say something or else this is gonna be awkward. "Do you want to hang out after school tomorrow?"

She looks behind her, which is hilarious because no one else is around. "Me?"

"Yeah, of course."

For the first time, she smiles. I've never seen her smile.

I guess I'm not that bad at making friends after all.

May 14

"Nonna, can you drive me to the park?" I ask.

"What for?" she asks.

"I'm going to hang out with a girl from school who doesn't have many friends."

She smiles. "Lucas can take my car. He can drive you."

Lucas opens the garage and backs out of the driveway. "So who's this girl you're meeting?"

"Joanie."

He slams on the brakes. "Joanie?"

"I know what you're thinking."

"Let me guess. You two are about to throw hands at the park and you invited the entire school to come watch."

"No. We're hanging out. She doesn't have any friends, so I'm gonna be one."

"You can't trust people so easily, K9. Maybe this is all a setup."

"You don't get it. I'm the one who invited her. She has nobody, which is why she bullies others. I need to change that. I want to be her friend."

He looks at me, then puts it in drive.

After parking in the lot, he says, "Call me when you need me to pick you up."

I approach Joanie, who's sitting at a picnic table.

"Hey," I say.

"Hey, Sol," she replies.

I take a seat across from her. "You don't have to call me Sol. You can call me Kalamiti."

She nods her head.

I wave at Lucas, and then he drives off.

Say something, Kalamiti. "So before I came to this school, I was pretty much homeless. Lucas and I were living with some other teenagers. I stole a car, got caught, and ended up in juvie. Then my grandma came and rescued me."

Plants are laid out in front of her. Grass. Dandelions. Henbit. Poppies. She separates and organizes them into piles. I'm not sure why she has all of that stuff, but maybe it was something to do while she waited for me.

She says, "I've always moved from school to school. This is my second year here, and it's the longest I've stayed in one place. My dad lost his job, so my family has been struggling this year."

"I'm sorry to hear that."

We continue to talk about school, our families, and music that we listen to. Joanie is such a cool person. We have a lot more in common than I thought.

"My friends Betsy and Annabelle are having a sleepover in a couple of days. You should join us," I say.

"I've never been to a sleepover. It seems like a girly idea."

"Me neither, but who knows, maybe it'll be fun."

She nods. "Okay, I'll go."

"Sweet."

May 15

Annabelle, Betsy, and I are having lunch in the cafeteria.

Griffin walks up to our table, holding a bouquet of roses. "Betsy, will you go to prom with me?"

Her eyes light up. "Yes!" She stands up and hugs Griffin.

I'm happy for Betsy. I always knew she had a crush on Griffin. We'll see if it turns into something more.

May 16

We had our sleepover at Betsy's place.

Initially, Annabelle and Betsy thought I was crazy for inviting Joanie. I think they ended up liking her. Hopefully we can all be friends and hang out more often.

Joanie was slow to open up, but eventually she started joining in the conversations, laughing, and smiling.

We played different board games, ate snacks, and watched a movie. They wanted to paint my nails, so I let them.

It's now 3 a.m. After a long night of fun, it's time for some sleep. Goodnight.

May 17

It's the championship soccer game at the rival school.

Betsy, Annabelle, and I are sporting Mayfield spirit wear. My friends even painted their faces. Griffin let me borrow a dark green and grey school hoodie.

Joanie was going to come with us, but her family is visiting from out of town. I invited Lucas, but he decided to stay home and catch up on schoolwork. At least he and Griffin are on good terms now.

The metal bleachers aren't very comfortable. The old people sitting a few rows below us are smart to have brought stadium chairs with them.

The game begins. At first, the opposing team is winning. Then things turn around.

They're at a tie, 2-2.

I'm literally on the edge of my seat.

Griffin steals the ball from one of the players. He's on his way to the other side of the field. There are only a couple of seconds left. He scores!

He and his team huddle up by the field. Spectators are on their feet, clapping and cheering.

Parents and students gather at the sidelines to congratulate the players. My friends and I join, but we stand off to the side.

The crowd soon starts to disperse. Griffin approaches us.

"Hey, ladies." He hugs us. "You're all welcome to come over to my house for the after party."

We congratulate him, and then he walks away to greet others.

"We've never been invited to any parties!" says Betsy.

"Let's go," I say.

"We need to dress up," says Annabelle.

"What? No," I say.

Betsy says to me, "I have a dress you can borrow."

I don't know how I feel about that.

We walk to the parking lot and wait for Annabelle's mom to pick us up.

After stopping at Annabelle's, we go over to Betsy's.

She takes a navy-blue dress out of her closet and tosses it at me. "Kalamiti, try this on."

I quickly change in the closet. I wish there was a mirror so I could look at myself first.

I step out.

"That looks great on you," says Annabelle.

Betsy goes into her closet and pulls out a leather jacket. She throws it at me and I put it on.

"Perfect. Let's go," says Betsy.

We pull into Griffin's neighborhood a little bit later.

As soon as we walk through his front door, I feel a little out of place. Populars are everywhere. Actually, after reanalyzing the room, there seems to be a good mix of people, including the team's family members.

The last time I wore a dress had to be when I lived with the Reeses, my former foster family. This navy-blue dress is reminding me of the glittery pink dresses they had forced me to wear. The smell of hairspray and Mrs. Reese's musky perfume swirl in my vicinity. At least the leather jacket is more my style.

Why did I decide to come? I guess it was because I could tell Betsy and Annabelle really wanted to, and sometimes we've got to make sacrifices for our friends. I'm glad they're with me and I'm not alone.

I've never really known what to do at parties and get-togethers. What am I supposed to do? Eat? Drink? Pet the family dog?

Annabelle tugs at my arm. "Kalamiti? Hey, let's go get something to drink."

I must've checked out for a minute.

We each grab a can of pop and stand in the corner together.

Griffin's mom makes her way around the room, talking to the guests. This is the first time I've met her. She's lovely, but something seems off. I can tell she's emotionally drained, as if she's putting on a mask for the party and everyone present. In a way, she reminds me of my mom.

As for Griffin's dad, I don't think I saw him. I would think he'd be supportive, but maybe he's got other things going on, or doesn't want to be around Griffin's mom.

"Do you guys want to come over to my place and have dinner there?" I ask them.

They say yes, so we get in the car and drive to Nonna's.

Lucas is home alone.

"Hey," he greets us. He stops me in my tracks. "Whoa. You look hot."

I turn red. I forgot I'm still wearing this outfit. "Thanks," I manage to say.

The three of them chill in the living room while I go and change. What a relief to be back in my usual clothes.

I join my friends in the living room.

"I heard Phoenix scored the winning goal," says Lucas.

"He did. It was impressive," says Betsy.

"I'll be right back." Lucas heads to the garage.

"What should we have for dinner?" I ask them.

Betsy suggests pizza. We begin to discuss what toppings to order.

Lucas hasn't come back yet. I wonder what he's doing. "I'm gonna go check on Lucas."

He's not in the garage. I return to the living room and walk through the back door that leads to the small patio. "Lucas?"

Water splashes me. I blink the water out of my eyes.

Lucas has a hose in his hand.

I can't help laughing. I grab the other hose nearby and I spray him back. Too bad it was on the mist setting.

"Ha," he says.

I quickly change the setting on the nozzle and spray him again. Two water guns are lying in the grass near us.

Betsy and Annabelle come out the door and pick up the water guns.

"This is war!" he yells. He changes the setting on the nozzle and sprays all of us.

We spray him back.

"Three against one! Give it up, Lucas!" I say.

"Never!" he responds.

I run farther out into the yard. Because the hose can't go any farther, I fall to the ground.

As I'm getting up, Lucas sprays me again. This time it's on the jet setting, because the water feels like a knife stabbing me in the back.

My friends spray Lucas. I'm finally able to get up.

Annabelle's gun is out of water.

While Annabelle and Betsy refill, I spray Lucas again.

I'm changing the setting, when Lucas coils his hose around my legs. He takes my hose from me and attempts to wrap my hands with it.

I try to pry the nozzle out of his hands, but I end up pressing it and spraying both of us. Water shoots up my nose. We're now soaked from head to toe.

Annabelle and Betsy return from inside and they spray Lucas down.

"Okay, I give up," says Lucas. "You guys win."

"What was all that for?" I ask.

He unwraps the hose from around my hands. "I thought it'd be fun. I needed a break from all the homework and studying I've been doing all day."

We laugh.

When Nonna comes home, she finds us all sitting at the dining table, towels wrapped around us, slices of pizza in our hands.

She stares at us. "You all look like you took a dip in the non-existent swimming pool in our backyard."

Everyone laughs.

She adds, "Don't tell me you actually swam in the pond." She holds out a hand. "Wait. I don't even want to know." With that, she walks off.

This day has been long. And fun. Can't wait to go to bed and rest.

May 18

Joanie has been joining me and my friends at our lunch table.

I'm glad I had the courage to talk to her. All she needed all along was a friend.

May 19

Lucas barges through my bedroom door, holding a suit.
"How's this for prom?" he asks.

I close my textbook and set it down next to me.

"Wait. We are going together, right?" he asks.

"Well, you didn't ask me in front of everyone at school, holding a bouquet in one hand and a cheesy poster in the other."

He stares at me with a blank expression.

"I'm kidding. We're totally going. And that suit looks great."

He laughs. "What a relief. Now you just need to get your dress."

I smile. "I'm working on it."

To be honest, I haven't even begun looking for a dress.

May 20

Annabelle is once again heartbroken.

The situation is pretty messed up. Derick broke up with her yesterday. They were supposed to go to prom together this Saturday.

The good thing is that even though we had dates, we all planned to hang out as a group. Griffin and Betsy. Me and Lucas. Since Joanie doesn't have a date either, Annabelle won't be the only one going without one.

The only issue is that the dance is for juniors and seniors. So, if you're a freshman or sophomore, you need a date or friend who's an upperclassman to get you in. The day of, we're going to ask two random dudes if they'll help out Joanie and Annabelle.

Anyway, I'm probably gonna get a call from Betsy any minute now about another emergency get-together. Hopefully I won't screw up and say something inconsiderate this time.

May 21

Let's be real, I eavesdrop on other people's conversations. I've lost braincells from the number of ridiculous conversations I've listened in on.

Students are going all out for prom. From what I've heard, some girls have spent $500 on their dresses. Guys are renting tuxes. I didn't know that was a thing. Don't get me started on the limos and party buses being booked for the night.

Some students were also persuading and guilt-tripping their friends into going to prom, saying things like, "If you don't go, you'll regret it for the rest of your life." It's a high school dance, not your sister's wedding.

Anyway, if my theme hadn't been picked, I probably wouldn't go. But it'll be like I'm finally having the birthday party I've always dreamed of. Since my friends are going and Lucas is my date, it won't be so bad either.

"Kalamiti, should I get this dress?" Betsy calls out from the fitting room.

She has on a beautiful, light green dress. It really compliments her skin and hair. "It's gorgeous. Take it," I say.

"I'm going to try on a few more and then make my final decision." She closes her fitting room door.

Annabelle is also trying on a few dresses. Joanie is looking at suits. I'm the only one who hasn't found a single dress I'd like to try on.

I continue to browse the overwhelming and disorganized

racks. Yellow dresses are hard to find. There needs to be a shade that isn't too bright or too pale.

Betsy is finished. She went with the light green dress.

Together, we look for yellow dresses.

"What about this one?" She holds up a bright yellow dress.

"Too bright," I reply.

I'm on the last rack in the store. This is it.

And there it is. The perfect yellow dress. Two are left. Juniors sizing is so inconsistent that I don't even know my size. I decide to try both on.

One of them fits me perfectly.

I take it. The thought of looking for other dresses seems so exhausting, anyway.

We go to the other side of the store, where Joanie is. She's sitting in a chair by the fitting room, empty-handed.

"Did you find a suit you liked?" I ask.

"No, I didn't," she says.

"We can go to a different store," says Annabelle.

Joanie looks at the ground. "I think I want to go home."

Betsy says, "What? But you haven't gotten a suit."

She sighs. "This is really embarrassing."

"What is?" I ask. "You can tell us."

"My parents didn't want to give me money for a suit. They said they would only give me money for a dress. And I don't want to wear a dress."

I look at Betsy and Annabelle. Then I say, "We can pay for your suit."

She raises her eyebrows. "I couldn't let you all do that."

"We insist," says Betsy.

Annabelle adds, "We want to help. That's what friends do."

Tears well up in her eyes. She stands up from her chair and we have a group hug.

As we pull away from each other, Joanie says, "I love you all. It's been a while since anyone's done something nice for me."

Together, we find a suit for Joanie.

Prom is gonna be rad.

May 22

Free time in French class. Ms. Adler is letting us catch up on all our schoolwork. If we don't have any work, we're free to use our phones or read a book or something.

Since it's almost the end of the semester, I think she's just tired of teaching us.

The bell rings. Everyone makes their way to the door. At the doorway, Summer stops next to me and Lucas.

She smiles at me. "It's awesome how they picked your theme. The Sunshine Dance. It's really cool."

"Oh, so now you want to talk to me?" I retort.

Lucas puts his arm around my shoulder and we walk away.

Take a hike, Summer.

May 23

It's the night we've all been waiting for. The Sunshine Dance.

Betsy, Annabelle, and I finish getting ready at Betsy's place. Luckily, Annabelle did my hair and makeup for me. I'm relieved I didn't have to curl my own hair, because I probably would have burned it all off.

Betsy's mom drives us to Joanie's place, so we can pick her up.

As we pull into the lot, Joanie is already waiting outside of her apartment. Except she isn't ready. She's sitting on the ground, tossing her phone between both hands.

Betsy's mom parks the car. I get out of the car and approach Joanie.

"Why aren't you ready yet?" I ask.

She sighs. "I don't think I'm gonna go anymore."

"Why?"

"My parents are pissed at me. Ever since I brought home the suit, they've been treating me different and distancing themselves."

"So?"

She looks at me. "I can't disappoint them. I need to just act like a normal girl around them. They even bought me a dress so that I wouldn't wear the suit tonight."

"You shouldn't have to pretend to be someone you're not. They need to accept you for who you are."

She shakes her head. "They're never going to accept me."

I take a second to think about what to say. "Would you rather have mad parents or be a happy you?" I start. "Either way, they can't be mad forever. And if they are, that's not healthy."

She nods. "You're right."

I hold out my hand to help her up. "Come on, you

already bought your ticket and they're already mad. Might as well enjoy your time at the prom."

She smiles. "Thanks, Kalamiti."

After Joanie finishes changing into her suit, she gets in the car.

Betsy's mom drives us to the venue, which is down the street from the school. We're meeting the guys there.

Limos, party buses, and other cars are lined up in the loop. Griffin opens the passenger door for Betsy. I'm about to open my door, when Lucas opens it for me. He holds out his hand and I take it.

He says, "You look great."

"So do you," I say.

The decorated venue is just like my vision. Beautiful and colorful decorations adorn the venue from floor to ceiling, consisting of balloons, streamers, and a giant sun in the center. There's a stage with a DJ, an area to take photos with friends, and tables stocked with various food and drinks. They even included the lemon bars, key lime pie, and lemonade. Beneath the giant sun sits the dance floor, surrounded by tables and chairs for guests.

Most students are eating and drinking. People continue to stagger in. The night is just getting started.

Our group reserves a table. Griffin and Lucas bring food and drinks over.

Upbeat music booms from the large speakers, making the entire room shake.

The dancing begins. An array of colors from students' outfits fills the dance floor.

Lucas and I are left at our table.

"Do you want to dance?" he asks me.

"I don't know how to," I say.

"Who cares?"

I observe the dance floor, where everyone is dancing and doing their own thing.

"Come on, it's a once in a lifetime opportunity to dance at the Sunshine Dance. This is your theme."

I smile. He takes my hand. As he leads me to the crowd of people, I start to feel sick and overwhelmed.

Our friends are dancing in a group on the other side of the crowd, waiting for us. We join their circle.

The sick sensation quickly dissipates. Dancing is actually quite fun. Individually, we take turns going in the center of our circle.

The upbeat music decrescendos and segues into a slow ballad. Groups of dancing students disperse, leaving behind couples.

Lucas whispers in my ear, "Let's dance."

As I wrap my arms around his neck, his hands meet my waist. I've never danced with anyone like this.

He takes my hand and spins me around. "So why do you keep a diary?"

"It's not a diary," I say. "It's a memory book. I decided to start documenting moments of my life."

"I read some of it. I like what you've written."

My eyes open wide. "You read it?"

"I only skimmed through it. I hope that was okay?"

My face turns red.

"I was curious why you were always writing in it. Sorry. I should've asked you first."

"It's cool," I say. "I just write whatever comes to mind, so I don't know if it's any good. I'm kind of embarrassed."

"Don't be. You have a way with words. After reading yours, I kind of want to start my own memory book. Look at how far you've come. You should be proud."

I smile. "Thanks, Lucas."

I wish the song would never end, and we could dance together all night under the giant sun.

May 24

I'm in my sacred space. My willow tree needed some company. A couple of sunflowers are standing tall.

"Hey."

It's Lucas, standing outside of the willow tree's embrace.

I smile. "Welcome to my sacred space. Come on in."

He pushes the curtain-like branches aside and takes a seat next to me. "So that's what you call this place."

"This is where I run off to when I want to be alone or recharge. I can spend hours here and it'll only feel like minutes. Consider yourself lucky, because I don't allow just anyone in."

His gaze wanders to the pond. He reaches out to touch the willow tree's branches and leaves. "This is marvelous," he starts. "The weeping willow holds your sorrow."

I smile softly, then look at him. "Yeah. It really does."

He leans his head back, his eyes gazing at the sky.

"I don't know what it is, but I've dreamt about my parents here." I place my hand on top of his. "Close your eyes."

He closes them and begins to breathe deeply.

Together, we sit in silence for a few minutes.

He opens his eyes. "That was amazing. I feel so relaxed now. I didn't dream about my parents, but it's like I went to a whole new world."

I smile. "Yup, this place is magical."

He gives the sunflowers a good look. "You've been trying to grow sunflowers here for a while, haven't you?"

I nod my head. "Yeah. Only a few have grown."

"Here's the problem. The seeds are planted too close to the pond's edge. This probably isn't the best place to plant them. The ground inclines into the pond."

"How do you know so much about this?"

"My mom loved to garden. At our old house, we always had flowers growing by the porch. Have you thought about having a garden bed out here?"

"No, actually, I never thought about that."

"Let's build one."

We spend the rest of the morning buying supplies from the hardware store and assembling. Nonna helps us, too.

Lucas places the bed where it's still close to the willow tree and pond.

Together, we fill it to the brim with soil. The three of us plant sunflower seeds in rows.

We stand around the garden bed and admire the finished product. Hard work pays off. As we hug each other, raindrops touch my head and shoulders. Soon it begins to drizzle.

"Let's go inside before it pours," says Nonna.

"Wait, let's dance," I say. "Let's soak in all the good things."

Nonna and Lucas look at each other, then the three of us

take each other's hands. We spin around and dance and jump under the rain. Laughter and smiles fill our circle.

Dancing in the rain is the best. I'm content.

May 25

We're in our last couple of weeks of school.

Finals are coming up.

Griffin is helping me prepare for my piano final. I'm not too worried about that one.

The good thing is that Lucas and I are caught up with our homework, so now we can focus on studying. Even though most of our classes are different, we've been quizzing each other.

Nonna has randomly brought us coffee and other snacks during our study sessions. We're in good hands.

Bring on the finals.

May 26

Lucas' birthday is this Sunday.

I have no idea what to get him.

I have a card picked out. All I need is a gift.

After browsing a couple of stores, I give up.

I board the city bus. Only a few other people fill the seats.

The bus brakes to a halt. A plastic bag on the sidewalk catches my eye. Something is moving inside of it.

Before the bus moves, I quickly get off.

It's a German Shepherd puppy. How dare someone abandon this adorable little guy? How could someone leave him inside of a plastic bag to die?

He comes home with me.

I need to keep him hidden for a couple of days. I hope Nonna will be okay with having a pet.

For now, he'll hide in my closet.

Lucas is gonna have the best seventeenth birthday.

May 27

Will I ever see The Crew again? Will I ever be reunited with Alessandro?

One thing I've begun to realize is that nothing will ever be the same. Things can't go back to the way they were. In a way, it's a good thing.

I guess Maci's prediction was right. We wouldn't be in The Hideout ten years from now. Either we'd get caught, we'd run into trouble, or we would all grow up and go our separate ways.

Change is inevitable.

May 28

I arrive home from an after school piano practice session. I ring the doorbell, and Nonna opens it. "Kalamiti, close your eyes."

"What?" I question.

"Just do it!"

I close them. Nonna and Lucas guide me through the house.

"Surprise!" they exclaim.

I open my eyes to a beautiful piano in the living room.

"Is that for me?" I ask.

"Of course. Now you can practice at home," says Nonna.

I'm shocked. Pianos are expensive. I can't believe Nonna got one for me. "I can't accept this. All I've done is hurt you and betray you. I've repeatedly run away and stolen your money. How can you trust me? How could you even give me a gift like this?"

"Forgiveness, Kalamiti. I forgive you for all you have done. You are learning and growing up, and we all make mistakes. You have been making better choices, and you'll continue down that path. I want to reward you. Piano is a hobby that you've picked up and you're good at it. Maybe you could even take lessons from Ms. Hayley."

"Thank you, Nonna." I give her a hug.

Months ago, I thought my life was over when she got me out of camp, separated me from The Crew, and brought me to California. It isn't until now that I realize my life was just beginning again when that all happened. I had another chance.

Without her, I would be nothing. She rescued me.

May 29

We're finished with most of our finals. The only one I'm worried about is French, which is the last one we need to take.

This has kind of been a stressful week. I wish the school

could measure our progress in a different way, instead of relying on tests.

Whatever happens, I'm sure Lucas and I will be able to pass all of our classes and move on to the next grade.

May 31

It's Lucas' birthday.

Yesterday he spent the day with his grandparents.

The first thing we did today was go to mass together. We've been accompanying Nonna every Sunday. Afterwards, we went out to eat at a restaurant. Then we took a walk around a park.

Lucas and I sit in the back row of the car, my head resting against his shoulder. Nonna turns into our neighborhood.

After pulling into the garage, I'm the first one out of the car.

"I have to go get something. Wait here," I tell them. I run to my room and fetch the puppy.

"Surprise." I hold him up.

"You got me a puppy? This is the best birthday present ever." He takes him from my hands.

"He was abandoned on the side of the road. I couldn't leave him there."

"Does he have a name?"

"No."

He smiles. "What about Bruno?"

"That's perfect."

Nonna barges into the conversation. "Did I ever mention dogs being allowed in the house?"

I forgot she was here, still sitting in the driver's seat of the car. "Um, no?"

"You can keep him in the laundry room for now. We'll have to buy him a bed and some other supplies."

"Thank you, Ms. DiAngelo," says Lucas.

Welcome to the family, Bruno.

June 1

Bruno is the cutest thing ever. He has a lot of energy. We're excited to start training him and teaching him tricks.

I'll write some more later.

June 2

Today was our last day of school. I can't believe I've managed to be here a whole semester. We survived. We did it.

Initially this school was like a prison, but it's grown on me.

Everyone went around and signed each other's yearbooks. I couldn't stop reading the kind messages some of my friends wrote, as well as others in my class who I never really talked to.

I'm going to miss the friends I've made. Low-key, I fear that I'll lose connection with them over the summer and that they'll forget about me. Who knows, maybe we'll be able to spend time with each other.

I'll miss some of the teachers and staff. I'll even miss the cafeteria food, which wasn't as bad as others made it out to be.

Despite summer classes, I'm hoping to have a productive summer. I'm going to start piano lessons with Ms. Hayley. After seeing my grandfather's artwork in the attic, I'm interested in doing art, too. I bought myself an oil paint set from the craft store.

Lucas is starting to research colleges. He's going to be a senior next year, and apparently college applications need to be filled out sooner rather than later. He still isn't sure what to do, and a part of him wants to become a police officer like his dad. I'm sure he'll figure it out, and whatever he does, he'll be good at it.

It's crazy that we're expected to figure out who we want to be and what we want to do by the time we're 18. I don't think anyone truly knows what they want to be when they grow up. As years pass, you'll always be learning more about yourself. You'll always be growing, and that's the way it should be.

June 4

My bedroom door opens. In walks Nonna.

"Kalamiti, can I talk to you?"

I nod my head. She sits down next to me on my bed.

"I don't want to keep anything from you." She pauses, as if she's trying to find the right words to say. "I know where your mom is. I've been in contact with her."

"What? Where is she?"

"She lives in Brookings, Oregon. She's doing well. She has a good job and she lives in her own apartment."

"I thought we weren't going to keep anything from each other anymore."

"I'm so sorry, Kalamiti. I promise I wasn't keeping this from you. I just found out a few days ago."

I kind of don't believe her. I'm doing everything I can to not throw my phone at the wall.

Nonna continues. "I now have her phone number. Would you like to talk to her?"

"No," I shake my head. "No, I don't want to. If she truly wanted to talk to me, she would've visited me by now."

"She cares about you. She's your mom. All she wanted was the best for you, which is why she left you with me."

"Well, if I ever talk to her again, it's going to be in person, so I can confront her about everything."

She sighs. "Someday." She leaves my room.

The day I'm reunited with my mom, I'm not even sure what I'll say to her. Should I hug her? Shake her hand? Imagine how long it'll take for the two of us to answer the simple question, "What have you been up to all these years?"

No matter how many times Nonna reminds me why I was left with her, that my mom loves me, and that it was for the best, it's still not enough. I need to know everything. What were the events that led up to my mom deciding to leave me with Nonna? What truly happened? Give me the details. Tell me why. I need to hear it from my own mom's voice, in person.

What I need is closure—closure from the past, for why things happened the way they did. Closure from my own foolishness of running away. Closure that'll make me realize that things are okay, and that the past won't determine my future.

June 5

Nonna has an event at church this evening.

"I'll be back around nine. Behave," she tells us.

Lucas is sitting in the recliner on the other side of the living room, watching a show on the TV.

"Lucas," I say.

"What's up?" he asks, his eyes fixed on the screen.

"Nonna admitted that she's recently been in contact with my mom."

He shuts off the TV. "No way."

"She lives in an apartment in Brookings, Oregon. Nonna says she's doing well, which is surprising."

"Do you think she'll come visit?"

"I doubt it. She probably started a brand-new life in Oregon without us."

He stares at the remote in his hands. "I'm sorry, K9."

I get up from the couch. "Come with me."

"What?"

"To Oregon. I need to find my mom."

"How are we gonna get there?"

"Hitchhike."

He gets up from the recliner and stands in front of me. "What if she doesn't want to see you?"

I never thought about that. He has a point, but I need to see her whether she wants to or not. "I don't care. I need to know why she abandoned me. I need to know everything." My hands take a hold of his. "We have a few days until summer school starts. Come with me. Please."

"Like right now?"

"Yes."

He looks away from me, then nods. "Let's pack."

I grab my shoes, pull them on, and put on a sweater. I grab my backpack and toss my belongings in it. Lucas does the same.

Our first stop is the nearest gas station.

Lucas points. "There's a truck. We can ride in the bed."

We approach the driver.

Lucas does the talking. "Could we get a ride to Oregon?"

He gives us a weird look. "Where exactly?"

"Brookings."

"Do you have any money?"

I chime in. "I do. I can give you a hundred bucks."

To be honest, I stole some money from Nonna. I shouldn't have done it, but we're not gonna get anywhere without it.

"Hop in," he says to us.

We get in the bed of the truck and lie down.

"Where did you get that money?" Lucas asks me.

"I kind of stole it from Nonna."

"Kalamiti," he starts, "you shouldn't have done that."

"Someday I'll pay her back for everything."

And we're off. Wind rushes past us. Road noise fills our ears.

The sun has set. I don't know how much time has passed. The bed of the truck isn't comfortable. We can feel every bump and pothole that we run over.

As I'm about to close my eyes and take a nap, the truck hits rough terrain. We're not on paved roads anymore. Not gonna lie, this is sketchy.

"Where's he taking us?" I ask Lucas.

He sits up and takes a quick glimpse. "Not sure."

Time passes by. At this point, who knows how long we've been traveling on this uncharted course.

"Let's jump out," I whisper.

He nods in agreement.

We wait for the truck to slow down, so it'll be safer to jump out. Finally, Lucas gives me the okay and beckons me to go first.

I peek over the ledge of the truck. Although it's like I'm in the middle of an intense scene from an action movie, this is terrifying. A million things could go wrong.

Lucas says, "We need to do this fast. Try not to scream or make any noise."

I place one leg over the side of the truck, then the other. It's impossible to see where I'm supposed to land.

"Go," says Lucas.

I jump. There's no shoulder to the road, because I fall straight into a ditch and roll down a hill, into the forest. As I tumble, my body runs over sticks and twigs. I keep my eyes shut and attempt to shield my face with my forearms. Lucas is close behind me, also tumbling down.

The forest flattens out and we come to a stop.

I open my eyes, but I'm dizzy. We sit up and take a second to breathe.

"Are you okay?" Lucas asks.

I fix my hair. "Yeah. What about you?"

"He braked right as I jumped out, so I fell pretty hard on the gravel road. I think I'm fine." He stands up and dusts himself off. "We do need to get going, though. The driver might come looking for us."

He helps me up. Flashlights in hand, we run deeper into the forest.

We're both breathing hard. Even with the flashlights, it's hard to see in the dense forest, filled with thin trees that are miles tall.

As we continue to run, I ask, "Where are we going to go from here?"

We both come to a stop.

He runs his hands through his hair. "I have no idea." He finally says the words I didn't want to hear.

The tall trees seem infinite. Is there an end to the forest? Where did it even begin?

We continue to walk in a random direction.

"Wait," I say, "do you hear that?"

Lucas stops in front of me. "No, what is it?"

"Listen. It sounds like water."

"Then we need to keep going. We're getting somewhere."

My ears guide us toward the sound of the cascading water.

It's now the middle of the night. I'm exhausted.

After what seems like miles of walking, the sound of the water resurfaces. It's closer than ever.

At last we arrive at a river. A metal and wood bridge lies in the distance. We climb the steps and walk to the center, where a fishing bridge leads off of it. Light posts are in the area, so we no longer need to use our flashlights.

We take our heavy backpacks off.

The breeze envelops me in a gentle hug. My hair is blowing all over the place. A sense of peace rushes over me as I peer over the bridge's ledge, into the bubbling water down below.

I pull my phone out. Upon pressing the power button, missed calls and messages from Nonna appear on the lock screen. I dismiss the notifications and check our location. "We're near the ocean. We're about forty-five miles from the Oregon border."

"So he was actually taking us in the right direction."

"Oh well. I saved myself a hundred bucks."

Lucas switches the subject. "I think you should call your grandma. Or text her. Let her know where we're going."

"No."

"You do realize you basically ran away from her again. She's going to be worried about us."

I cross my arms. "I'm not going to contact her. Not until I've made it to Oregon. Not until I see my mom and talk to her. If I contact her now, she's going to come get us before we even reach the border."

Lucas stares off into the river.

We stand in silence, listening to the water. An owl hoots in the distance.

I say, "*L'appel du vide.*"

Lucas takes a second to reply. "Wait. That's French."

"It's the call of the void. You never read that book from the library that I told you about, did you?"

"Honestly, no."

"Self-sabotage. It's that voice in our heads that tells us to do something wrong. It's impulsive. Like, jump off this bridge."

Lucas puts his hand on my shoulder. "Don't tell me you're actually going to jump off right now."

"No. The idea is running through my mind, but these

kinds of thoughts can happen to anyone. It's normal. There's so much more to this phenomenon. Research it, Lucas. Read the book. It's fascinating."

"Why are you bringing this up all of a sudden?"

"I don't know. It just came up in my mind," I start. "Don't you ever get those thoughts? Like what if I jumped off the top of a building? What if I stab myself with this knife? What if I swerve into the other lane while I'm driving? What if I make this decision?"

He slowly nods. "Yeah, I guess I do."

I stretch my arms across the bridge's ledge and rest my chin on my hands. I could stay in this exact spot for hours.

My eyes can't help wondering about the river. What kind of fish and creatures call this river their home? How deep is the water, and is it warm or cold? Are there any sharp rocks in it? Where does the river lead to?

As I tilt my head back up, my necklace unlatches. Before I can catch it, it makes its way to the river.

"My necklace!" I hoist myself over the ledge and dive in. "Kalamiti!"

* * *

I'm floating.

When I open my eyes, slowly and slightly, they're greeted by Lucas' chest. Feet off the ground, he carries me in his arms, through the mysterious forest.

* * *

A crackling fire wakes me.

I'm lying down on my side with Lucas' jacket draped

over me. We're now in an area of the forest that isn't so dense with trees.

Lucas pokes the fire with a stick and adds more kindling. I sit up.

"You're awake," he says. "You scared the shit out of me."

"What happened? All I remember is opening my eyes for a second. We were soaked and you were carrying me." My hair is still wet, but for the most part, the fire has helped me dry.

Lucas takes a seat next to me. "You yelled something about a necklace and then you jumped off the bridge. We had just finished talking about *l'appel du vide,* or however you pronounce it. Were you trying to kill yourself?"

My hand reaches for my neck, which is bare. "It's gone."

Lucas stands up, walks over to his backpack, and unzips one of the pockets. He returns to my side. "You mean this?" He opens his fist, revealing my necklace.

I gasp and take it from his hand. "No way."

"What's so special about it that you risked your life for it? I've never seen you take it off, so it must mean a lot to you."

I stare at the necklace between my hands. "My dad gave it to me before he died. It's *un sol* with my initials on the back." I show him. "It's the last memory I have of him."

"Luck was on your side, Kalamiti," he starts. "When you jumped, I jumped right after you. You were having trouble staying afloat. I pulled you out of the water and the necklace was wrapped around your ankle."

"Dad intervened." I smile. "What are the odds?"

Lucas points at the necklace. "The clasp is broken. We should put it in your backpack until we can get it fixed."

I nod. "Thank you, Lucas. You saved my life."

He smiles. "I'm always here for you."

I swallow. "I've come close to death many times, but I think this is the first time I'm actually happy to still be alive."

As he looks at me, his eyes water. He hugs me, then kisses me on the forehead. "Let's rest up. Tomorrow we'll make it to Oregon."

June 6

9 a.m.

We leave our makeshift campsite and walk alongside a road that cuts through the forest.

The ocean is in sight.

After we step over some rocks, our feet meet the sand. We set our stuff down and take a seat.

"This is beautiful." I stare off into the ocean.

"It is," he says.

Waves ebb and flow. The occasional seagull flies by. We have the whole area to ourselves.

Lucas sighs. "We need to go home."

I sift sand through my hands. "We've come so far. We can't go back yet."

"Your mom lives in Brookings, Oregon, but we don't even know her address. How are we gonna find her?"

"I don't care if I have to knock on every single door."

"I admire your determination and persistence, K9, but there comes a point when you need to be realistic."

He's right. I never think things through. It's like a repeat of me running away as a kid, trying to find my mom in the city, when she was never missing in the first place. "You're right. I didn't think this through."

He touches my shoulder. "Let her come to you."

I look at him. "Why did you bother coming with me if you already knew we weren't going to find her?"

"Because I knew you were going to end up going anyway. I couldn't let you come by yourself."

I smile.

"Let's grab something to eat. Then we can figure out a way to get home," he says.

We walk to the closest diner we can find. We eat as much as we can and sneak whatever's possible into our backpacks for snacking later. We've got a long way to go.

"Let's head to a travel center. We'll have a lot of hitchhiking options there," says Lucas.

By the time we arrive at the travel center, it's early afternoon. The lot is packed with cars and semis. Our phones are dead.

At the edge of the lot, a red and white rusted truck with an open driver's side door reveals a blond haired, green-eyed guy. He looks rather young. One of his ears has a chrome piercing in it. This dude is trying too hard to look cool.

We stare at him, until he finally notices. "Can I help you?"

"We were wondering if we could hitch a ride with you," says Lucas.

"Sure. There's enough space in here for both of you." He hops out and slams the door. "I'm heading inside, but we can leave when I get back."

The moment he walks into the convenience store, I say, "I'm not sure why, but I'm getting a bad feeling about him."

"Yeah. Let's go see if someone else can give us a lift."

We skip the car lot and try the semis. The first semi

driver tells us he's going east. The second driver claims there's no space for us. One of them pulls out a machete. Another one says he's going to Canada. Then, another tells us we'd have to ride in the back, but there's no way we're going to be locked up in there.

"Let's try that last one over there," says Lucas.

We veer to the end of the lot. Lucas knocks on the door. An old man with a full beard opens it.

"Yes?"

"We were wondering if we could hitch a ride to San Jose."

"Sorry, no can do. I can lose my job for that."

"Please," I add in.

He looks back and forth at us. "I'm sorry, kids." He closes his door.

Behind us, the sound of footsteps hit the asphalt. It's the young guy, wearing flip flops. He smells like he just finished smoking a cigarette behind the convenience store. For a second, I thought there was a joint hanging out of his mouth, but it turns out it's a lollipop. I guess I'm pretty tired.

He pulls the lollipop out of his mouth. "I've been looking for you two. Let's get going."

He beckons us to follow him. I swear this guy is weird.

Lucas opens the passenger door. The young guy apologizes for the mess and commences to move a pack of cigarettes, a blanket, dirty clothes, a toothbrush, and other random junk from the seats.

Once clear, Lucas climbs in first, and I sit by the window. We're on the road.

As the young guy pulls the lollipop out of his mouth, his lips make a "pop" sound, and the artificial cherry scent reaches my nostrils. I hope this won't be taken the wrong way, but I could really go for a cherry-flavored lollipop. My mouth and lips are drier than a desert.

After a bit of driving, the young guy initiates a conversation. His lips and teeth are now stained red. "What are your names?"

Lucas answers for us. "I'm Duke and this is Roxy."

"Roxy. That's a gorgeous name."

"Um, thanks," I say.

"My name's Lawrence. I'm 23. I just got my license back a few months ago…"

This is going to be a long ride.

* * *

The sun is beginning to set.

We're on a highway with nothing to see out of the window except fields. No buildings in sight. If you need to fuel up or hit the toilet, you're kind of screwed for who knows how many miles.

Flashing lights reflect off of the rearview mirror on my side. "Lawrence, there's a cop behind you," I say.

"Damn it." He pulls over.

The officer approaches the driver's side and asks Lawrence for his license and other documents. He doesn't question why Lucas and I are in the vehicle.

He writes a ticket, hands it to Lawrence, then leaves. Apparently, he was going thirty over the limit. I wonder what he did to get his license suspended in the first place.

I'm exhausted. I want to take a nap, but I don't feel comfortable sleeping.

Lawrence talks so much he could have his own show called "Late Night with Lawrence." He could even do stand-up. To be honest, if I were one of the audience members, I would probably throw tomatoes at him. Except that would be a waste of food. You'd think he'd take a hint by the fact that we're not responding to anything he's saying.

But guess what. He spots one nice car, so he and Lucas dive into a whole conversation about cars.

They keep pointing out the window and discussing rims and tires. I don't understand what they're talking about once they bring up modifications.

I'm so annoyed. "Will you guys hush? I'm trying to sleep." Not really. It's just that sometimes I don't want to hear people talk.

They both look at me. "You got a problem, K9?" Lucas immediately covers his mouth.

Great, he revealed my real nickname.

"Bro, what's your problem? She's a girl, not a dog," says Lawrence.

"No, it's cool, that's her nickname."

"Really? You call a beautiful girl like her 'canine'?"

Gross.

Absolute silence.

Lawrence fumbles with the radio knobs. "So are you two brother and sister?"

Lucas rolls his eyes and bangs his head against the back window. "No. Not even close."

I always think I'm awkward, so I end up overthinking things. But then I meet people like him, and it makes me realize I'm not so bad.

Can San Jose be any closer?

* * *

Lawrence pulls into a gas station. Bathroom break.

The second he shuts his door, I turn to Lucas. "We need to get out of here. I don't care if I have to walk the rest of the way to San Jose. I'd rather do that than sit here for another five minutes."

"No, I agree. Let's go."

I open the glove box, revealing cherry-flavored lollipops. "Might as well take a few."

We gather our belongings and head down the road.

It's dark out. A small gas station is on the horizon.

We ask the cashier where we're at. She looks at us as if we're stupid. "This is Reno."

Lucas and I turn to look at each other. We then walk out the glass door and plop down on the curb.

"Lawrence was a bad idea," he says.

"At least we're not stranded in the middle of nowhere."

He runs his hands through his hair. "Were we really sitting in his truck that long?"

I stretch my arms. "It felt like the longest drive of my life."

"Let's find a place to stay for the night. We need to get some sleep."

We continue down the same dark road. Hardly any cars pass by.

With every step we take, the night seems to drag on. My energy is depleted.

And then it's like night and day. Restaurants, hotels, fast food, gas stations, schools, housing, and more buildings and lights brighten the dreary night.

The first motel we spot, we book a room.
Until tomorrow.

June 7

1 p.m. Just woke up. Our sleep schedules are jacked up.

Now that my phone is charged, I have even more missed calls and texts from Nonna. I haven't bothered reading any of them, nor have I updated her on our whereabouts.

I stare at my image in the full body mirror in our room. Dirt and scratches cover my face. Oily, tangled hair makes my scalp itch, begging for shampoo and conditioner. Chapped lips crave a moisturizing coat of peppermint lip balm. I run my tongue over my teeth. I'm dying to scrub the thin, grimy coating off. My clothes are filthy, sending a cry for help to the washer. I won't even go into detail on how I smell. I barely recognize myself.

And just like that, I'm transported back to homelessness.

Was this really how I was living for years?

Months ago, the Kalamiti I was with The Crew had no purpose, no will to live. She thought she'd live in The Hideout forever. Although she was surrounded by The Crew, she still felt like there was something missing.

I've come so far. I've accomplished so much in so little time. And that's how I intend to keep going at it. We may not have made it to Oregon or seen my mom, but I'll get there someday.

I've changed. Not just physically, but all around.

Time to call Nonna. Home is where I need to be.

"Nonna, I'm sorry I haven't picked up or texted you back."

"Have you read any of my messages?"

My heart drops. "No, I haven't."

"I'm on my way to Oregon. I assume you've made it to your mom's?"

I gasp. "Wait, don't go over there! Come to Reno. It's a long story, but I'll explain everything when you get here. I'll send you the location."

She chuckles. "My goodness, you two have quite the adventures."

That's a first. I thought she'd be mad or would punish us by not picking us up after all.

Lucas is out of the shower.

"Nonna's coming to rescue us. She'll be here in a few hours."

He kisses me on the lips. I'm surprised he's not disgusted with the state I'm in.

After I finish taking a shower, we eat lunch and lounge in the motel room.

"What a crazy few days it's been," says Lucas. "Hitchhiking is not at all easy like I thought it would be. How did you manage getting to Chicago on your own as a kid?"

I sigh. "I didn't exactly hitchhike like what we did this time around. I snuck onto a Greyhound. People were starting to get suspicious, so as soon as we made it to the bus station, I ran off. Two weeks later I was caught, which is why I was placed in a foster home."

"I'm glad nothing happened to you. That could've been so dangerous."

Before we know it, a car honks in the parking lot.

We check out of the motel and meet Nonna in the lot.

"Kalamiti! Lucas! I'm so glad you guys are okay." She hugs us.

"I'm sorry," I say.

"It's okay. Let's go home."

While in her car, Lucas and I take turns explaining everything that happened. Her reactions are hilarious. They're a mixture of laughing, smiling, and disciplining us.

She says, "That Lawrence guy is something else."

We all laugh.

The conversation turns serious again. "If you wanted to see your mom, you should've asked me. I would rather take you than risk something happening to the both of you." She glances at Lucas. "And how did you wind up going with her? You should've talked her out of it."

Lucas smirks. "Kalamiti is determined. Once she wants to do something, there's no talking her out of it."

Nonna smiles, then sighs. "You don't have to do everything on your own. Sometimes it's okay to ask for help. We need to be more open with each other, and not be sneaking around and doing things in secrecy."

I nod. "I know. I'm working on it."

The rest of the car ride results in Nonna playing us different genres of music she enjoys.

I'm glad Reno wasn't too far of a drive from home.

June 8

Patterson, California. It's good to be back.

While I missed out on many of Nonna's messages, I came

home to another missed message on social media, from June. She's currently in a foster home in Wilmette, Illinois. This is the first foster home that she feels she belongs in, and she's hoping to be adopted by them. I'm so happy for her.

I may never see her in person again, but at least I still have a connection with her online.

June 9

It's our first day of summer school.

Instead of having six different classes and hours, we stay in the same room. Four classrooms are open, one for each grade.

Ms. Adler is my summer school teacher. Maybe I should stop giving her such a hard time.

We didn't do much today. It was mostly introductions, going over classroom rules, and the syllabus.

This is gonna be a piece of cake.

June 10

I've been keeping in touch with Betsy, Annabelle, Joanie, and Griffin.

Betsy's and Annabelle's families are both going on vacation this month, but they said they're down to hang out in July.

Joanie is actually in summer school with me, so I get to see her during the day.

Griffin's preparing for college music auditions and staying busy with his other hobbies. He mentioned something about studying for college entrance exams, too. We're hoping to get together to practice piano soon.

He and Ms. Hayley mentioned a piano camp in San Francisco that they want me to attend next year, so I'm going to begin preparing for it.

Sofia and Turner asked me if I wanted to go hiking sometime. Of course I said yes.

It's gonna be a great summer.

June 11

Do teachers even want to work during summer break?

I'm pretty sure Ms. Adler has been hungover this whole week. She's done with everyone. She even went off on the principal the other day.

She should probably just retire already, although she doesn't seem that old. Maybe she's in her forties? A career change would be good for her.

Summer school is kind of a joke. All we've been doing is fill-in-the-blank worksheets, the kind that copy the exact paragraphs out of a textbook. How are we supposed to learn from that? I'd rather spend the day reading books at the library, where I can actually retain interesting information.

Oh well, it is what it is. Anything to pass this grade.

June 13

Dinnertime.

We're eating in silence.

Nonna speaks. "We're leaving for Sacramento tomorrow."

I stop eating. "What for?"

"We have a funeral to attend."

"Who died?"

I still need to learn how to properly respond to things.

Lucas nearly spits out his water.

Nonna looks at me strangely with her eyebrows furrowed. "One of our family members. Your Great-Aunt Violet."

"Oh. I'm sorry to hear she passed. I didn't even know we had other family around."

"Of course. Your aunt, uncle, and cousins live in Sacramento."

I never knew I had other family in California. Nonna mentioned in the past that my dad's extended family is near Chicago. "How am I related to them?"

"Your Great-Aunt Violet is my sister. She had a daughter named Regina, who was cousins with your mother. Regina married your Uncle George and they had your cousins, Cora and Stella."

"Why have I never met them?"

"You have met them, Kalamiti. The very first time you lived with me. They would visit often. Cora and Stella were older than you, so you girls didn't play much. We don't visit each other because we're not as close as we used to be."

Now I remember. "Actually, yeah, I do remember them."

"Can I go to Sacramento with you two?" asks Lucas.

"Yes, absolutely. I can drive us there. We can stay at a hotel tomorrow night," says Nonna.

It's gonna be bittersweet seeing them after so many years.

June 14

We're currently driving to Sacramento so we can rest up tonight. Great-Aunt Violet's funeral is tomorrow.

I'm scared and anxious about seeing my extended family after so many years. What if they see me as the infamous missing granddaughter? What if they think negatively of me?

At least I'm not alone. I have Lucas and Nonna with me. Let's hope I make a good impression.

June 15

Today is my great-aunt's funeral.

After mass, we all head straight to the cemetery.

Everyone's dressed in all black.

The weather is beautiful. It's sunny, but not too hot.

People around us are crying. I feel a bit uneasy. I didn't really know her, and Lucas has never even met her.

Seeing Nonna cry is making me want to cry. I think Lucas can tell I'm a bit anxious because he takes a hold of my hand.

The crowd huddles in a circle around the casket. They begin lowering it into the ground. Prayers are being murmured, both in English and Italian.

I need to step away for a second. "I'll be right back," I tell Lucas.

I walk down a gravel path. A pond is up ahead, which reminds me of my sacred space back home.

I kneel by the pond's edge and gaze into my reflection. For the first time, I think I actually recognize myself and know who I am.

A voice in my head tells me to look up.

There's a woman, dressed in all black, standing next to a tree. Her gaze is fixed on the pond water.

Is it me? Did my reflection come to life? Am I imagining this?

Our eyes meet.

Mom.

I run toward her and I throw myself in her arms.

* * *

Mom and I take a seat on a bench near the pond.

After a moment of silence, she initiates a conversation. "Kalamiti, I'm so sorry."

"You have a lot of explaining to do. Every time I think of you, I just wonder why. Why things happened the way they did. Why you left. Why Nonna lied about it all."

"I do have a lot of explaining to do," she starts. "I was doing a lot of drugs and alcohol. I lost touch with reality and motherhood. I wasn't giving you the life you deserved, so I thought Nonna would be a better provider. As soon as I left, I went straight to rehab. I was there for a few months. Once I was released, I was doing well, but I relapsed. That time I ended up in prison."

I look into her eyes. As soon as she said those words, I could see the pain she's gone through. The bad memories resurfaced.

She continues. "I was in prison for a few years, Kalamiti. It was awful. Everything seemed to be over for me at that point. That's why I wasn't able to reach out to you." She pauses. "After I served my time, I went back to rehab. I'm doing better now. I'm sober, living in Brookings in my own apartment. I have a stable job."

I believe her about being sober. She's no longer slurring her words. She's not checked out. Life has returned in her eyes.

"We shouldn't have lied to you. Since you were just a kid, we didn't want to tell you about my drug addiction. But now we've realized we should've been more honest."

"Nonna told you about everything that I did, right?"

"Yes. On the phone, a few weeks ago." She pauses, then softly says, "I don't want you to end up like me."

I stare at the pond without blinking. My eyes mist over. "There was a time where I was experimenting with different drugs in Chicago. The only reason I did it was to see what you saw in them, to see why you always preferred them over me."

Mom begins to cry. "I'm so sorry, Kalamiti. If I could go back in time, I wish I would have never touched them."

I finally blink. "All that matters now is that you got through that part. We've both learned from our pasts."

She nods. "I understand if you hate me and never want to see me again. I understand if you don't want me to be a part of your life. You have every right to be angry at me."

I take a deep breath. "I was angry. And sad. But above

all, I've always wanted to reconnect with you. You failed me in the past, but that doesn't mean you'll fail me in the future."

"Do you forgive me?"

Nonna's words about forgiveness flash in my mind. "I forgive you, Mom. We can start over."

She hugs me tight. "I've been trying to get custody of Alessandro."

"Where is he?"

"His dad and the girlfriend moved to Iowa with him. But as you know, it hasn't been a good home. After I win custody, I want to return to California. I want us all to be a family again."

I smile. "We would all like that."

She smiles. "We have a lot to catch up on. So what do you like to do in your free time? And what's your favorite color and number?"

I lean back in the bench and begin sharing all the little details of my life.

June 16

We're back in California.

Yesterday still feels so surreal. I keep thinking it was a dream from my sacred space.

After summer school ends mid-July, I'm going up to Oregon to spend the rest of the summer with Mom. We still have a lot of catching up to do.

Lucas is going to do the same. He's planning on going back to Denver to spend time with both his mom and aunt before school starts back up.

This is a summer of reuniting.

June 17

I'm in my sacred space, leaning against the willow tree. The trip to Sacramento was a lot to process.

The branches and leaves rustle.

It's Lucas. "Can I come in?"

I nod. He gently moves the branches aside and takes a seat next to me.

A cotton candy sky reflects off the pond. Shades of pink, purple, orange, and blue mix together with the few clouds scattered about.

I lean my head against his shoulder. "Hey, Lucas?"

"Yeah?"

"Remember when we were in that greenhouse in Denver and you asked me to visualize a sunflower field?"

"Yeah, I remember."

"When I visualized it, I was there dressed in white. But it wasn't just me. You were there, too. We were like king and queen."

He smiles. "That's amazing."

"And remember when you told me that in order to find my brighter path, I needed to add up all my components?"

"Yeah, what about that?"

"I used to think I didn't have any. But I've come to realize that you're one of my components. A vital component. I'm a sunflower that needs sunshine. You're my sunshine, Lucas. Nonna is my nutrients. The Crew is my water. Friends are my soil. Mom and family are my roots. The little moments in life, whether good or bad, are full of meaning. They're the sky and air. I wouldn't be able to blossom and grow without all of them."

He looks at me with his kind eyes. He smiles. "That's perfect. I love how you put it. You're my sunshine, too, Kalamiti. *Eres mi sol.*"

We sit in silence under the comfort of the willow tree, watching the sunset.

I used to think I was alone. I used to think I never had anyone. Turns out they were here all along, enjoying the ride with me.

As I fill the final page in my memory book, I'd like to leave a message to my future self. There will be moments of sadness and anger up ahead, so this will serve as a reminder for when I'm feeling down. This message is also for anyone who ends up reading my memory book from the time capsule. I know if it would make me happier, that it would do the same for other people.

You're never truly alone on your quest to finding a brighter path. You just need to find your truth and go for it. Trust that whatever choices you make, they'll take you exactly where you need to be.

Acknowledgments

When I first wrote The Girl with No Sol, I originally planned to do the entire project on my own. I realized I needed help after all.

First off, I'd like to thank my mom and dad, for instilling hard work in me from a young age. Shout out to my sibs: Denise, Freddy, and Emily, for being supportive. Denise, thank you for letting me borrow your laptop many summers ago so I could finally take my manuscript from paper to screen. To my nephew Toby, for being adorable, and just because. Shout out to my dogs, Tiny and Luna. All the experiences in my life, whether good or bad, shaped me into who I am today and inspired many of the events in this book. I'm thankful for all the resources available online to learn more about writing, editing, and the publishing industry. To nature, for being incredible and inspiring me daily. Everything from the sky, to the clouds, to the trees, plants, and even water.

Many thanks to my editor, Beth Rodgers, for her feedback and guidance. Not to mention answering the millions of questions that were on my mind. Throughout the editing process, I listened to music from Tracey Chattaway, Jonny Southard, and Anthony Greninger, as well as the "World's Most Breathtaking Piano Pieces Contemporary Music Mix Vol. 1" playlist on Spotify. Thank you to Jonny Southard, for responding to my email and giving me permission to use his track "Who You Are" in my book. If you haven't listened to his music, go check it out. Katie Larabee did a lovely job with my cover's artwork. The sun is just incredible, and I couldn't stop smiling when I first saw the design. Emily Fritz took care of my book's interior and cover file. I was blown away when I received the sample of the interior, and it was better than I imagined it in my head. Thank you for working with me and for your patience. I couldn't have done this without you all.

To my family, friends, and colleagues: Thank you.

Thank you to all the people who read excerpts of The Girl with No Sol and continued to encourage me and cheer me on to the finish line. A million thanks to anyone who ever bothered even listening to me talk about my book. You all know who you are.

About the Author

PC: *Christopher Ramirez*

Karen Vega is a Mexican American author. She finds inspiration for her writing from everyday life, just taking in all observations. The Girl with No Sol is her debut young adult fiction novel. Originally from a Chicago suburb, Karen now resides in Tulsa, Oklahoma. She has a bachelor's degree in music and plays many instruments, including the flute. In her free time, she enjoys drinking coffee and tea, meditating, being in nature, and spending time with family. You will most likely find her laughing in serious situations and at the most random things. Check out her website www.karenvegawrites.com and social media @karenvegawrites